THE GRAND SEX TOUR Murders

DANIEL M. JAFFE

Rattling Good Yarns Press
33490 Date Palm Drive 3065
Cathedral City CA 92235
USA
www.rattlinggoodyarns.com

Cover Design: Rattling Good Yarns Press

Library of Congress Control Number: 2022950877
ISBN: 978-1-955826-29-7

Second Edition

To the boys who didn't make it.

Acknowledgments

While I was writing this tell-all, I didn't know if anyone would have the guts to publish it. But then I met Ian Henzel and St Sukie de la Croix of Rattling Good Yarns Press. Those two editors have got balls the size of Palm Springs grapefruits. Thanks, guys—you're great.

Oh yeah—and thanks to my hubby who shares the laughs.

Paulie Hahnemann

First Words From Me, But Not The Asshole

Here's my book you lucky bastards have been waiting for: *The Grand Sex Tour Murders*—the behind-the-scenes lowdown on all the sex and murders both, all the nitty-gritty how-to's and what-the-hell-happened's sure to get you wet. My story, the boys' stories (may half of 'em rest in peace), and…the killer's story, that sick fuck. I conducted tons of interviews with him in his German prison so you could get a bird's-eye view of all the shit that went down during the Tour in Europe.

Of course, I didn't know what he was up to 'til near the end of the Tour—there's no way I could have known he was stalking us, right? Nobody in my position could possibly have had a fucking clue, so don't go blaming me. But I—we—won out in the end, caught him and locked him up a year ago. Too late for half the boys, but in the nick of time for the rest. It was my plan that caught him, don'tcha know. Mine. So don't you go blaming me for anything.

I did every single thing I promised from the get-go: I hired the boys; took 'em to Europe; arranged for their hotels, transportation and sightseeing tours; wined and dined 'em; taught 'em the do's and don't's of earning orgy points. I (well, Burt and I) set up the video van, the online streaming, the gambling, the whole shebang. So why should I feel guilty because some stalker pops up out of nowhere and goes after my good boys? He could have attacked Burt or me, too, don't forget. We were just as much at risk as the boys. My own life was on the line, for God's sake. So, no, I don't feel guilty for shit. Not at all.

You've no clue how hard I worked to put the Tour together. It was on me (well, me and Burt) to raise all the dough. Every last penny. You think I was born shitting golden eggs? In order to get the investment bucks, I had to spend months setting up a website. Then weeks drafting the investor prospectus. I had to make it sound like a once-in-a-lifetime chance for investors to get in on the ground floor of a brilliant plan sure to come in a real gusher. Hell yeah, I'm proud of that prospectus because it made us a fucking mint, which is the good old U.S. of A. way. In case you missed it, here it is, the magic-of-my-mind that got the whole ball of wax rolling, even if it did lead to the murders, but remember—they're not my fault:

The Grand Sex Tour Investor Prospectus:

Are you ready to make a fortune?

Are you ready to invest in the most brilliant venture since the internet?

Am I talking Silicon Valley start-up investments?
—Nickel and dime waste of time.

Hollywood celebrity Instagram endorsements?
—Chicken feed.

Drug muling?
—Horseshit.

The real money is in sex.
Sex sex sex.

Millions are addicted to reality TV, right?
Millions are addicted to the internet, right?
Milllions are addicted to gambling, right?
And millions are addicted to gay porn.

We blend these addictions into **an internet live-streaming gay bathhouse reality sex competition that allows betting on who'll score the most tricks.**

We'll advertise on dating apps of all kinds, officially marketing the show to gays. But of course, all sorts of closeted bi's and "straight" married cuckolds will go ga-ga over the show. And everyone knows straight women get hot for gay porn. Gays, Bi's, Straight men and women—a fucking money machine.

THIS IS YOUR CHANCE!!!!

Will you be one of the forward-thinkers rewarded for investing in the boldest entertainment show of the 21st century? Or will you be left in the dust, sweltering in a roach-infested Death Valley trailer park instead of lounging poolside at your luxury Palm Springs mansion?

Want to spend your retirement years working as a destitute bagger in the local Winn-Dixie grocery store just so you can afford a single hit of Viagra once a month, hoping to score some homeless young junkie willing to lick you in exchange for a dirty-needle fix? Or do you want to spend those golden years as a rich sugar daddy/mommy hiring any Mr. America escort you damn well please any time of day or night? Hire two escorts at a time. Hire a dozen to hang by your pool and perform at the snap of your fingers, to fill your every orifice with so much youthful spunk that your cells will spontaneously rejuvenate—discover the fountain of youth Ponce de León died for!

For your initial investment of $250,000 (or more?), you'll become rich beyond your wildest dreams! (This statement has not been vetted by the SEC…hah hah hah.) Act now—space is as limited as the inside of an evangelical WASP's clamped-shut asshole.

But hurry—only a limited number of investor slots remain.

Here's How It Works:

The Show

Are you bored with run-of-the-mill gay porn where tweaking actors mouth wooden dialogue like so many dickless Pinocchios? Are you tired of formulaic cries of "Oh, fuck!" and "Yeah!" and "Give it to me!" that every stoned porn actor recites over and over like some empty mantra on the porno path to never-gonna-reach-it sexual nirvana? Are you sick of the phony ripping off of breakaway prop clothes, the obviously forced kissing of the other guy's hangover-stink mouth, the robotic suck-and-fucks with an occasional lousy reluctant rim-job of zit-covered butt cheeks?

Fuck that phony self-conscious shit. Our sex is real! Our boys are unscripted and horny, well-groomed, and Triple X hot. Our boys show you the spiciest sex in the world because they're competing for a Grand Prize. (Capitalist incentive at its best.)

For our first season, we'll film five different orgies (a/k/a FuckFests), each in a different European city's bathhouse (a/k/a sauna), so you'll get to travel the world while you watch and jerk off from the comfort of your own home.

The Boys Boys Boys

Well...the men, actually—all our "boys" are consenting adults certified to be at least 21 years old. Also, they sign waivers against any liability on our part—medical, legal, and any other kind imaginable. So...investors undertake zero risk exposure.

Why, you wonder, would the boys sign those waivers? A trade-off for potential riches (to say nothing of the fun fun fun!). Your investment provides financial security for gorgeous virile young men. Don't you want to support gay youth?

Contestants are so gorgeous, we won't need airbrushing or other computer-generated bullshit to adjust their multi-cultural physiques or...ahem...dimensions...on film. I personally guarantee a racial rainbow of boys, and an ideal mix of smooth muscle guys, bears, and lean swimmers' build twink types. Nobody smaller than seven inches, a mix of cut and uncut, mushroom heads, tapering heads, arrow-straight shafts, and curved ones (I personally inspect all these stats when doing the hiring—a tedious job, but I'm willing to sacrifice for you investors...hah hah hah). And of course, our boys are a mix of tops, bottoms, and versatiles.

The Technology

We hired moonlighting CIA staff to develop remote video technology capable of filming in shadows (although not in pitch black dark rooms—we're not miracle workers). We've implanted our revolutionary video technology in fashion-forward headbands that appear to onlookers like run-of-the-mill red-white-and-blue striped terrycloth sweatbands. (We're nothing if not patriotic.) Each headband bulges with a cluster of absorbent terry threads tipped by fiber optic video cameras working together like a fly's eye, providing multiple angles of simultaneous footage. Then, our supercomputers synthesize them into a unified image so crystal clear it makes High Def look like cave paintings.

To supplement the boys' hidden headband cameras, our professional cameraman roams around, directing his own hidden headband camera at the hottest action. How does he know where to film? Our highly experienced porn producer—yours truly— sits in a discreet van outside the orgy venue watching a wall of computer screens, each displaying a different boy's headband footage. As I view the screens, I direct the cameraman, through his remote-access micro ear receiver, to film the most intense action. All the footage that I see—you'll see: we'll live-stream it all on our website displaying multiple screens simultaneously so that subscribers (and you investors) can follow their (your) favorites.

Once we return to Hollywood after a season of filming, we'll edit the humongous amount of footage the way any good reality show does—to highlight the best of the best, intersplicing the boys' downtime tourist fun in Europe in order to provide a well-rounded and entertaining specHOTular director's cut film—fifteen hours worth that we'll break up into a series we'll sell to Amazon, Netflix, Apple, Hulu, or Disney (can you just picture The Grand Sex Tour showing up on a TV screen right after Snow White and Bambi? Better check those parental controls, folks!).

Your Money Stream

How, you might ask, do you earn a return on your investment? For starters: from the millions upon millions of subscribers we're sure to attract, and from the sale of the final edited director's cut film.

We'll offer three tiers of subscriber viewership: Six-Inchers, who pay $50 a season, get to see the weekly live-stream FuckFest broadcasts, and are eligible to purchase the director's cut film at a 10% discount. King Dongs, who pay $100 per season, can also watch the live-streaming FuckFests; in addition, they get the director's cut for free. Super Shlongs, who pay $500 per season, get all the above plus autographed used jockstraps from their three favorite contestants. Needless to say, you initial investors of $250,000 each get free Super Shlong subscriptions in addition to your profit share.

And then we'll encourage each subscriber to gamble on which boy will win the season. "The house," of course, takes a cut of every bet—full disclosure. The gambler who picks the Grand Prize-winning boy gets a free, all-expenses paid week with the winner in a five-star hotel with a king-size bed and all the condoms and lube they can possibly use. In case more than one gambler selects the actual season winner, the prize goes to the gambler who bet the highest amount. If there's a tie, then the winning boy decides, after reviewing the gambler's list of fetishes.

The competition's winner is chosen based on the number and kind of sex acts performed during each FuckFest, all tallied by a point system per a secret proprietary computerized algorithm developed by a team of pervy Silicon Valley geniuses. The algorithm is so secret that even I don't understand how it works. All initial $250,000 investors are guaranteed a minimum 20% return on your investment within a year plus a proportionate share of actual profit above that 20%. Of course, if you invest more than $250,000 for a larger profit share, then you'll become super-duper rich.

All You Need Do…

…is contact me at the email address at the bottom of this web prospectus and wire money into my personal bank account at.…

The rest of the ad was technical stuff that's none of your goddamn business. Like I'm really gonna publish my bank account info in this book so you readers can hack into it now that you know I'm filthy rich. Bad enough I had to publish the info online to attract the dough in the first place. That was a mega risk, although until the dinero started pouring in, there was nothing in my account anyone could filch. Things're different now.

Everything's different now—just ask the dead boys. Sorry, bad joke.

Anyway, a super prospectus, right? I came up with it all by myself. Every fucking word. Well… maybe Burt suggested a word or two, or a phrase, or maybe even a coupla paragraphs, but basically, it was all mine.

You're probably wondering where this whole Grand Sex Tour idea came from. For a good long time, Burt and I made a decent living filming porn flicks. Burt's a wiz with cameras. We used to do it the old-fashioned way, on videotapes sold through bookstores and the mails. Once the internet got going, I saw an opportunity, and took it. At first, we made a mint selling online porn subscriptions. But, little by little, too many other porn makers jumped in, and price competition ruined profit margins. Then thanks to fucking cell phone cameras, amateurs started posting their own films online for free. They're mostly crap, but would-be customers of ours really went for 'em because they're "real." That put the kibosh on professional products like Burt's and mine. Burt started filming weddings and quinceañeras and bar mitzvahs to make ends meet, but he hates that sugary shit.

One day he and I were doing our usual grousing while watching our favorite movie, *Gypsy*, about strippers. After taking a few tokes, we followed Mama Rose's instructions to "sing out, Louise." We belted along with the three strippers as they sang, "You Gotta Get a Gimmick," that song about how you gotta find your own shtick if you wanna stand out from the crowd. We laughed so hard, I sorta pissed a little on the sofa, but we didn't really give a crap. Then we watched a lousy reality TV baking competition show (Burt and I both got the bellies to prove we like cake), and I joked that our gimmick should be filming a reality TV sex contest. Burt jumped up, grabbed me by the jowls, and kissed me smack on the lips. He even slipped me some tongue. He hadn't done that in I don't know how many years. "I married a genius!" he cried.

I figured it was the Mary Jane, but a coupla hours later, when we were sobering up, he took out a pen and pad and made notes. The Grand Sex Tour was born. So that's the history for you pervy Film Studies professors who're reading this book for the kicks while pretending "to do scholarly research."

Now, the way this book's gonna go is I'll include three kinds of material. Most important will be my memories of what happened when and how—the real facts. The second kind of stuff will be transcripts of some of the secret boy conversations; more about them…later. And third, I'll include transcripts of the interviews I conducted with that asshole serial killer after we finally caught him and stuck him in prison. I tape-recorded those interviews so's I could get 'em all down right. Good thing I did because that snooty patootie gabs in a way I could never remember just from notes. I had to cut out a ton from those interviews—that fucker's got such a diarrhea mouth that after the first interview, I wanted to shove a butt plug in it. But then I decided I might as well let him spray his shit every which way so he'd get it out of his system. Then I could hose everything down—it's not like some law says I gotta put every piece of his crap into this book, right? Just the chunky parts. You'll see what I mean soon enough. I won't waste your time with my questions to him. Or arguments with him, that nasty fuck. I just want you to get a pure feel for his twisted mind.

You probably got lotsa what-the-crap-are-you-talking-about's going through your heads right now. By the time you finish this amazing book, all your questions'll be answered. And if not—tough shit, I already got your money for the book, so the joke's on you.

Copenhagen

My Memories: Copenhagen—Queen's Birthday

I purposely booked us to arrive in Copenhagen early morning on April 16, Queen Margrethe's birthday. After all, what better way for a group of fags to start an adventure than on a "queen's" birthday? I asked the pimply bimbo hotel check-in clerk about celebration festivities. "Well, the Queen will wave from the Radhuis balcony at 2:00." Then she shrugged and giggled like the Queen was stupid touristy shit. Fuck her (the clerk, not the Queen).

That's when I introduced the boys to my Burt, who looks like everybody's uncle—pot belly, bald, wispy brown-and-white hair on the sides of his head, a light-bulb nose over a thick-lipped grin. Such a hot daddy type—still turns me on after thirty years together. But at the same time, I knew he'd be the perfect Mr. Bland to blend into bathhouse backgrounds and film the boys with his headband camera.

I explained to the boys that Burt had flown to Copenhagen a week earlier to rent and outfit the van I'd be using in Europe. Each week, Burt'd drive the van ahead of us to each destination so he could "arrange things." Of course I didn't tell the boys that the real reason Burt would be traveling ahead was so he could set up hidden cameras in the boys' hotel rooms.

By the way, our Copenhagen rooms were great—royal blue carpet, royal blue curtains, royal blue or gold comforters—all looking out across the Nyhavn canal at old buildings and restaurants. One of those postcard Copenhagen views.

Everyone quickly showered. At noon, we gathered in the hotel's big lobby and found Radhuis (Town Hall) Square on a map. Hell, we'd really have to haul ass across town. "Follow the bicyclers," advised the bimbo check-in clerk. There were so many cyclists the street looked like one of those AIDS/LifeCycle events back home, but without any leather daddy monitors keeping the cyclists in line. Those Danes just naturally respect traffic lights and pedestrians. And thanks to all that bike riding, Danish men have amazing muscular asses and thighs. Toto, I mumbled, we ain't in fucking L.A. anymore.

Soon we spotted a unit of "hussars"—men and women both—in bright blue uniforms with white braiding, white gloves, red capes over left shoulders, black caps with chin straps, and white horsehair pompomy things on top, black boots. The Wicked Witch of the West's flying monkey soldiers, but on horseback. The brown and black horses clippity-clopped in unison, right through town.

The parade cued our only flaming twink, Irish Tommy (wavy red hair, pale skin with freckles, skinny swimmer's build, and BIG uncut dick bulging under the worn crotch of his jeans). He took to marching with his knees kicked up high while his right hand pumped up and down like some grand marshal with a baton (or some sex-crazed Jack jerking off his beanstalk giant). Then Tommy started singing "Before the Parade Passes By" from *Hello Dolly*. He ain't no Streisand. More like Carol Channing the night she croaked. Or the night after.

A coupla other boys joined in with their "la la la's," but not Sam—curly black hair and beard scruff, a pudgy bear with a jiggly ass you just wanna bury your tongue in. He's a real Jewish sexpot that'd give Mandy Patinkin a run for his money in *Yentl*. (And don't go breaking my balls about that money remark. It's just an expression for fuck's sake, not at all anti-Semitic, so lighten up.) Then he shook his head and said, "a chorus of queens for the Queen. Lame."

Tommy, the redheaded twink, glared at him—if looks could kill, right?— then belted the song even louder, Ethel Merman style.

Danes on sidewalks stared like the circus was in town. With a regular video cam, Burt filmed the boys serenading the marching hussars, who didn't react jack shit. Not even a whinny from their horses. They might as well have been stone-faced Buckingham Palace Queen's Guard in London. I guess it's a queen thing.

I was disappointed when we reached Radhuis Square—not fancy like I expected. Just a dull brown brick Town Hall with a few turrets and a small gilded relief sculpture of some old king or saint above the central balcony. Giant photos of the Queen at different ages plastered a red wall at the opposite side of the Square. But only a coupla hundred people were milling around. Didn't the Danes love their Queen?

From a vendor on the Square, Little Frenchie (our petit blond Montrealer who really lived up to his nickname, lick lick) bought each of the boys a "Franks" hot dog: the middle-aged woman vendor took stubby, hollowed-out rolls, pumped in some ketchup, then stuck a long hot dog into each, leaving a third of the meat sticking out. The boys all thanked Little Frenchie, said what a good little guy he was.

I nudged Burt to get his video cam ready because what was coming next was predictable, not that I knew from which boy, but then: Flaming Tommy, of course, I should have known. He made a crack about the vendor not being able to stick the meat all the way in. Then Tommy clamped his left hand against the back of his own head, forced his mouth down onto the sticking-out hot dog in his right hand, and gagged. Most of the boys chuckled, but Sam said, "Could you be less gross in public?"

"What's the matter, girlfriend?" replied Tommy. "Jealous of a hot dog?"

"We're like American ambassadors in a foreign country. At a celebration for their Queen, for God's sake. Show some respect."

"Respect this," said Tommy, shimmying his shoulders like he was jiggling tits.

"Fairy."

"Self-hating homophobe."

I felt glad I made those two New Yorkers roomies here in Europe. Who knew what fag drama would show up on their hidden hotel room cams? Bitchy shit sells subscriptions, and this whole project was about the money, right? (Not just for me, but for the boys too, so don't go calling me selfish.)

I hoped Tommy and Sam would go on sniping, but a blond cop (navy blue uniform stating "*Politi*" in white) was giving us the eye. The last thing we needed was trouble, so I stepped between the boys and directed 'em to opposite sides of the Square, which was finally filling with more people.

A giant video screen showed the Queen at some to-do inside Town Hall. At 2:00 on the dot—not 1:59, not 2:01, but 2:00—a marching band (red jackets, white pants with blue stripes on the side, furry black hats) began playing and Queen Margrethe—blond in a pale blue Chanel kind of suit and Jackie O pillboxy hat—stepped onto that balcony and waved. The crowd cheered while she held onto her hat against the wind. A coupla more waves, a coupla more cheers. Then she went back inside.

That was it? No speech? No thank-you's?

A big nothing unless Chanel suits make you hot.

Okay, so maybe the hotel check-in clerk wasn't a total idiot, after all.

Killer Interview 1

I wish to thank you, Mr. Hahnemann, for undertaking this series of interviews so that I may express feelings and thoughts. I have always been a rather contemplative sort, and now that I find myself residing, presumably for the rest of my days, in solitary confinement, my inner world is the only expanse available for exploration. How lovely—the opportunity to share memories and insights with you and your readers, whom I regard as my public.

. . .

What's that you say, Mr. Hahnemann? You deem the readers to be exclusively *your* public? I'll grant you that if not for your Grand Sex Tour, there would be no readers. However, I venture to assert that if not for the maimings and murders—my maimings and murders—there would be no readers, either. So, I propose that we bask in the glory jointly, shall we?

. . .

Thank you, Mr. Hahnemann, for at least considering my proposal.

. . .

As you wish, I shall commence at the beginning. You wish me to explain how I came to invest in, and become, as it were, a camp follower of your Grand Sex Tour boys. A laughably simple chronology: one evening after a session of self-pleasurement inspired by one of your "best of" online porn film compilations—I have spent a fortune on your B-porn flicks over the years, insipid as they are—I came upon your prospectus solicitation for investment in The Grand Sex Tour, the text of which solicitation you have assured me would accompany the textual transcription of these, my interviews, so as to provide our readers appropriate context for understanding my reasoning. I do wish to be understood. As well as appreciated. And remembered.

You are a P.T. Barnum of investment capital, Mr. Hahnemann. Despite the proven feebleness of your past film efforts, your prospectus seduced me utterly.

Although not initially. My initial reaction was one of disdain: as if sexual interaction could ever be competition, should be competition, were anything but competition whether in an alley, bar, sex club, or bedroom. As if we of greatest experience were not sidelined every single day because the world is run by the inexperienced young. Oh, if only to live in Japan, a society respecting experience and wisdom! But one is *in* the West and *of* the West, in and of a culture that denigrates white hair and paunch. How enraging is Western disrespect for an older gentleman's natural flaccidity that is erroneously assumed a reaction to hormonal decline attending certain age. One's occasionally prolonged state of penile repose is actually a physiological response to decades of high-demand experience and over-use that should be venerated the way we glorify withered athletes renowned for once having broken records for hits, tackles, baskets, and holes in one.

Oh, you wonder with cynicism typical of the low entrepreneurial class: if I could undertake to fly to Europe from Boston, then why did I not purchase a ticket to Japan and be done with it? Given that I possessed sufficient funds to invest in The Grand Sex Tour, why not spend the money on moving to the East instead, even applying for citizenship there? I will tell you, Mr. Hahnemann: because at age sixty, I cannot learn another language with the same alacrity as when younger—my brain is the organ displaying the most significant signs of wear. Because I am allergic to soy and seafood, and my back cannot handle even a single night's sleep on a floor. Because I do not wish to serve as North Korean missile target practice. Because my ancestral spermatozoa swam out of intersections of European genetic pools, so is it any wonder that my loin-compass points primarily, albeit not exclusively, salmon-like in the direction of my spawning? Do you regard my Western genetic hormonal predisposition to be racist? Complain to my endocrinologist.

I spent weeks contemplating this investment opportunity, concluded it to be a means both of providing better for my nearer-rather-than-farther old age and of enjoying some naughty, voyeuristic fun—my *eyes* have continued to function with the same vigor as in the bloom of youth. Moreover, investment in a high-tech, culturally engaging, pornographic internet gambling venture designed to appeal to the basest desires of a broad swath of the population struck me as exceptionally astute—Mr. Hahnemann, the porn producer, has matured, I thought and has advanced to a higher plateau of artistic-entrepreneurial endeavor. So I invested.

In receipt for the 1.5 million dollar investment, you sent a certificate of financial involvement delineating the percentage of profits eventually due to me as a major investor. Wonderful. You also sent a Major Investor's Itinerary of cities in which filming would take place during Season One. Excellent. And you satisfactorily specified that the first—excuse my language, but such is your jargon—that the first "FuckFest" would take place at Buddies Sauna in Copenhagen. Appropriately specific.

To my frustration, however, each subsequent entry on the itinerary stated merely the city of FuckFest, noting "particular sauna to be determined." I ask your readers, Mr. Hahnemann, to consider: had they invested $1.5 million, the entirety of their retirement savings, would they not feel a tad uncomfortable at such vagueness? All I knew of you, Mr. Hahnemann, were your prospectus, your past titillating yet poorly crafted porn films, and the web-posted copy of a diploma certifying your completion of a Film Studies degree from the University of California, Santa Barbara, a credential which, even if valid, guaranteed nothing of your ability to make good on any but the most theoretical aspects of your proposed venture.

With the sobriety so typical of post-investment regret, I asked myself: what had I done, investing my entire nest egg with you? Why on Earth had I flung caution to the winds, departing utterly and resoundingly from the Aesopian tortoise-rather-than-hare, slow-and-steady-wins-the-race approach previously guiding my lifetime of investment decisions? I reasoned that the libidinous fantasy stimulated by your prospectus must have short-circuited my usual cold logic, prompting me to abandon tried and true practices of due diligence and principles of diversification. Alas, whatever the reasoning (or lack thereof), I was forced to acknowledge that my investment had been made. I grew increasingly anxious.

Also, in my defense, I should suggest that the frailty of my decision-making could also be explained by the nervous exhaustion resulting from my having been terminated after thirty-five years of employment at a Boston mutual fund complex where I had, for decades, dutifully drafted literature promoting newly designed financial vehicles whose genuine objectives bore less relation to their touted goals of enriching investors, than to their aggregation of clients' money into a pool from which my employer, the investment advisor, could extract a variety of questionably legitimate fees. One late winter morning, my boss, a clean-shaven relatively recent Wharton graduate whose ostentatious gold Rolex watch was clearly intended to boast the size of his anticipated annual bonus, summoned me from my cubicle into his corner office, only to inform me that the company had decided to take promotional literature "in a new direction," one that "would certainly rub you the wrong way," so "we're showing you the kindness of allowing early retirement." And, "remember that you're fully vested in our Defined Contribution Plan, so you'll be rich as Croesus" (as if that moron understood the classical source of this cliché reference).

I felt at that moment an impulse to lunge over the surface of his tidy faux walnut desk, clasp his anorexic neck in my grip and squeeze as if ringing out a wet t-shirt of the kind he had surely worn in Acapulco during many a spring break to shield his pasty shoulders from being kissed by the sun or any other south-of-the-border deity, that sexless little closet case. However, knowing that others would see through his office's glass wall and most likely rush to intervene, thereby frustrating my efforts and landing me in prison without my at least having achieved sufficient satisfaction to make the loss of freedom worthwhile, I restrained myself.

Nevertheless, the impulse lingered, the desire, the secret longing. That night of my firing and every day for weeks, I fantasized vengeance—should I leave threats on his office voicemail, for example, and then binocular-watch his tremulous saliva-drooling expressions of trepidation? Gun him down in the produce section of the local Stop-and-Shop and enjoy his spurts of blood onto ripening cantaloupes? Perhaps tamper with the brakes on his hot pink Mercedes, then tailgate him down Rte. 9 during an ice storm until he crashed so that I could enjoy yanking his severed limbs from the wreckage? Lie in wait and follow him to his suburban, wooded, Chestnut Hill home, force my way through his front door and shove him down his kitchen garbage disposal piece by piece in mimicry of that British serial killer, Denis Nilsen, who was caught after having clumsily clogged his toilet plumbing with too many body parts? Set fire to that mock Tudor house, then revel in peeling charred barbecued flesh from bone?

. . .

I see how you cringe, Mr. Hahnemann. How delicate your sensibilities must be. But you have sought my truth, have you not? And my truth is what it is. So I advise you to gird your loins unless you wish me to cease explication of the text that is myself. Shall I continue?

. . .

Thank you.

Of course, none of those murder fantasies were practical, given how traceable all proper revenge attacks have become nowadays, what with hidden video cameras, DNA swabs, digital fingerprints, and the teachings of television's *Forensic Files* about the magical properties of blood-detecting luminol. Nevertheless, as I fantasized, I was vaguely reminded of pubescent erections pressed against a mattress when feeling an urge one could not even identify with clarity, let alone satisfy. I could not yet appreciate the extent to which repressed adolescent longings were slowly being set to simmer.

During my forced early retirement, I spent day after day pacing around my Back Bay condo, strolling through Boston's snow-crunchy Public Garden, taking amusement in ill-clad shivering tourists roaming Paul Revere's historic North End, gorging on cheap eats at Faneuil Hall and along Boston Harbor's redesigned waterfront. How much satisfaction could one garner from feeding returning pigeons day after day? How many times could one indulge in the abundance of Sargents and Copley's and Japanese armaments at the Museum of Fine Arts, exquisite as they may be?

Oh, I know what you're thinking—another highly cultured killer, *très* cliché. Let me remind you that the vast majority of murderers throughout history (a lumpen among whom the to-and-fros of history have tossed me) have not at all been aficionados of high culture. Besides, my primary cultural "vice," if you deem connoisseurship as such, is not at all opera, which is the standard Hollywood cliché killer's penchant. So, I am not in any way a stereotype.

You see, Mr. Hahnemann, for me, the epitome of artistic expression is visual art, the successful capturing of human visage and/or emotion and/or hope, desire, fear, longing on canvas or textile, in clay or stone, the manipulation of color and shape and form, especially 20th-century art with its cubist manipulation of torso and face, its post-Rodin twisting, its location of beauty in the tortured distortion of human form—

. . .

What's that you say, Mr. Hahnemann?

. . .

You, yourself, attended art history classes at university? So there you have it: a basis for mutual understanding, don't you think? Perhaps even kindred esthetic sensibilities? How I could expound upon the value of artistic—

. . .

Ah, yes…well…fine. I beg pardon for the digression, although the elaboration of my mindset does provide illumination of my psyche in general. The point, Mr. Hahnemann, that I began to make a moment ago is that I grew increasingly anxious as I contemplated the investment of my life savings—$1.5 million!—with you. What had I done? How could I be certain that you truly would produce The Grand Sex Tour in the first place? That the contestants you had vowed to gather actually existed? That they were hot enough to generate broad interest and income? After all, I'd watched enough of your porn films to know the unevenness of your casting eye. What assurance had I that your proposed hidden cameras would function as claimed? That they even existed? That the competition would, indeed, be live-streamed online? That gambling would ensue? That I would eventually receive my proper due, rather than some unaccounted-for, meager royalty or—horrors—total loss? If this were a scam, could I take my case to court and insist upon the return of my investment? I ask you, Mr. Hahnemann: which judge would deign to hear a case concerning an investment in a series of furtively filmed "FuckFests"?!

Yes, I certainly should have taken all these doubts into consideration before investing in the first place. Still, I had been, as I indicated earlier, swept up by your seductive prospectus, only afterward to be overcome by—not exactly buyer's remorse, but buyer's worry. Exhausted from sleep loss due to my increasingly obsessive worry, I decided to rely upon the only person I could trust—myself. I would track you personally by following you and your boys around Europe, and I would attend the FuckFests in person.

Certainly, I would not announce to the boys at the various saunas that I was one of their prime patrons. To do so would be to distract them, to inspire them to faun upon me, thereby potentially causing them to lose opportunities to score a maximum number of tricks—my money was riding on the success of their promiscuity during competition, after all. But I did wish to be *among* their tricks. Was I not entitled to sample my investments? What was the harm in pinching the grapes one was placing in bins for sale? In sniffing a handful of coffee beans whose roasting one had financed? Was I not entitled to the same right as any other entrepreneur? The investor's right? Yes, the excursion to Europe would allow me to keep an eye on my investment as well as to enjoy modest pleasure, the chance to be rescued from depression by both the muse of art (whom I picture draped in ancient Greek robes, breastless like the Columbia Pictures logo woman) and the muse of sex (whom I picture as a disembodied, ever-spewing phallus of enormous proportion).

I embarked upon my trip. The rest, as the saying goes, is history.

My Memories: Copenhagen—Tivoli

I slept in and missed breakfast (jet lag), then sent the boys off with Burt. He rented 'em all bicycles to spend the day cycling in the countryside—gotta keep 'em fit. But I needed a relaxing day just for myself because I'm so fucking L.A.—me me me me me. So I spent the day shopping alone on Strøget, Copenhagen's pedestrian shopping mall. Pretty damn amazing and way bigger than Rodeo Drive: five connected avenues paved in cobblestones with old buildings everywhere, green copper roofs, big and small shops selling clothes, silver, porcelain, Legos, jewelry, everything. Bought a coupla Samsøe & Samsøe t-shirts and scarves as souvenirs at Magnus Department Store, then a big burger and strawberry shake at Café Norden.

Later, I met Burt and the boys in front of Tivoli Gardens—that's the amusement park that gave Disney the idea for Disneyland way back when.

Only 99DKK admission ($15)—mucho cheaper than Disney—so not a big splurge even for the ten of us.

I didn't want the boys to do any of the wild rides because what if a gear broke or something and the boys crashed and burned—literally? I cared about those boys even though I hardly knew 'em. I was kinda like their coach. They counted on me to take care of 'em. Besides, if I had to cancel the Tour after I already laid out all the expenses, how could I explain to our Italian and Russian Mafia investors, the Mexican drug cartel investors, the Al-Qaeda arms dealer investors, the secret Wall Street brokerage investors, and Kim Jong Un (shhh!) that the show's canceled and their money's gone? I'd be on an international (s)hitlist with nowhere to hide. (Burt told me that the Russians and Wall Streeters were already emailing about interest payments even though I'd explained upfront there'd be at least half a year lag-time. Why is it that those who've already got money are the greediest?)

But the boys whined about wanting to go on the rides, and Burt promised good video footage we could splice into the final director's cut of the competition. Okay, I gave in. During the Golden Tower ride (not Golden Shower ride, you pervs), when those seat compartments made a sudden drop from high up, our Big Bill (think Paul Bunyan on steroids) held tiny Little Frenchie on his lap. Bill's massive arms wrapped around him, snuggling him tight like a poodle. Both roared all the way down.

But not Manny, our Puerto Rican fresh off the boat from San Juan (lean, wiry, jet black goatee, café-con-leche complexion I just wanted to lick all over 'til I guzzled his *crema*). Manny sat rigid and silent the whole ride, kept getting paler and paler, stepped off after, and puked in the grass. Yuki (our only Asian, with a lean swimmer's build so perfect I just knew he could win an Olympic medal if he tried) supported puking Manny with an arm across his chest and a hand on his forehead. Yuki even tugged a tissue from his pocket and wiped Manny's mouth. I never met any other Japanese immigrants, but if they're all as nice as Yuki, then I'm feeling really bad that Roosevelt stuck 'em in concentration camps during WWII.

Keeping up with our multi-culti international image, we ate dinner at Belgrade Buffet. Burt got the manager's permission to video the buffet "for our Hollywood sports team film:" salads, goulash soup, sausages, potato pie, dumplings, mushroom stew, roast lamb, potatoes, porks, greens, desserts, breads. Carlesberg beer. Super footage for foodie interludes in the final director's cut film. A real doll of a waitress brought us soup and drinks. Philipa. She flirted a little with a coupla the boys. Waste of her time, poor kid. I wanted to say, "Honey, save your cleavage for men who notice," but left a thirty percent tip instead, even though we served most of the meal to ourselves from the buffet. Ain't I decent?

During the whole meal, we kept hearing screaming from outside like someone was being mauled. Creepy-scary. Turned out it was peacocks in a tree, screeching like crazy. If I was superstitious, I'd think they were sounding an alarm warning about what was gonna happen here in Copenhagen, something like, "Get out now! Get out now!" But I didn't know. I couldn't possibly have known, okay? So don't go blaming me!

By the time we left the restaurant, it was dark outside, and Tivoli was all lit up: red-blue-green lights outlined the small lake; multi-colored lights draped a Chinese pagoda; white lights hung on other buildings. The rides were partly lit up, too. Fairy tale magical.

Lotsa people of all ages. A pathetic classic pop concert. Then Motown onstage that was a little better. The boys wanted to stay, so we did, and Burt filmed. On my cell phone, I made a *Note to Self: don't wait 'til the final director's cut, just post tourism footage on our website between FuckFests to keep subscribers coming back all week. We want audiences to get to know the boys, to get crushes on 'em, to care about what happens to each one. That'll raise subscribers' interest in betting on which boy'll earn the most orgy points at each FuckFest, and that'll turn into more dough for us.*

As the evening went on, Big Bill and Little Frenchie looked at each other more and more in *that* way. Then Big Bill started marching around with Little Frenchie sitting on his shoulders and bopping other boys on top of their heads with a soup ladle he'd stolen from the restaurant. That made me nervous. Not the bopping or the stealing (hey, I'd left a great tip), but the heat you could just feel growing between those two. And I'd assigned them to be roommates! If Big Bill fucked Little Frenchie, he'd split him like firewood. So, after we got back to the hotel, I reminded the boys of my no-fucking-each-other rule because they gotta save every drop of energy for the FuckFests.

Soon as we got to our hotel room, Burt and I switched on the closed-circuit hidden camera from Big Bill's-Little Frenchie's room to make sure we didn't lose the little guy.

Hidden Camera Transcript: Big Bill and Little Frenchie

They're naked but for Bill's pale blue boxers and Frenchie's red thong. Their two single beds are shoved together, and their gold comforters have been turned down. "I'm so happy we're roommates," says Little Frenchie, curling up like a puppy on Big Bill's broad, smooth, muscular chest.

With eyes closed, Big Bill plants a kiss on Little Frenchie's straight blond hair. "Your hair tastes sweet."

"It's my hair gel. Want me to suck you?" Little Frenchie reaches down and gropes.

"Against the rules." Big Bill pulls Little Frenchie's hand up to his lips and kisses the fingers' small tips. "Just lemme hold you."

"Will you get jealous when you see me sucking lots of men at the FuckFest?"

"Do you want me to be jealous?"

"I wouldn't mind."

Another kiss on top of Frenchie's head. "I'll get jealous if I see you cuddling some other guy. But sucking? Nah."

"Do you have a thing for small blonds?"

"Maybe I just have a thing for Canadians."

"Really?" Little Frenchie lifts his head, looks into Big Bill's brown eyes.

"Just kidding." Big Bill squeezes him. "Or maybe not. You Canadians are friendlier than most Americans."

Little Frenchie again reaches down and gropes Big Bill, who's getting thicker.

Big Bill again retrieves Little Frenchie's hand. "Rules are rules. I learned that from body-building competitions. We shouldn't blow our wads before tomorrow's FuckFest. I've been saving up for a week."

"So romantic." Little Frenchie strokes Big Bill's biceps. "I always wanted a big muscle hunk all for my own."

"Now you got one." Big Bill rolls Little Frenchie off his chest and onto the bed, looks down into his eyes, kisses him deeply. "Mmmm, peppermint toothpaste."

"Please, Bill? I need you. You don't have to cum."

"Like I could stop myself. Better not start. I love cuddling you, don't get me wrong. But if my heart goes too lovey-dovey, I'll never be able to compete."

"Fine," says Little Frenchie, wriggling out from under Big Bill's embrace. "Have it your own way, as you Americans always do." He slides off the bed.

"C'mmon Frenchie, don't get pissed."

"Just because I'm small doesn't mean I don't get frustrated." Little Frenchie minces into the bathroom with an exaggerated wiggle of his uplifted butt. He slams the door shut.

Big Bill mutters, "What the fuck?" He stares at the bathroom door, does not follow.

My Memories: Copenhagen—Post-FuckFest

At 4:00 AM, when I returned to the hotel, I was totally jacked. The first FuckFest episode was a whopping success! (Except, of course, for the murder, but I didn't know about that yet, so don't get on my case for being excited at first.)

I'd been so damn nervous because everything was riding on this "gamble" (pun intended). Great in theory, but in practice? Yes! Yippee! Burt was right—I was a genius! It'd only be a matter of time before the money'd come rolling in, and I could pay off the investors and get 'em off my back. Everything else'd be gravy for Burt and me. And the boys, of course.

Weird name for a bathhouse in Denmark—"Buddies"—but it was the perfect decision (mine, by the way) to use the city's largest "sauna" (what Europeans call bathhouses) for our first episode. It was in a university neighborhood, so I knew there'd be tons of hot young studs on a Saturday night. I love Europe, where you don't need IDs to enter saunas, just money. Europeans've got their priorities straight: they don't give a crap who cocksuckers are as long as they pay and swallow.

Good ol' Burt had gotten me a non-descript beige van so I could park anywhere without attracting attention. In the van, I followed the hotel shuttle driving Burt and the boys to Buddies. Then I drove the van round and round, nearly puked at first when I couldn't find a parking spot close enough for the remote video camming to work. It wasn't like I could ask the police for a special permit to park close "because, officer, I need to secretly film a gay FuckFest that I'll be broadcasting live-stream online for a shitload of money, which probably isn't exactly a legal thing to do in your country, but I'm an American and you wouldn't want me to complain to my congressman and recommend that the U.S. stick tariffs on Danish pastry, would you, so just be a doll and give me a permit, okay?" Finally, I found a spot only a few blocks away alongside Vor Frue Kirke (Church of Our Lady), the city's main cathedral. A quick glance at the van's live-stream video screens showed that the boys were still checking in at Buddies and getting their locker key wristbands, so I had a few minutes.

I got an incredible idea for additional Denmark footage, so I jumped outta the van and walked right through the cathedral's wide-open doors. According to entrance posters in English, this was some free-to-the-public evening called "God Bless You Deep," with airy-fairy electronic music playing from the altar. The church was 19th-century, neo-classical style. White pillars and Thorvaldsen's famous gigantic white marble statues of apostles lined both sides of the nave. (My college art history courses dozens of moons ago were finally paying off.) Candles were lit all around the church. Incense. Red lights focused on the altar's colossal Jesus statue mixed with a blue light to give the illusion that his outstretched arms were moving. Whoa! I found the caretaker and asked if the cathedral could ever be rented for private Hollywood filming. He gave me the email address to write to. But we'd have no time for that in our remaining two days here.

I jotted down *Another Note to Self: if we return to Copenhagen for some future season, request filming permission in the cathedral, but don't explain specifics, just say, "Hollywood reality TV show featuring churches of Europe." The real idea would be to film the boys frolicking naked inside the cathedral in front of Jesus, whose outstretched arms would look like he was blessing our show. Burt could film the boys clinging naked onto the supersized apostle statues.*

Another Note to Self: check with a lawyer if the Danish Church could sue.

I climbed back into the van and started watching the live-stream screens just as the boys got to roaming around Buddies in their white towels. The footage was all streaky in the showers, but that didn't matter because nobody was fucking around in there. I was pissed that their headband cameras didn't work so well in the first-floor steam room—I couldn't see shit for the steam. But thank God the filming worked perfectly in the second-floor private cabin shadows. Filming was a little dark in the third-floor maze where I could hear the clinking of a sling's chains and lotsa grunts, but clear enough. The only problem was that the boys didn't always tilt their headband cameras at the best angles to capture all the juicy parts. *Note to Self: arrange for Burt to give a tutorial on positioning cameras during sex to get the best footage. And for future seasons, give the tutorial before the first FuckFest.*

A good thing Burt was in the sauna: I directed him via his micro ear receiver to film extra shots with his own headband camera. He got super shots of Tommy fucking half a dozen different guys in the third-floor sling. Even though Tommy'd written on the contestant application that he was a top, I didn't really believe it because he's so fey—just goes to show, you never can tell a top from a bottom just by looking. A real stud fairy queen. After Tommy left, our Jewish bear, Sam, jumped into the sling to be gang-banged by a bunch of Danes. *Note to Self: remind Sam there are no extra points for getting fisted.*

Then I wrote *Another Note to Self* that totally freaks me out now because it was like I could see the future even though I didn't know I could. So here's the note*: if I ever wanna write a murder mystery, set it in Buddies's third-floor maze— nearly pitch black with dead-end corners. Easy to strangle or stab. Death rattle would sound like sex grunts or chains. If any cruising guy stumbled on the corpse in the dark, he'd assume it was some drunk or junkie or maybe just kinky shit and would move on. Plenty of time for the murderer to escape into shadows—and remember, no ID check to enter a sauna, so the murderer could get off scot-free.* Like I said, this note freaks me out now. Maybe I should get a job with Walter Mercado's Psychic Friends Network or something if that shit's still going on. Maybe Manny'd know since he and Mercado are both from Puerto Rico. (But Manny's not talking to me anymore, so forget that inside connection.)

I also wrote an *Additional Note to Self: coach Manny not to waste time on affection. He's a sweet kid, but he wastes time hugging, caressing, even kissing each trick right after he gets 'em to cum. Like he really cares. Cute, but better to use the time for more jerking and sucking although maybe: are all PR's like him? All Latinos? Maybe keep him the way he is so we capture the Latin audience better, and Republican fetishists? Think about it.*

Everyone wanted Freddy. No surprise—how many Black men showed up in Copenhagen? Besides, he could'a been pink with purple polka dots and he'd still have been fucking gorgeous: his smooth flat chest muscles and rippled abs made him look steel-plated, his broad back was shaped a perfect "V." Massive, muscled arms, thighs, calves. Thick dimpled butt cheeks. To keep things interesting, he wore kelly green contact lenses that made his eyes look practically like neon signs, and he dyed his short fuzzy Afro strawberry red. His seven-inch cut cock was always hard with the kind of gentle curve that you just knew would hit a fuckee's prostate at the perfect spot to make him shoot a whopper load.

Older men flocked to him like hummingbirds to red sugar water, and he went with it. He sucked as much as he got sucked. Fucked as much as he got fucked. He always managed to whip a condom outta nowhere. Where did he carry 'em? The weird thing was he walked around with no expression on his face even when cumming. Hey, Freddy, it's okay to show pleasure! *Note to Self: coach Freddy to show joy…or is it better to leave him naturally stony so the ice queen subscribers can relate?*

Big Bill stormed through the second floor like some Tom of Finland sketch come-to-life, grabbing anyone he wanted, shoving 'em into a cubicle and to their knees or pretzeling 'em and rutting like Paul Bunyan plowing a virgin field. He held his camera overhead like a pro. *Note to Self: during Burt's camera tutorial, use Bill as an example.*

Little Frenchie was better than any Dyson vacuum cleaner—sucked like a champ. He was so small he kept crawling through legs in the third-floor maze, popping up and cock-gobbling guys before they even knew he was there. Gotta give him loads of points for that. How is it his jaw didn't get tired? Even with a small mouth, he deep-throated giant cocks to the root. Amazing. *Note to Self: before the season ends, try out Little Frenchie yourself if you can.*

Our blond WASP, Dean, seemed beyond a cold fish. Lutefisk. Green-eyed Freddy seemed indifferent, and Big Bill was aggressive, but blond Dean was downright mean, especially when he set his jutting square jaw hard. He'd just stand there, all tall string bean lean with those thick eraser nips, like he didn't give a flying fuck and was waiting for men to notice the outline of ten inches through his towel. And waiting for them to kneel. Which they did, one after another. He probably slayed the twinks in those Chicago Boystown bars and baths back home. I caught him spitting on half a dozen cocksuckers, slapping a few who said something in Danish ("yes, master"?). Spit and slaps made 'em suck faster, gagging and loving it. One sucker pulled Dean's hands around his throat. That's the only time I saw a smile on Dean's face—as he slowly squeezed. The sucker sucked and jerked himself off and spurted all over the floor, but Dean held his grip. Then the sucker's eyes started bulging, and he had to pry hard to get Dean's fingers off. He coughed a lot and cursed something in Danish before skulking away, looking over his shoulder. Dean's smile lingered. Creeped me out big time.

Thank God for Yuki. When he grinned, you melted and forgot he was foreign. Lean muscular, and practically no body hair of course. Totally versatile. Especially affectionate to all the silver daddies and other oldies who groped and licked him like he was one head-to-toe cock. He'd make a fortune being a private escort in a gay old-age home. *Note to Self: for my next project, consider providing escorts to gay senior centers in pervy rich places like West Palm Beach.*

Audio from the boys' cams picked up the loud thumpity-thump music with strong bass rhythms all night. Lotsa grunts and moans and sometimes even screams—natural sound effects. *Note to Self: I didn't think about this before, but I can save money on music tracks for the final director's cut film by using each sauna's music and sex sounds. Super! Just add music to cover the touristy scenes. You're so smart, Paulie boy, you didn't even know you were figuring out a way to save time and money, but you were.*

Finally, after the van footage showed Burt leading the boys down to the locker room at 4:00 AM—good old Burt, adhering to schedule even when exhausted—I flipped off the van's video feeds, left Burt to get the boys back to the hotel, drove the van back myself, and flopped into bed with a laptop to type up my *Notes to Self.* Burt arrived, collapsed into bed beside me and, in seconds, was snoring up an earthquake.

I snuggled up close to my chubby hubby. We'd sure as hell come a long way, baby. I'd started in the business world as a kid way back when, spending summers selling salt-water taffy in Dad's Atlantic City Boardwalk shop. Back then, I thought that was gonna be my whole future. Then Ma, who was forever tinkering with toys in the basement instead of fixing us dinner, got a job designing radio-controlled toy airplanes for ToyMaker out in SoCal where we all moved when I was fourteen. "Turn your hobbies into your passions," Ma taught me, "and one day you'll make a mint. But first you gotta stop diddling your peepee every chance you get. No son of mine's gonna turn into an f-ing sex maniac."

Ma was sharp as shit.

After the move, Dad spent years trying and failing to get a salt-water taffy business off the ground on the Santa Monica Pier. Spring of my senior year in high school, the week after I turned eighteen, Ma got canned because the memos she wrote trying to explain her sophisticated designs weren't up to snuff. "So what if I ain't no English major?" she whined. They both went on benders most afternoons, which I guess was how one of Ma's soldering irons started a house fire.

Rushing outta the school bus, I couldn't get into the house for all the firemen, police, EMTs. Kinda freaked me out to tell you the truth. That fire practically burned 'em into charcoal. After that, I could never eat at a barbecue without balling my eyes out, which the high school psychologist said was a good thing because "you're otherwise not displaying proper grief, Paulie, but seem to be developing a defensive shell."

Whatever. I just wish they'd lived long enough to see me hitting it big with this Grand Sex Tour idea. Hey, Ma, I'm a success! Look at me, Dad, I'm making it rich! But I kinda think they'd shit all over the sex part of the project, so maybe it's just as well they're six feet under.

At least I've got my Burt. The two of us showing the world what we can do. Who'd have imagined when we got started back in college? My first two years at the University of California, Santa Barbara didn't go so great because the profs kept telling me I had the brains—like I needed 'em to tell me that— but that my writing was kinda fucked up, like it was "from two different sides of the track that fail to sync up in the middle." Over and over, I heard crap like, "I don't know how to grade this essay because your ideas are so good, but your writing's so bad." Yeah, well, blame my Atlantic City, NJ elementary school that didn't teach me shit, followed by SoCal's El Segundo Unified School District where high school English classes were all about self-expression and self-esteem, not "proper academic prose tone and register," like those UCSB douchebag profs were on my case about.

Ma was right—what the hell difference did it make if my papers sounded like Shakespeare or some kid hollering to his homies while rollerblading down the Venice Beach boardwalk, as long as my ideas were aces? Those profs thought because they lived down the road from Montecito multi-millionaire celebs and exiled British royalty, that they were special. Whose book are you kicking back and reading now, Herr Professors? Each other's? No, you're reading *mine*! With me using "proper grammar, diction, register, and tone" when I feel like it, but not busting my balls all the time because sometimes I feel like writing the way normal people talk. Like Ma did.

By the way, at least one of *your* colleagues thought my language was top-notch. She was the coolest prof on the faculty by far, a feminist lesbian. Film Studies. She got tenure for a book about "porn as an expression of popular cultural oppression, a reaction to capitalist imposition of body-commodification as labor recourse for those in a society lacking Marxist dignification options." After one class with her junior year, I knew I wanted to major in Film Studies. That's where I met Burt. We'd just spent a three-hour class watching a homo gangbang compilation that, the professor explained, "manifested the versatility and fluidity of male-male power dynamics in marked contrast to the normative male-female domination scenarios prevalent in hetero porn (except for dominatrix films involving rigid role-playing)."

Seeing me stare at his boner as we stepped out of the dark lecture hall into sunlight, Burt asked if I wanted to go study with him in his dorm. "My roommate's out at a lab all afternoon," he said, practically dripping saliva. Soon as we reached his room, he dropped to his knees.

We signed up to be roomies for senior year. The first day of fall quarter, while we were watching a porn video and jerking each other off, Burt shot a lubed "Eureka!" finger up in the air as he spurted the idea of us doing a joint independent study: "Let's make our own porn film!" That feminist lesbian porn professor was thrilled to be our advisor, and said we could make any film we wanted as long as we wrote up an analysis of how it compared/contrasted with contemporary porn norms. "I want your analysis to reflect both the freshness of your ideas as well as the diction of the lumpenproletariat masses. There's no reason to separate art and scholarship from real life."

We didn't wanna make just another phony porn film with a director moving actors around like chess pieces. So, I came up with the idea of filming reality scenes like the Loud family'd done some years before in their PBS series, "An American Family." In case you're too young to remember: they filmed their family's daily lives in Santa Barbara—divorce, a faggot son, the whole reality shebang. *TV Guide* said it was one of the 50 greatest TV shows of all time. Good enough for *TV Guide* and PBS, good enough for Burt and me.

Since half the campus spent Saturday nights fucking anyway, why not get exhibitionist Theater Department majors to let us film 'em at their frat parties so they could get an independent film credit on their résumés? A whole group let us tag along weekend after weekend so Burt could film 'em chugging beer, tossing back vodka shots, puffing weed, popping pills, sucking and fucking their brains out. Burt and I edited it together, with me having the final say because I was the official director. I wrote up an analysis that Burt okay'd.

The professor loved our film and said our analysis, "written in an occasionally jarring juxtaposition of highbrow formal grammar and lowbrow Jersey Shore colloquialisms was nothing less than post-modern eclectic, linguistically revolutionary, a heterodoxical act of rebellion against straight white patriarchal orthodoxy insistent upon straitjacketing language as well as any other primal source of non-conformist expression. Your film and analysis are refreshingly transgressive in their naturalistic use of improvisational, illicit modalities that seek to fill the gap between legality and legitimacy." Yeah, well, whatever. As long as we got our A+.

We graduated summa cum laude, and she pulled strings to get us a joint internship with a porn production company in Van Nuys out in the San Fernando Valley. We spent a coupla years getting experience under our sticky belts, then started up our own porn production company. The rest is history.

Killer Interview 2

Excellent question, Mr. Hahnemann, as to how I recognized your boys. You correctly surmise that although I had invested in your Grand Sex Tour venture, I had never before seen the boys, nor they—me. It was thanks to the detailed prospectus you had posted online to solicit investment that I knew precisely how to find them. At Buddies Sauna, they were easily identifiable by those red-white-and-blue terrycloth headbands with small hidden micro-fiber video cameras bulging ever-so-slightly on their foreheads like so many miniaturized miners' lamps. I could monitor my investments, as hoped. And such a varied display of male pulchritude! One's mouth watered. You fulfilled your casting commitment, after all, Mr. Hahnemann. A true racial rainbow of the finest the male gender has to offer. I applaud you.

At the sauna, I observed how the various boys clumsily positioned their heads and cameras. I also spotted that lumbering slug of a cameraman who followed them around, directing his own camera headband in supplemental filming. To observe is to know is to understand how to avoid.

As a sixty-year-old man of experience, I am acutely aware that my appearance no longer lures young men as once it had. Most young men fail to recognize male-pattern baldness fringed with white hair as a testament to increased testosterone flow, just as they fail to appreciate the textural contrast of soft fatty tissue layer over decades-strong pectorals and well-exercised waist. Nor do they recognize the Samsonesque significance of a trimmed white mustache purposely waxed so that lengthy end curls protrude from the face in a metaphorical double-ended erection. Instead, these youngsters are likely to assume that a man my age is, by definition, unable to sustain the rigorous performance of younger years. Although this has often been true in my case, I have had my moments, particularly after receipt of patient oral stimulation: where do you think Maya Angelou found inspiration for her poem, "Still I Rise"?

. . .

Very well, Mr. Hahnemann, I grasp your impatience as well as your questioning whether my remarks are intended as serious commentary or flippant irony. If the latter, then I ask: must mayhem and murder always be regarded with absolute solemnity? Do you find utterly unbearable the lightness of my being?

. . .

Fine fine fine. To the point: I bided my time at Buddies. And I did my best to quell the constant irritation arising in reaction to the sauna's stereotypically brash background music—why not soothing melodies or moody jazz rather than fast-paced heavy bass beats? As if all sexual experience need be frenetic.

I noticed that several of your boys engaged in play with community elders. Hmmm…had I a chance, after all? However, not yet wishing their cameras to focus upon me—was one ready to be seen by the internet world while mid-fornication?—I held back, took pleasure in observing from a safe distance while noting which boy was enjoying what with whom. I saw that the little blond fellow—petite and smooth-skinned—spent the entire evening dropping to his knees, pleasuring one after another in this dark corner and that, squirreling among legs of orgiastic mobs. Such determination, such agility! Yet no one reached for the blond's own disproportionately large endowment. Not once did I see him issue release.

At approximately 4:00 AM, as I watched him attempt to suck his sweets in a corner from a tall and enormous Dane—how did he fit such girth down his narrow throat?—I noticed your slug of a supplemental cameraman round up your other boys. Wearily, they dragged themselves down the steep third-floor stairs. The evening's FuckFest had apparently come to a close. To be sure, the sauna's overall crowd had thinned considerably.

I followed them down a second flight of steep stairs to the first-floor locker room. Yes, your boys were dressing in preparation for departure. But they seemed to have forgotten their comrade, the little blond oralist. Admittedly, they were exhausted and bleary-eyed, but how forget one of their party? Was this the care shown to my investment assets? Clearly, your entourage lacked the ethics of U.S. marines.

I thought to say something, but doing so would have elicited unwanted attention and revealed myself as a knowledgeable investor. Perhaps the wisest course would be to scurry back to the third floor and interrupt the little blond, thereby prompting him to look around and realize the absence of his peers and, perhaps, to notice my modest need before joining his associates.

In the third-floor maze, he remained kneeling in the very same corner gorging on the very same Great Dane who, presumably having already gushed several times this evening, was now quite slow to achieving yet another eruption. The little blond continued bobbing head up and down, his hair wet with sweat and his headband askew with the camera directed up and left. I recall thinking, "As long as I stand to his right, the camera won't capture me." I tapped his shoulder. He shrugged my finger away. I yanked his shoulder, unintentionally pulling his mouth off his prize.

He glared up at me and said, "What the hell? Go away!" Just as he turned back to continue his thwurping, the Dane patted him on the head and left.

"You cost me a cum," the little blond hurled at me. "I was working hard for those cum points!" As if a Danish stranger would have the slightest clue as to his meaning, even assuming understanding of crude English slang. The fool.

He stood, yanked off his headband camera and clutched it in a tight angry fist, stomped toward the steep staircase leading down.

Irritated at having been thusly treated when my intention had been to show him a kindness, I followed across what was now a completely empty third floor. At the top of the stairs, I reached him, grabbed his shoulder once more, and spun him to face me. "You can earn your points from me," I said, unhitching my towel and displaying myself in pre-stimulation flaccidity.

He actually snickered and sneered.

I ask you, Mr. Hahnemann, was such callousness necessary? Wouldn't a soft, "no thank you" have been sufficient?

I did not at that moment reason the pros and cons of my ensuing action there at the top of the steep staircase. At certain times, one reacts to stimulus with unexamined reflex rather than with measured calculation. I readily acknowledge that I reacted spontaneously the way any man would to such a degrading insult: while re-hitching my towel with one hand, I gave the ungrateful little bugger a hard shoulder shove backwards with the other.

I doubt that he actually floated for a prolonged instant suspended in mid-air, but this is how memory records the moment: as he lost his footing, his blue eyes opened wide in surprise, his lips parted in the default circular shape so typical of avid cocksuckers, his arms flung out at his sides as if positioning for impalement upon a crucifix while he momentarily hovered…so angelic…before falling backward and down the steep stairs, somersaulting Humpty Dumpty thumpity thump thump thump, slamming his head again and again and again until he lay completely prone in an expanding pool of cranial blood.

I tiptoed down that steep staircase, my heart racing faster and faster.

He lay inert and twisted, his legs at odd angles to torso as if in some painting by Austria's Schiele, whose remarkable expressionistic oeuvre I hoped to see at Vienna's Belvedere, which houses a finer collection, from what I'd read, than the more popular Leopold Museum.

I touched fingers to the broken body's neck pulse point. To his inner wrist. I brought cheek to his nose and lips. No pulse, no breath. However, I could not help but notice the delicious pungent scent of so many gargled ejaculates emanating from his mouth. And those alluring bits of dried white crust flaking from the corners of his lips. He was a veritable seductor even in such a prone state.

Holding onto his wrist in vain search for a resurgent pulse, I found none. But, I did feel his skin gradually cool, grow clammy. Or was that my imagination?

Oh my, Mr. Hahnemann, I must admit that these sensory memories are serving even now, as I speak with you, to inspire a twinge of nostalgic arousal. Yes, to my surprise, while kneeling beside the deceased fellow, I suddenly sported a huge erection. Without any of the typically essential foreplay. It simply sprang up of its own accord: a huge woody distending my towel like a proverbial tent pole.

A startling revelation.

One felt an irrational impulse to bring that boy's clammy hand to oneself, to wrap the cooling flesh around one's own throbbing heat in soothing. However, one's desire was trumped by practical considerations: was anybody watching? I looked around: no one. The sauna's brash background music had most likely muffled, beyond the immediate vicinity of the staircase, the crashes of his fall. Where was his camera? The headband had flown away mid-flight, the camera's fiber-optic bulge now face down on a middle step. I stomped my heel upon it. Bits of wire protruded through cloth. I set it by his side.

Removing his towel, I sopped its corner in blood. Unable to resist a sudden, surprising urge, I gave the towel corner a quick suck, tasted the blood and felt my arousal intensify. As my heartbeat raced, I smeared the little whore's shoulders and knuckles clean of my fingerprints, not that they could serve law enforcement any comparative purpose because no prints of mine were on file with any law enforcement agency anywhere, this being my first "crime" (for which I should have been absolved under the legal justification of self-defense of dignity). I tossed his towel beside him—mightn't a towel quite naturally have flown off during such a tragic fall?

After tiptoeing over his remains, I sauntered with measured casualness down the next staircase to the first-floor locker room, where I looked around. No sign of the other boys who must have departed.

Still aroused beyond measure at the lingering sensation of that dead fellow's clammy skin, the coppery taste of his blood, and the unfulfilled fantasy the experience had inspired, I relieved myself in the shower…in body-shuddering orgasm. Oh, Mr. Hahnemann, one nearly shudders now in the re-telling. Such is the power of vivid memory.

After completing my cleansing, I dressed and left, all the while thinking, "One hopes that Mr. Hahnemann will not use the loss of his contestant as an excuse to delay investor re-payments."

. . .

Ah, you ask after one's conscience, Mr. Hahnemann: was I initially horrified? Did I feel at all guilty? Had murder been my intention? No and no and no.

I certainly felt sorry not to have been able to enjoy the little man's obviously talented oral skills. I felt sorry to have missed the chance of scolding him further. Yet I was not devoid of compassion, and felt sorry, too, for his having been so arrogant as to assume he never risked suffering repercussion for his gross rudeness to an elder. There are risks inherent in all misbehaviors. He'd undertaken his risk and now suffered for it. A lesson for the ages.

In ensuing days, as I reflected upon what some might deem my first ever "murder," inadvertent as it was, I found myself in a constant state of startled bemusement at the ecstatic nature of my physiological response not only at the time but also upon subsequent recollection: when poking about a Skagen store on Strøget in search of a souvenir wristwatch, while mingling among a crowd of tourists ogling the bronze sculpture of Hans Christian Andersen's fictitious Little Mermaid seated on a rock by the Langelinie promenade, even when strolling through the ramshackle, heavily graffitied, outdated hippie enclave of Christiania—each time I recalled the taste of blood and speculated as to the feel of that little blond's cold clammy hand upon my hot throbbing erection, I spontaneously threw another. I am not unproud to acknowledge, Mr. Hahnemann, that in those ensuing days, I sported erection after erection as I had not done since adolescence when mortified by my body's betrayal of hormone-induced gazing at this algebra teacher's muscular pectorals on display beneath a thin white shirt, or that gym teacher's thick hairy thighs protruding from white cotton running shorts. I had suddenly become, in older years, a wildly sexualized pubescent.

Was I now, at the age of sixty, discovering a new dimension of eroticism?

I grew curious as to whether my near-constant state of arousal had been sourced in my having (inadvertently) caused a death, having witnessed a death, or having pressed my flesh against that of a newly deceased cold, clammy, seductive corpse and having tasted blood. All of the above? Or was one ingredient in this newly discovered pleasure recipe more essential than the others? Furthermore, had my prior diminution of libido been the result of boredom with archaic, biblical only-with-the-living sexual straightjacketing? Oh, the tyranny of organized religion.

Armed with such questions, I wondered whether it might be possible to re-create circumstances sufficiently so as to re-encounter such joy. As any Lacanian sophisticate or adolescent masturbator knows, one fulfilling sexual experience leads to an endless string of others. (This, Dr. Stephen Hawking, is *my* string theory.) My point, Mr. Hahnemann, is that repetition and anticipation of repetition are the driving forces behind many a fulfilling human experience. I am human, *ipso facto*....

And one additional question arose in consciousness: was I prepared to undertake the risk inherent in facilitating another death? The very instant I posed this question, Mr. Hahnemann, I was struck by a realization as if by a Zeus thunderbolt: my recent remarkable arousal experience had not at all been entirely novel after all. Rather, it turned out to have been a vaguely familiar one that I had, for decades, been repressing, but that had now bubbled over the sealed yet roiling psychological pot, so to speak, had surged to the forefront of my psyche in a volcanic eruption of freedom.

Permit me to explain:

During childhood, I was shuttled from one foster home to another. At age thirteen, I spent a good year in one such home with a remarkably sexy foster father. He resided in the woods of upstate New York with a voluptuous wife who enjoyed clutching me to her more than ample bosom, whether from frustrated maternal instinct or pederastical inclination, I cannot say, but her pheromones sparked in me not an iota of lust. He, on the other hand, with his brawny chest and upper arms, full mustache, square jaw, wavy brown hair, underarm hint of faded Old Spice deodorant, and breath frequently smelling of cigars and beer, quickened my pulse with the slightest pat on the shoulder or tussle of my own then-curly locks.

Yet at the same time, I resented the chores with which he overburdened adolescent me—clearing out poison ivy and other underbrush, pruning branches, destroying rat nests, scraping rat turds off the wooden porch railing, burying poisoned rats, and on and on as though I were a slave laborer rather than a child to be bounced upon his lap and cuddled while watching professional wrestling together on television and ogling thick muscular sweaty bodies engaged in macho gladiator combat. Subliminally frustrated both by his sexual indifference and imposition of exhausting and revolting physical demands, I felt an ever-growing mix of pent-up desire and resentful rage, not that I could, at age thirteen, identify my confused psychological state as such.

Is it any wonder that one Sunday afternoon, the axe Freudian-slipped from my hand just at the moment I was swinging it down toward the log he was showing me how to chop, such that my axe severed toes from his foot? As he screamed "My left foot!" and collapsed, clutching at those severed bloody toes rolling out from his sliced boot, I fled to my room. Of course, I would later assert traumatic regret and shame, but what I actually felt at that moment was intense inexplicable arousal. In my room behind my shut door as Mrs. rushed Mr. to the hospital, I repeatedly masturbated feverishly while picturing myself shoving his dismembered bloody hairy little piggies into my mouth and rolling them around my tongue, feeling them cool and become clammy as every coppery drop of masculinity drained down my throat, as I swallowed that blood, ingested, digested so that Mr. would become part of me, so that I could carry him within myself always, so that one day I could grow up as big and strong and manly as he. The fantasy shocked me even as it thrilled me. The shock enhanced the thrill that, in turn, enhanced the shock that, in turn, intensified the thrill, etc. *ad spurtum infinitum.*

Fortunately for Mr., the reattachment surgery was successful, and he would eventually be able even to play soccer with his pals. However, during his initial months of incapacity, he increased my chores as a means for me to offer recompense for the consequences of "the accident."

Mrs., a pious sort, grew suspicious, and frequently reminded me of the Bible's cautionary verses about an eye for an eye and a tooth for a tooth. "There's nothing in there about a toe for a toe, so you might get off scot-free. Just the same, you better behave." She meant, of course, to issue a warning, but her teaching inspired a line of reasoning that justified my budding inclinations: if God Himself sanctioned mutilation and/or dismemberment under certain conditions, who was I to argue? Apparently, the maiming of others was biblically condoned. The only question remained: under which circumstances?

It seemed to me that maiming for the purpose of achieving ecstatic joy was as acceptable a circumstance as any other. Had I not been taught in history class that "the pursuit of happiness" was a fundamental American right?

Nevertheless, even at that tender age, I was savvy enough in the ways of the world to recognize that, regardless of my private theological justifications, my fantasies would meet with severe social disapproval if ever actualized. A timid sort, I feared prison, especially since, being a delicate young man, I would certainly be mauled if thrown into a lion's den; although I longed for the intimacy of men, the prospect of becoming a bloodied pulp of a vessel for indiscriminate, older male brutalization horrified me. No, I would do nothing to risk capture.

In order to prevent myself from succumbing to bloody desires and risking engagement in arrest-prompting behavior, I had to expunge lustful longings even from the realm of fantasy. Lying in bed as a teenager, masturbating to images of high school athletes I'd observed in the locker room with their various hardnesses and bulges, I shoved out of mind visions of myself biting off nipples and chewing them throughout the day as others might chew gum, of sucking in an entire testicle and severing it before chomping as if it were a hard-boiled egg (egg salad sandwiches being my all-time favorite picnic lunch). I stopped myself mid-fantasy from jabbing a knife into a lover's jugular and lapping the spurting blood during fornication, of mounting a giant and throttling him until his eyes bulged and tongue lolled at the very moment of mutual orgasmic ecstasy followed by a cuddle of his cold dead flesh throughout the night in the knowledge that such a lover could never flee my embrace. And so on.

Over time, I repressed these fantasies so successfully that I actually forgot about them, Mr. Hahnemann. How remarkable the power of the human mind.

No wonder my dating life was ever a source of dissatisfaction. No ordinary sexual experience could possibly satisfy, whether I were top, bottom, or somewhere in-between. I was forever seeking, but never finding because I would never permit myself to explore the natural predilections I'd so effectively buried below consciousness.

But then—that fortuitous encounter with the little blond fellow in Buddies served as a release of steam from the tightly sealed pressure cooker of my psyche. His death—the clamminess of his skin, the copperiness of his blood—somehow jolted a sense memory within, one connected to my primal adolescent sexuality. His death and the lust it inspired began a gradual resurrection of self. Of course, during my European foray, I did not wish arrest and confinement; however, as a man of sixty, I need no longer fear, as I had feared so profoundly in youth, becoming the object of incarceration gang-rape. My age freed me from the worst of my worries. Consequently, throughout my European adventure, I roused not so much from profound libidinous sleep as from self-induced sexual stupor. My true nature increasingly asserted itself, awakened. And so I embraced it, reveling in a Whitmanesque song of myself. I do hope you understand.

And that, in answer to your question, Mr. Hahnemann, has been the reaction of my conscience.

My Memories: Copenhagen—Post-FuckFest (cont'd)

My plan was to review the hours and hours of footage from all the hidden cameras in the boys' hotel rooms once we got back Stateside. Then I'd pick and choose for the director's cut film. But, once in a while, I spot-checked just to keep an eye on things, like I said before about Little Frenchie and Big Bill—to make sure the boys weren't fucking each other.

The morning after the first FuckFest, I got a surprise from the Tommy-Sam hidden camera. From the looks of things, they'd been together in the past, which was kind of against my rules although not exactly. I'd told the boys I didn't want couples in a relationship. But they weren't anymore, so I let it go. Too late to do anything about it now, anyway. If they'd had a bad break-up, that'd explain their sniping on the Queen's birthday. More divorce bitchiness would be great for the director's cut film, so maybe there was an upside.

Hidden Camera Transcript: Tommy and Sam

Naked but for his white towel, Tommy stands by the hotel room's blue curtains and looks out the window, speaking as if to the 17th-century, orange-roofed buildings across the canal. "Did I do okay last night? Macho enough?"

"You kidding? You looked like your feet were nailed to the floor in front of that sling. The man who fucked a thousand asses."

"Not yours."

"We don't get points for sexing each other," says Sam in bed, scratching his scruffy beard and rubbing his oily bald spot. He yawns. "And besides…you know."

"Yeah, I know."

"Anyone try to fuck you?" asks Sam.

"No, which is a first. Usually everyone assumes that because I sometimes embrace my feminine nature—"

"You can't blame them, Toms, the way you camp it up. And the way you comb your wavy red hair into—whatchamacallit, wings—sometimes you look totally fem."

"True, my lean pre-pubescent girlish figure doesn't help."

"Exactly. If you want everyone to take you as a top all the time, you need to act like it, just the way—"

"That attitude pisses me off. Why can't a female spirit in an androgynous man's body also be an aggressive top?"

"He can. You can. You were last night."

"Yeah, but only because I butched it up so I could score. I want to be desired as the complex mass of seeming contradictions that I am."

Sam stands naked from the bed, steps over to Tommy, wraps his thick hairy arms around him. "I used to desire you for the weirdo you are. For a long time."

"But not anymore, right?"

Sam steps back. "Toms, we've been through this."

"Why won't you let me fuck you? Last night you opened your furry ass more times than the automatic doors at Bloomingdale's during a post-Christmas sale. But you won't open up for me anymore."

"Come on, Toms."

"And then you go insult me when the whole group's together."

"To throw them off track, you know that. We agreed. So nobody knows we've got a history.   Paulie doesn't want contestants who are in a relationship."

"We *aren't*. We *were*."

"I still love you, Toms, but I'm just not *in* love with you anymore."

"Fine…but do you have to come down on me so hard in public? Like when I was having fun singing on the Queen's birthday?"

"To throw them off track, Toms. But I guess I don't have to be actively hostile. Just not lovey-dovey."

"Like ordinary friends in public, okay? Can you at least give me that?" Tommy presses against Sam.

"How can you possibly get a hard-on this morning after cumming so many times last night?"

"I only came twice. Besides, you're the only hairy pudge I want to sink into." Tommy lets his white towel drop. "I can't get enough of you. That's what love is, right?" He reaches around, caresses Sam's cheeks, squeezes. "God, you're so thick and beautiful. Your furry ass drives me crazy. Your scent."

Sam reaches a hand down to Tommy's crotch, slowly pumps him up and down.

"You know how to jerk an uncut cock better than anyone," says Tommy, nearly breathless.

"And you're the only female-spirited twink top man to drive me wild." Sam lifts his hand, wipes Tommy's slickness on his belly, backs away. "Who used to drive me wild. But not anymore, Toms."

"Fucking cocktease."

"I'm sorry." Sam turns, tugs on a pair of gray sweatpants, picks up the remote control and clicks at the TV.

Tommy turns back toward the window, looks out again, places a splayed palm on the glass as if grasping at something.

My Memories: Copenhagen—Post-FuckFest Brunch

The morning after the FuckFest, Burt panned his video camera over the post-FuckFest hotel brunch buffet table, getting great foodie footage for both the director's cut film and touristy website interludes: "Wanna know how to feed your sexual energy? Watch what our sex stars eat to fuel their stamina and lust!" Baskets of white rolls (crispy outside, fluffy inside), pumpernickels with sunflower seeds on top, and croissants. Loaves of crusty white bread half-wrapped in cloth tea towels so you could hold it and cut your own slice without touching it with your ass-wipe dirty fingers. Trays of Danishes—some with custard or a fruit center, others swirled with cinnamon or chocolate. Paté loaves, hard and soft cheeses, three kinds of marmalade, gold-wrapped tabs of organic butter, reduced-fat spread, honey, preserves. A platter of cold cuts. Porridge with bananas and chocolate sauce mixed in. Cold cereals. Bowls of hard-boiled eggs, sliced cucumbers, carrots, tomatoes. Cut-up melons, pineapple, oranges, and bowls of fresh plums and pears. Huge punch bowls filled with fruit yogurt and plain; side bowls of toppings—granolas, seeds, dried fruits. Coffee, teas, dispensers for milk and juices—apple, orange, water. So healthy!

Most of the boys sat with Burt and me at a big round table (I know about team-building): Manny and Yuki, Dean, Tommy and Sam, Bill. But no Little Frenchie—I figured he must be sleeping in. Then I noticed that green-eyed Freddy was sitting off at a little table by himself.

I went over to him because...well.... "Hey, Freddy." I tussled his strawberry red hair, then massaged his muscled back a few minutes. "How you doing this morning?" I sat down across from him.

"Fine, Mr. Hahnemann, thanks."

"What's with the 'Mr.' crap? I told you guys, I'm Paulie. Call me Paulie."

"Sure thing, Paulie."

"Why're you sitting alone here, Freddy, instead of at the big table with the rest of us? Your roommate Yuki doesn't like you? Maybe the other boys are jealous?"

"Yuki's a sweetheart, always asking if I want to use the john before him, the shower before him, if it's okay to keep the light on a few more minutes so he can read. The other guys are okay, too, I guess. I just need a little quiet time, you know? Last night was intense."

"For sure. In that case, I'll leave you be. But before I shove off—you gotta eat more than a coupla rolls, Freddy. Keep up your strength after all the energy you put out last night. How's about some hard-boiled eggs? Protein. Of the chicken kind—I know you swallowed gobs of the human kind, but that's not proper nutrition." I forced a guffaw.

He didn't laugh, just said, "Yeah," and dropped his head. "Yeah."

"You're tops, Freddy, tops. One of the best guys. I can tell already after just our first FuckFest. Nobody sexed more men than you."

"Thanks, Paulie." His voice got soft, almost like he didn't wanna speak.

"You seem kinda down, Freddy. Anybody hurt you last night and I didn't see? Or say something…you know…nasty about…well…? I know you Black guys get dumped on a lot back home. But I don't know how it all goes down here in Europe."

Freddy looked up at me then. "No problems like that. But thanks. Really—thanks."

"Any of our other boys bothers you that way, you send him to me and I'll set him straight, you hear? You're a good man, and I won't put up with racist shit."

Did his eyes get a little red? "My dad used to say things like that. Worrying about how other people treated me, especially the police, you know? Especially after I came out. Dad worried a lot on my account."

"I'm old enough to be your pops, that's for sure." I tugged on my gray sideburns. "But I'd need to work on my tan first, don'tcha think?"

That got a grin out of him.

"You're all my boys, you hear me? Each of you. You included. I'm here if something's eating at you."

He nodded and looked down. "Thanks, Paulie." Then he breathed in deep through his nostrils, sighed the air all out, shoved his seat back hard. "Time to go grab those eggs." He stood and walked to the buffet table. *Note to Self: keep an eye on Freddy. If he gets depressed, you could lose one of your big draws. Missing his pops?*

Back at the main table, the boys were all teasing each other about who'd swallowed the most jizz last night, whose ass must be sorest, whose dick must be totally used-up limp.

"Who's in the lead according to the computer?" asked Tommy. A few granola flakes fell out of his mouth when he talked.

I'd prepped for this question, was ready to lie through my teeth. Of course there was no computerized algorithm calculating sex competition points like I'd advertised. C'mmon, let's get real. The only "algorithm" was my sense of how to manipulate betting. One week one boy, the next week another. Totally random and unpredictable. I took a cut of every bet, so the important thing was that online subscribers just kept betting on their favs.

"According to the secret proprietary algorithm," I answered Tommy, "it's neck-and-neck between Manny, Freddy, and Little Frenchie."

Manny, the goateed Rican, beamed as all the boys except Dean congratulated him. "Thanks, guys," Manny said. "Hey, Paulie, too bad you couldn't whore around with us last night. I bet you got one hot *culito.*"

"Want to try it, Manny, our Paulie's ass?" asked strong-jawed Dean Lutefisk, Mr. Undiscovered Author. He'd started his whining on the flight over: "The world doesn't appreciate me." "I'm before my time." "They'll love my avant-garde fiction once I'm dead." So I told him, "Yeah, well, don't get any ideas about jumping outta the plane so your books'll get appreciated any sooner." Dean gave a laugh, but not a happy one. A bitter laugh. I started to worry about that kid but then reminded myself his moods were none of my business as long as he fucked like a champ. "I bet," Dean said to Manny, "you'd love to pump those salsa hips against Paulie's ass."

Manny's jaw twitched for a second like he was deciding whether to say something angry or hold off. "No thanks," was all he said.

"I bet you'd fuck him if he paid you," said Dean, flicking back his long straight blond bangs, "the way any *puta* would."

"Who you calling a whore, asshole?" Manny spat out. "You got a problem with me? Or is it all Puerto Ricans that piss you off?"

"Now, boys," I said. "We've got a lota breakfasts to get through together, so let's play nice. Dean—behave yourself."

Dean stood, bowed in a mocking kind of way, first at me and then at Manny. "Manuelito, I'm heading to the pastry corner. Can I bring you back a Danish to stuff in your *boca loca?*"

"*Gracias, cabrón,*" Manny replied. "An apricot Danish, hold the poison."

"But that's where all the flavor is." Dean turned and left for the buffet table.

"As for me," chimed Sam, our bear, "I'm proud to be a whore. Yummy yummy yummy, I got cum in my tummy."

"Such a poet," said Tommy in a smarmy-queeny way.

"Sam," I said, "you just oozed joy last night."

"That wasn't joy he was oozing," said Tommy.

Sam gave him a wink, but I couldn't tell if it meant "fuck you" or "way to go."

When Burt and I were choosing boys for the Tour, my first thought—to be honest, my reflex without really thinking about it at all—was to hire a bunch of White guys of various shapes and sizes. After all, most of the actors in our porn flicks, Burt's and mine, had always been White. But then I got to thinking that maybe this was a chance to open things up a little, to do our porn part to make the world a better place. "Burtie-boy," I asked, "you enjoy watching hot Black, Latino, and Asian guys as much as White guys, don't you?"

"A juicy dick is a juicy dick is a juicy dick."

"Exactly," I said. "So let's expand our casting call so's we can advertise a 'rainbow mix' of boys. Whattaya think?"

"Super idea to ride the Woke Political Correctness gravy train. Just make sure we've got at least one cut cock in the bunch."

"Good reminder. So we should probably be sure to include a Jew or a Muslim."

"But not both," said Burt, "or we'll risk some Mid-East sex war in the middle of the Tour."

"Good point."

After breakfast, I gathered the boys in the hotel lobby seating area, a semi-circle of sofas and armchairs. Still no Little Frenchie. "Hey, Bill, go wake up your roomie, would you?"

"Frenchie?" said Bill. "He's not asleep. He never came back to the room last night."

"What? And you didn't tell me? You didn't worry about your roommate?"

"I'd sort of hurt his feelings the day before the FuckFest, so when I woke up and he wasn't in our room, I figured he'd crashed with a couple other guys."

I asked if anybody'd seen Frenchie at the hotel—the others all shook their heads. I looked at Burt, asked, "Was Little Frenchie on the shuttle bus home?"

Burt turned deep red, mumbled, "I was so exhausted, Paulie, I didn't count. I saw the boys pile into the shuttle, and just assumed."

"He was still going strong at the baths when we were leaving," said Bill. "I thought about telling him, but didn't want to piss him off anymore, so I let him be and figured he'd come back when he was ready."

"He probably slept in a cubicle at Buddies," said Burt. "I'll go back and check. After filming this little confab."

I wanted to ream Burt out for not making sure Frenchie'd arrived safe at the hotel—did I have to do fucking everything? What if Little Frenchie got mugged walking back on his own? He was a small guy, after all. But I couldn't afford to piss Burt off. Without him, the whole project'd fall apart. And you don't exactly tell your husband he's a lazy piece of shit, even if that's what you think sometimes. Especially if he acts all agreeable when sober, but turns into a mean drunk, who might flatten you with one good sock in the jaw when he gets riled. So, I just nodded.

Standing in the center of the semi-circle, I gave a pep talk about "What a super FuckFest, boys, the best sex I ever saw. You guys are studs, every last one of you. The hottest sucking and fucking—" Before I could say more, the pimply hotel check-in clerk stomped over with a what-the-hell look on her plastic face and said, "Perhaps you would feel greater comfort in one of our small conference rooms instead of this lobby where parents are walking with children who hear every inappropriate word you speak?" She pointed in the direction of a conference room. Fine, we moved. The boys enjoyed swiveling in black chairs around a rectangular glossy wood-topped table.

I thanked 'em for not bringing their cell phones or laptops or other electronic shit on the trip because we couldn't risk any of 'em secretly filming or pasting social media pics or whatever because that'd mess up the website gambling (and my monopoly on filming). "I know it's hard on your generation to give up the gizmos, so you're all aces for handing 'em over at JFK. They'll be right in that airport locker when we get back. Now let's talk about some of the other guidelines. I don't think all you boys read 'em carefully."

"We're here to fuck, Paulie, not to read," said Dean.

"The rules," I continued, "for points programmed into our computerized algorithm." I was using the algorithm bullshit to make sure they gave the kind of sex I thought'd appeal to the broadest range of subscribers. After decades directing porn, I knew a thing or two. "You all wanna have the best shot at winning, right? So you don't wanna waste time on sex that doesn't count."

"Maybe you should have explained all this before the first FuckFest?" asked Dean.

I wouldn't let him get my goat. "I wanted you boys to express yourselves naturally the first time, before I put restraints on you."

"Some guys love restraints," said Tommy, looking at Sam, who looked away and blushed.

I looked toward Sam, said, "As fun as it is to take a forearm up your ass, you don't wanna risk anal fissure or hemorrhage that'll bench you for the rest of the season, right? So, according to the rules, fisting doesn't count. No extra points for BDSM. Including spitting."

"You saying spitting's prohibited?" asked Dean.

"No, just no points for it 'cause it turns a lot of guys off."

"It turns a lot of guys on. How about piss play or boot-licking?"

What a prick. Was Dean serious or jerking my chain? I said calmly, "No."

"How about gerbiling?" he asked with a smirk.

Best thing to do was ignore him. "Sex between contestants doesn't count, of course, because we don't want you boys colluding to earn points. And no points for participating in the same threesome. And remember that any sex act has gotta last five minutes for it qualify."

"But I can make men cum super fast," said Sam, licking his lips.

"We programmed into the computer algorithm that if you suck or fuck for less than five minutes, you get points for the cumshot, but not for the suck or fuck itself."

"I'll slow down," said Sam.

"And remember," I continued, "you'll get double points for your own cum shot. We draw no point distinction between topping and bottoming, so just do what comes naturally. Rimming earns, too, either way. The highest point values are if you're skewered at both ends or otherwise got two or more guys working on you at the same time."

"Nip play counts, right?" asked Sam whose perky little boys were pointing through his blue t-shirt.

"Low points, but yes, unless nip play leads to a cumshot, then you get added points. And kissing gets one point, but not more." I looked casually back at Manny and added, "Vanilla's okay—lotsa viewers will enjoy seeing a feel of connection, even affection, but we don't wanna overdo it."

Manny gave a small wink. "Gotcha."

"We're not a romance show. Keep that in mind."

"Okay, Paulie, I said I got it," said Manny, annoyed now.

"I have question if permitted," asked Yuki, raising his hand halfway.

"Shoot."

"What?" He looked confused.

"Ask your question."

"Do we earn extra for special position?"

"How special?"

"I can fuck while doing one-hand push-ups."

"Whoa," I said. "That's mighty special, for sure. I hadn't thought of that. But, no extra points because I don't want you using up energy on stunts—this isn't a gymnastics tournament. And if you do try an unusual position, remember that your own headband cameras might not catch it, so be sure to do it in an open area where you see Burt or one of the other boys filming, not in a private room."

Yuki gave a quick bow of his head. So polite and respectful, I coulda creamed right there.

"And one last thing—we put bottles of RID lice shampoo in each of your bathrooms. Shampoo your crotches and butts after each FuckFest, just in case. Oh yeah, and if I catch any of you doing poppers or any other drugs, I'll boot your ass outta here with no return ticket home. Last thing we need is a drug bust or something. And keep remembering the Grand Prize: $250,000 and a contract to star in ten porn flicks as top, bottom, or both, depending on your preference. Also, a year's supply of hair gels, body hair laser removal coupons—"

"Thanks," said Sam, our hairy bear, "I'll skip it."

"Sam, if you win, we'll throw in a year's worth of RID instead."

"Deal."

"And the last prize is one free cosmetic implant of your choice with free follow-up doctor visits in case anything goes wonky. Okay, boys, rest up while Burt goes back to Buddies to wake up Little Frenchie. After they return, Burt'll drive our precious camera/computer van ahead to Munich and make arrangements there. The rest of us'll spend the afternoon on a guided tour of some palaces while li'l ol' me'll take film footage we can post of everyone looking ga-ga at the royalty-shmoyalty shit. Gotta keep our fan base interested between FuckFests. Tomorrow'll be a shopping day for everyone—the shopping here's super—and then…on to Munich!"

My Memories: Copenhagen—Shitty News

When I got back to our hotel room at the end of the sightseeing afternoon, Burt filled me in.

"Holy Christ Almighty," I said, dropping onto the bed.

Little Frenchie was dead. Dead dead dead.

Dead dead dead dead dead fucking dead.

Poor Little Frenchie.

Burt explained: back at Buddies, he asked the sauna's wrinkly old check-in clerk if he could remember if a little blond guy left sometime after 4:00 AM? Or maybe he'd seen some little blond guy hunker down and sleep in a corner somewhere upstairs? The clerk got all antsy, stammered a lot of "um um um's," then said to wait, made a phone call. Not five minutes later, two cops showed up. The fucking police!

The cops asked why Burt was asking about a little blond guy—was one missing? An American? Would Burt come with them to the morgue to identify a little blond American who'd died last night at Buddies?

Burt started to sweat and stammer, "Me, officer? Me?"

Turned out that after the cops had taken the locker key from the "dead man's" wristband and opened his locker, they found Little Frenchie's wallet with his U.S. driver's license (I'd told the boys to leave their passports at the hotel) and his room key with no hotel name on it. They'd begun calling hotels, but I guess they hadn't gotten to ours yet.

The cops wouldn't give Burt the dead blond's name because they wanted Burt to confirm the corpse's identity with no prompting.

Burt could barely speak—that's what he told me: "My mouth dried up and nearly froze shut." At the morgue, they yanked out a shelf from a wall fridge, and there he was, Little Frenchie, "so pale he looked plastic," Burt told me, "but peaceful." Burt confirmed his identity, told the cops that Frenchie was with our "gay group tour" and "boys will be boys, they all wanted to go to Buddies last night."

The cops explained they hadn't found anyone who'd witnessed the fall, but when the sauna's custodian was mopping around 5:00 AM, he nearly tripped over Frenchie and screamed bloody murder. The cops found him with his towel slipped off—he'd probably tripped on a corner of it, gotten tangled and fell, they said, smashed his head over and over on the steps. His neck snapped like a twig, and he bled out besides. The coroner confirmed no drugs or alcohol in his system. They said they'd release the body after the paperwork was done.

I don't know where Burt got the balls (he's got unusually big avocado balls I used to love to lick and suck way back when): before I got back to the hotel, Burt had already called Little Frenchie's mother in Montreal. "She shrieked like a banshee. Didn't even know her son was in Europe in the first place." Burt muttered something to her about us leading a "wholesome young men's tour of European churches," and then he cursed out the steep, narrow staircases in European hotels and promised we'd pay to ship Little Frenchie's corpse home "out of loving respect for his memory, may his soul rest among the angels of which he surely is one."

"How much'll that cost, Burt, to ship him back?"

"I don't know, but we gotta pay whatever."

"That could be thousands of bucks. I'm sorry for the kid, but why should we shell out thousands just because Little Frenchie was stupid enough to trip on his own fucking towel?"

Burt told me to calm down, and that of course it was my grief speaking. (He called it grief, but I called it wallet.) "Listen, Paulie, it's better this way, to hush it up. Sure, we got all the boys to sign liability waivers, so Little Frenchie's mother can't sue. But still, we don't want her raising holy hell, do we? Whining to some snoopy Canadian law firm that'll sniff around and threaten to shut us down unless we pay a fortune in hush money to avoid a publicity stink? Better to spend a few thousand dollars shipping him home to show goodwill so we can move on, save more in the long run and keep earning, no?"

Of course he was right. So I asked, "What the hell do we put on the website to explain that Little Frenchie's out of the competition?" Betting had already started. And after the live feed showed him sucking away all night, lotsa subscribers had bet on him. I'd have to post some explanation. But saying he died could put subscribers out of the mood.

Burt said, "Start with the truth: Little Frenchie slipped on the stairs—emphasize his own fault. Then just say he broke an ankle so he can't continue the tour—how could he compete all gimpy in a cast and on crutches? So we'll be sending him home to the loving arms of his Montreal *maman* who'll cure him with garlicky snails and broiled frogs. We'll say it'll cost us a shitload but that's just the sort of generous people we are."

"What about the gamblers who already bet on him? What if they ask for their money back?"

"No fucking way," said Burt. "It's *gambling*, for fuck's sake. They bet on a clumsy idiot, so they lost. The house keeps the money. Tough shit."

Made sense. "But what about the other boys? How'll they react?"

"We'll just tell 'em the same broken ankle story and say that Frenchie's docs shot him up with morphine so he's in intensive care and completely out of it, no visitors allowed for a week—weird Danish customs, right?—and we've gotta stick to our schedule and shove off for Munich, so there's no chance to say goodbye, *c'est la vie*, or however they say it in Denmark. The boys can write all the get-well notes they want and I'll deliver 'em to the nurse on duty who'll pass 'em along when Little Frenchie wakes out of his morphine stupor."

Burt's advice sounded good, but what if one of the boys insisted on calling the hospital? Then the truth'd come out and it'd be worse for us trying to cover it up. "Maybe we should tell 'em the real truth: he slipped, fell, and— brace yourselves, boys—he died."

Burt liked that, especially since it'd make the boys extra careful in other saunas. "We can't afford to lose anyone else."

So, we went with that. After we told 'em, I added, "I'm paying to ship our poor Little Frenchie back home, boys, no need to thank me, that's just the kind of guy I am because you boys are special to me like my own sons, gosh darn it, and I wanna make sure you're all well taken care of…. Stop thanking me, boys, I'm glad to do it, glad to do it. So let's think of the future. Burt'll give you a short lesson on the best ways to film using your headband cams, okay? Then, onward to the next FuckFest where Little Frenchie will be cheering us on from heaven."

Hidden Camera Transcript: Big Bill

Standing by his hotel room window, Big Bill looks out over the canal, at a couple of docked sailboats gently swaying, at the orange-roofed red, yellow, and blue buildings across the water. He turns, steps over to the two single beds shoved together, glides a hand across the gold comforter spread where he'd lain with Little Frenchie just a few days before.

He leans over, places a soft kiss on one white pillow, straightens. He walks into the bathroom, picks up from the white countertop a black comb and sniffs it. He unscrews the plastic top of a travel-size tube of yellow hair gel, squeezes a dab onto his thick thumb, rubs it with his forefinger, licks it. He picks up a pink toothbrush coated in sparkles, shoves it into his mouth and swishes it around while mumbling, "My poor Little Frenchie. If only I'd…"

Munich

Killer Interview 3

Munich appealed not only as situs of your second FuckFest, Mr. Hahnemann, but as one of Europe's art museum capitals. Most particularly: glory to the German Expressionists, those pre-World War II renderers of soul who tugged the heartstrings via paintings of pain. Otto Dix with his horrific portrayals of First World War wounds, mutilations, cripplings of body and soul. Kirchner and Nolde's startlingly colorful depictions reflecting inner, spiritual agony and despair. The art of these, Hitler's so-called "decadents," has always brought tears to my eyes. Perhaps you are familiar with them, Mr. Hahnemann.

I have not considered until this very moment: were not my recent undertakings a logical extension of my artistic esthetic? Should I, too, not be considered artist of a different sort? Did I not also create human distress both for my intimate victims and their horrified peers? True, I possess no skill at painting nor molding clay, but still, I discovered in Europe my ability to *do*. To transform a human being at rest—or in the throes of ecstatic pursuit—into an inert lump of gore still possessed of the capacity to provide a modicum of joy to one increasingly sensitive to the erotic quality of cold dead flesh.

Every great artist has sought to satisfy self, the rest of humanity be damned. Is my art any less unique than that of the famous? Could one not even argue my art—my manipulation of an actual human form—to be of greater achievement than mere daubs on canvas or squeezings of clay?

To grant you your due, Mr. Hahnemann, I would posit that your past porn films were analogous artistic expressions of your own personal esthetic. Fellow artistic types, you and I. Comrades-in-arms.

. . .

Very well, back to chronology and logistics: completely unaware of the hotel at which you and your boys were staying in Munich, I decided to enjoy my own, one mere blocks from the Hauptbanhof, the central train station. My first morning, I arrived downstairs before other guests at the hotel's sumptuous buffet of—

. . .

Mr. Hahnemann, I beg you to indulge my savory memories that serve as unparalleled escape from the solitary confinement prison repasts of current and future circumstance: the hotel's sumptuous buffet of scrambled eggs and various sausages, including the famous München *Weisswurst*, white sausages, whose spongy insides one teased out of their skins with front teeth (does not sexual imagery come to mind?) and then daubed with sweet mustard. Absolutely delicious. Baskets of rolls seeded with poppy or sesame, croissants, sliced cheeses, cucumbers and tomatoes, stewed prunes, assorted pastries.

Heaping my plate high, I sat at a white-clothed table where a woman about forty in black slacks, white shirt, and maroon vest sporting a gold name badge declaring "Fatima" stepped over to inquire as to my choice of beverage. Moments later, as she brought the cappuccino, I examined her exotic non-Aryan appearance: light brown complexion, almond eyes, high cheekbones, wavy jet-black hair. Neither East nor South Asian, a touch of the Middle East about her, yet not quite Arab. "Please don't take offense," I implored with my warmest smile, "I see your wedding ring and intend no disrespect. But I've never before observed your particular form of beauty."

As her face reddened, she held my gaze for a moment, then offered a tentative smile. "I thank you for your complimentation."

"Are you from here?"

"Don't be daft." Giggling, she explained in surprisingly decent English that she had immigrated years before from Turkmenistan. "Formerly one republic of Soviet Union. My beloved husband is skilled anesthesiologist— he began career back home in Ashgabat responsible for surgery on Communist Party leaders." She leaned down to whisper, "One mistake and—" she dragged a finger across her throat. We shared a laugh. "I managed restaurant there. And you?" Did she genuinely wish to engage in conversation, or was she simply passing time before other hotel guests arrived and distracted her attention? Was she lonely? Did she sense that I was? "Are you from Britain or America?" she asked.

"The United States, yes."

"The land of golden streets. Our son attends medical school in Florida. One day he will earn citizenship so we may join."

"You don't look old enough to have a grown-up son."

"Again, my appreciation for your complimentation. My husband and I grew enamored in youth, married in late teens, and were blessed with son before I turned twenty. We immigrated to Munich ago eight years and received kind welcoming, but in light of recent immigrations, the atmosphere here…" her face clouded, "has modified for those of certain origins."

"I hope I will have the chance to welcome you and your husband to America one day."

She gave a bow of her head. "Other guests are arriving. You will kindly excuse me?"

"Until tomorrow morning."

"I shall look forward."

I grew rather sullen while eating my poppy seed roll with a slice of mild yellow cheese. Not every child is blessed with Ozzie-and-Harriet Turkoman parents who struggle to put them through medical school, whose lives are so tightly bound with one another's that they plan trans-continental moves as a cohesive unit. Some of us were raised by a series of indifferent foster parents because our junkie biologicals were unable to keep needles out of their arms long enough to change a diaper or fill a tit with milk, let alone kiss a forehead to soothe our incessant screaming that prompted neighbors to summon police who broke down our apartment front door, handkerchief-covered their mouths and noses against the fecal-vomitous stench, and immediately shunted us into the hands of poorly paid, overworked social workers who did their best to place us in meagerly acceptable foster homes with woodsmen who eventually tired of us and shifted us onto other couples in need of state-provided child support payments, all of whom filled our befuddled heads with bittersweet fantasies of potential loving adoptions and Cinderella endings never to be. Some of us, against all odds, managed to put ourselves through university and learn enough about the intricacies of finance so as to develop a skillset offering the opportunity to tuck away a nest egg, which is the least we deserved in this world of betrayal and neglect.

A lovely cappuccino.

After breakfast, I strolled to Marienplatz, the medieval center of town and now an extended outdoor shopping mall. Progress. A spired town hall with its seemingly lifesize Glockenspiel figurines no longer on the move. One old church after another, gray and yellow buildings ornamented by red and white geraniumed window boxes, bakeries featuring soft pretzels so large they surely violated Olympic Committee rules prohibiting steroids.

What a contrast—the overwhelming numbers of Arab women in traditional dress. Some wore head-to-toe black coverings and sneakers, walking the cobbled streets alongside gorgeous swarthy men in t-shirts, shorts and sandals. Other women revealed eyes through black veil slits; still others wore copper metal masks that shielded only noses and mouths, reminding of Halloween jack-o-lanterns. Where had they come from, all these women? Still others showed their faces openly, their hair wrapped in fashionable, flowery cloth turbans. I thought of Fatima, the morning's waitress with no head-covering whatsoever. How diverse the variations of oppression.

The saddest of women was not one of the walking black shrouds. Rather, this particular woman stood with exposed face under an olive green headscarf matching her olive green, ankle-length caftan. She stood staring before a two-story-high Benneton ad of a muscular young blond man in a tank top, depicted tastefully from the waist up with hands behind head. So beautiful was he that I pictured myself licking that chest, those sweet pits displaying blond fluff, and every inch of those window-sized biceps. I imagined giving his muscular ass (not on the billboard, but one could extrapolate) an extended rimming, which was not one of my usual predilections, and I even licked my own saliva-covered lips as I fantasized nipping his flesh with teeth and discovering the taste of young handsome blood.

This Arab woman's face expressed not mere fascination, nor the cheap lust presumably emblazoned upon mine. Rather, hers implied a puzzled inability to comprehend: how could a man appear so sexual in public and beautiful and available for fantasy and able to smile without the slightest hint of shame? I imagined her thinking, 'So this is what the mullahs declare to be decadent Western indecency…but can something so exquisite be so wrong? Are there not worse things in the world than physical beauty and sexual allure? Allahu akhbar.'

"He's really something, isn't he?" I said to her, in offer of empathetic understanding.

Visibly startled, she turned her head abruptly to me, opened her mouth, shut it, spun on her sneakered heels and scurried away.

Damn, I'd ruined her moment. Whether she understood my English or not. She probably had not even realized herself to be gawking, had simply grown so lost in male beauty and fantasy that she forgot she was in a public space demanding adherence to all the shoulds and shouldn't's her father and brothers and husband had perhaps beaten into her. If word of her gawking reached those men, would she be stoned to death in a so-called honor killing? Poor woman. Here I was, another man inflicting shame.

My Memories—Munich Beer Garden

I was glad I followed Burt's advice and shipped Little Frenchie's corpse back to Montreal. Out of sight, out of mind. (What the hell else was I supposed to do with it—stuff it at a taxidermist's and lug it around Europe like a mascot?)

Burt told me not to worry too much about those emails from our shadier investors asking when their money was coming in. "Paulie," he said, "they want us to succeed so's they can get their dough. They'll give us time." I understood, but maybe we shouldn't have followed the businessmen in that movie, *The Producers*, and oversold to our half-dozen "institutional" investors. We told all six of 'em they'd each get fifty percent of the profits. *Note to Self made on the plane from Copenhagen to Munich: maybe I can cook the books well enough so investors'll never know we're scamming 'em?*

Another Note to Self on the plane: look into merchandising deals ("I'm a Grand Sex Tour-ist" t-shirts and mugs, DVDs autographed by the contestants, dildoes modeled on their dicks, etc.). Maybe do Grand Sex Tour Asia next so I can visit merchandise factories in Hong Kong while I'm there.

Another Note to Self on the plane: when putting together the director's cut film, save cutting-room-floor sex scenes for purchase by gay travel agencies…to entice clients to book Euro travel. They can create tours that follow our Grand Sex Tour itinerary, city by city, sauna by sauna. Figure out how to get a percentage of those tours—file for trademark in the U.S.? Better yet: create my own tour company with ex-contestants as (sex) tour guides!

And another: create a reunion orgy film after the season's winner is chosen, with all the boys sitting around gabbing and teasing each other. And after half a dozen seasons, I can bring back all the winners for a Champion of Champions Grand Sex Tour competition. I could even have a Losers Re-match Grand Sex Tour competition. Endless monetizing options!!!

And another (is there no end to my brilliance?): after the filming's all done and edited, to keep up subscriber interest, we can include a pop-up section on our website where the boys can earn extra for doing real-time chat rooms (of course I'll get a fifty percent cut).

Our first Munich dinner was at a beer garden down a main avenue alongside the Hauptbanhof. Far down the block. Soon as we walked through the brick wall entryway, it was like we'd stepped into the woods and back in time. Awesome, as the boys said. Long wooden tables were set up among the (linden?) trees, with green checkered tablecloths stretched in diamond shapes on the middle. Cool breezes, some flies, no aromas, but the soft chatter of a coupla thousand people, all muffled by the trees. A waiter took us to a table on a central restaurant porch. Lucky for me I picked a waiter wearing a pin with British and Italian flags—symbols of languages he spoke. He said it'd be okay for Burt to film our table, but not any others, so Burt got to work while we drank from beer steins. Burt skipped the beer—thank God because sometimes beer makes him downright nasty—and I got a *halb* (half) liter, so I could keep sharp, but the boys each got a whole. Dean, Tommy, Bill kept leaving the table to go piss, big surprise.

I ordered sampler plates (*Schmackenplattes*, or something like that) for everyone. A sampler for 20.50 euros (less than $25) per person. Roast duck (crispy), roast suckling pig slice (heavy with a rind I didn't like), pig's knuckle—super crisp skin but way too much fat. Small smoked sausage, warm sauerkraut with juniper berries, steamed (boiled?) carrots and parsnips. Lotsa gravy and a *Knödel*—a heavy potato dumpling.

By the end of the meal when the beer really kicked in, the boys were hamming it up, swaying with arms around shoulders, and singing from *Cabaret*. Even Freddy got into it, which made me glad. He did a heartfelt version of "Maybe This Time," that song when Liza Minelli/Sally Bowles was hoping love'd stay for fucking once. Burt got 'em all on film—perfect! But I had to stop Sam, our bear, when he stood and started in on "Tomorrow Belongs to Me," that Nazi beer garden rally song. He even made with the *sieg heil* salute.

"What the hell are you doing?" asked Tommy. "You're Jewish, for God's sake! Don't you have any self-respect?"

Folks at nearby tables stared and grumbled. Our waiter rushed over with the check and said, "time to depart, please."

Sam gave me a big wink at that and gave Tommy a slurpy kiss, so maybe Sam was fucking with the Germans on purpose. What a pisser.

During the ten-fifteen-minute walk back to our hotel, drunk Bill, that giant muscleman, got weepy about how much "my poor Little Frenchie" would have loved this dinner. Like Bill could really know that. And how much "my poor Little Frenchie" would have loved the Glockenspiel and shops, and everything else in Munich. On and on. Yeah, it was sad that Little Frenchie'd broken his neck, but let's get real—Big Bill had only met him like a week before he died. How close could they have gotten?

Yuki handed Bill tissues and literally held his giant hand. Decency wasn't dead, after all.

Hidden Camera Transcript:
Manny and Dean

"What the fuck? You trying to rape me or something?" Dean shoves naked Manny away and yanks the gold blanket high beneath his neck.

"I woke you because you were screaming, *pendejo*," says Manny as he climbs back into his own bed. "And you're sweating like a pig."

"Shit. I do that sometimes." Dean sits up, rubs spittle off his prominent chin. "Did I say anything, or was it screams?"

"At first you were just moaning, but then you yelled, 'No no no!' And then, it was hard to make out, but sounded like 'Go back! No no no!' and more moaning."

"Shit," Dean mumbles. "Sorry."

"What's going on?"

"Sometimes I—" Dean covers his eyes. "Shit shit shit."

Manny gets out of bed again and, naked, sits beside Dean, who's covered waist down by the gold blanket. Manny places a hand flat on the center of Dean's naked chest. "It's okay, man, whatever. It's okay."

Dean drops hands from face, focuses his red eyes on Manny's clear ones, says nothing.

"What the hell, dude?" With one finger, Manny strokes the outline of Dean's unusually prominent chin, then tucks a few of Dean's stray blond hairs behind his ear the way a father might soothe a child.

Dean mumbles, "Afghanistan."

"No shit."

"Yeah, my best buddy. On a mission in the middle of bumfucknowhere hills. We got separated a couple days, and I was afraid maybe he got captured. I was about to head back to base, then saw him running over a hill toward my position. I jumped up and waved, and he waved and kept running and that's when—"

"They shot him?"

"Exploded. A hundred pieces. Ran right onto an IED. His fucking head flew off. I saw his fucking head fly off. My best buddy's fucking head."

"It's okay, bro'," says Manny, scooping Dean to himself as if he were a toddler. "I got you. I got you."

Dean sits numbly as Manny rocks him. Then Manny lays Dean back down, pulls the gold blanket up to his neck, lies on top of the blanket beside him, holds him.

For the rest of the night.

In the morning, Dean turns to him. "I can't believe you did that for me."

"You wouldn't do that for somebody?" asks Manny.

"For a buddy, sure."

"But not for a Puerto Rican."

Dean grabs Manny by his face, kisses him full on the lips. "That's a thank-you. And an apology. But nothing else."

"Your breath fucking stinks," Manny says, rolling out of Dean's bed and climbing back into his own.

Dean stands, walks to their bathroom, stops at the door. "We don't need to tell the other guys about this, do we?"

"You think I want anyone to know your gross WASPy lips touched mine?"

My Memories—Munich Sightseeing

I let the boys poke around town by themselves a coupla days. Then this A.M., I gave 'em a mini-lecture in the hotel lobby about going to art museums with Burt so he could film 'em. "We need to attract snooty fags to our website—they're the ones with big bucks. No matter which of you wins or loses—after our show's over, sophisticated old millionaire queens worldwide will clamor to become your paying clients. Most'll just want a quick celebrity fuck, but some'll whisk you off to their Mid-eastern palaces, Alps chalets, Borneo estates, Argentinian haciendas, Park Avenue penthouses, or whatever. You've at least gotta be able to bullshit your way through a dinner party where your client'll try to pass you off as a sophisticated kept boy from an Ivy League school. I took art courses in college and read lotsa travel guides, so I know where Burt should take you."

"You're not coming with?" asked blond Dean.

"I'm already highbrow enough."

"Yeah, right."

"If you mention to some sugar daddy art collector that you were in Munich, he might test you and ask if you know about Der Blaue Reiter group.

After today's trip to the museums, you can comment casually, 'You mean the permanent collection at the Lenbach Haus? Their use of color and composition was so incredible I nearly creamed right on the gallery hardwood floors, don'tcha know.' Talk to 'em like that, boys, and they'll be on their knees with their wallets out in no time."

The boys chuckled, but only Yuki and Freddy agreed to go with Burt. Those two roomies were our sophisticates, I guess.

The rest of the boys went shopping with me. The next day, Saturday, there'd be a gay festival in Munich's gay neighborhood—had I planned this trip well, or had I planned this trip well? We'd attend the festival in the afternoon and then go right into our second FuckFest.

Hidden Camera Transcript: Freddy and Yuki

After removing his kelly green contact lenses, Freddy stands in front of the hotel room's full-length mirror, admiring himself in nothing but red running shorts. He flexes, examines his ripped abs and thick bulging arms, all as if he were alone.

Across the room, Yuki, naked but for black jockstrap, watches while doing gentle lunges, stretching thighs and calves. "You will win competition, I think. Everybody loves muscles. Yours are like black onyx. Is alright for me to say 'black'?"

"That's what I am."

"Not many Black men in Kyoto."

"But there are lots in San Francisco."

"I am living in San Francisco only two years. You are my first Black friend."

"Friends, are we?"

"So sorry—roommate."

"'Friends' is fine. I was just yanking your chain. You seem like an okay dude, Yuki my man."

"Thank you. You go to gym every day, yes?"

"Usually. I can't believe there's no weight room in our hotel, though."

"I do weights, too, but not like you."

"Yeah, you're a swimmer's build guy. You could help me out if you sit on my back while I do push-ups."

Yuki grins, "You know Paulie rule—no roommate sex."

"Exercise, not sex. Seriously."

"You want to show me your strength."

"Well, maybe that, too. Whattaya say?"

Freddy drops to push-up position, Yuki straddles his lower back and sits. Freddy pushes up and down in a steady rhythm.

"Very strong," says Yuki.

After pushing up again, Freddy gives a quick clap before re-positioning his hands and lowering down.

"Wow," says Yuki.

After twenty-five push-ups, Freddy lies flat on his stomach on the gold carpet. Yuki leans forward and massages his shoulders. "That feels so good," says Freddy.

"Only massage," says Yuki.

"My ass could use some massaging too."

"Only shoulders!"

"Hah hah."

"I glad to see you in better mood. You very quiet at museums today. I think you are sad these days."

Freddy flips around so that Yuki now straddles Freddy's stomach. "You make me smile, Yuki. Something about you. You're a good guy."

"Want to talk about sadness?"

Freddy shakes his head. "Some other time. But if you need to talk about anything…"

"Maybe."

"Really? What's up?"

Yuki sighs, slides off and sits cross-legged on the carpet. "If I say, you will not tell others or Paulie?"

"No, man, of course not. Just between us."

"I am thinking maybe I made mistake with this contest. The week before I saw advertisement to apply as contestant, I came out to parents. Mother cried, but hugged me. Then she blamed my father because he moved us from

Kyoto to San Francisco 'homosexual city.' Father slapped her face then mine. He called me whore. Ordered me to leave house."

"No way."

"I stayed with friends and looked for apartment, but then saw ad for Grand Sex Tour competition and thought, 'you think I am whore, father? I will show you whore.'"

"Heavy father-son stuff, for sure. Sorry about that, Yuki. But, I've got to say—I saw you in Copenhagen. You were a regular fuck machine."

"Is that good thing?"

"It's not a bad thing."

"I am not certain. Now I am thinking I am in contest for wrong reason. Maybe I should leave. I do not wish to fuck because of father. I wish to fuck because I wish to fuck."

"I can respect that, man. But don't drop out of the competition. You'd have to pay Paulie a huge dropout penalty, remember. And think about the money you'll earn if you stay. Even if you don't win, you'll get a shitload. We all will. You're gonna need the money, right?"

"Of course. I am having two more years of college to pay, and apartment in San Francisco."

"So, stay."

"Probably right. Probably I should continue to fuck for money. Like real whore."

Killer Interview 4

On Saturday afternoon, I strolled toward the Viktualienmarkt, an open-air market of rows upon rows of stalls and shops selling gustatory delights from produce to cheeses to sausages to honey and spices…endless amusement for the palate and eyes. But my ultimate destination lay several blocks south, in the upscale Glockenbachviertel neighborhood where I'd read that a gay street festival would be taking place close to the city's grandest sauna. Surely the next FuckFest would be held in that very sauna. (The city's other two were, per online reviews, considerably smaller.)

As anticipated, Hans-Sacher Street was blocked off. Folk music blared from behind barriers. After passing through the police security checkpoint, I found myself amidst a gay block party not all that dissimilar to those I'd attended in Boston on Gay Pride Day: clusters of thirty-forty somethings chatting and drinking beer, munching hot dogs wrapped in puff pastry, sausage chunks, cheese-covered fried dough vaguely resembling pizza. A withered old man, holding an open black umbrella against the sun, minced about on black high heels and nodded à la Queen Elizabeth while garnering attention for his black corseted red silk Chinese Dragon Lady dress. Everyone else appeared gay-normal in t-shirts, shorts, jeans, an assortment of tattoos and nose rings. More beards on one block than I'd noticed so far in all of Munich. Joyful yet somehow subdued compared to U.S. such parties, except for a group I heard speaking English.

I turned my head—yes, your Grand Sex Tour boys, Mr. Hahnemann. I recognized them from Copenhagen's Buddies Sauna. And the bald fat middle-aged cameraman presumably there as chaperone. Quaint.

I squeezed through the crowd to overhear any possible remarks about the loss of their little blond friend—admittedly, a week had passed since I'd encountered him at Buddies. Perhaps they had already forgotten him. Here today, gone tomorrow—are not we all?

Initially, as they ogled the German crowd, I listened to ordinary small talk about this one's basket and that one's pecs, how they'd like to grab that bulging cock over there and plug this chunky ass over here. Normal naughty boy talk comparable to the sort occasionally engaged in by heterosexual U.S. presidents. Then, to my surprise, the giant in the group, a hulk of a man with arm muscles the size of footballs, grew teary-eyed and murmured that he "missed Little Frenchie, my cute little buddy." Might that be the name of the late little blond?

The giant actually shed tears. Such sentiment in the heart of a bruiser surprised me. The group's bearded chubby bear—from the aquilinity of nose, curliness of dark hair, disorderliness of close-cropped beard, and overall pudginess, one presumed him a Jew—hugged the giant while the dark-complexioned, goateed Latino gently took the weeper's beer from his hand. "Maybe you've had enough for today, Bill."

Bill, the name of the inveterate gambler in *Showboat*. Bill, the name of the crippled and embittered romantic lead in *Carnival*. Surely these gay boys would share in dishing about old Broadway/Hollywood musicals? One could use some compatriot company. Time to make my approach and ingratiate myself through witty American-centric reactions to Munich. Certainly, I could come up with my share of harmless *achtung*-Brunhilde-*Wienerschnitzel* jokes à la *Hogan's Heroes* and *The Great Escape*. The boys would welcome me into their fold, invite me to tag along on their European adventures, thereby inadvertently facilitating my primary objective of maintaining an eye on my investment.

I tapped the shoulder of a tall, bored-looking fellow with long blond hair and a protruding Habsburg sort of jaw almost—but not quite—inviting surgical correction. So close are the extremes of beauty and ugliness. In Buddies, a number of men had fawned on him, and I'd seen him top a good half dozen with a degree of brutality. Admirable passionate ferocity.

"Howdy there!" I said. "Fellow Yank, I presume?" He eyed me with a suspicious look of the sort one might hurl at a spangly earringed, long-skirted Gypsy tugging on one's elbow and begging for alms with her right hand while simultaneously slipping her left into one's back pocket. I added, "It's great to run into Americans here."

"Whatever."

Foolishly, I continued in my best colloquial phrasing, "I don't generally mind being on my own. I mean, that's how I like to travel, seeing whichever museums I want when I want, you know? But in a crowd like this, when everyone else stands in cliques with friends, well, it would be nice to celebrate our pride with others. Okay for me to hang with you guys a little?"

It was his look that flint-sparked anger within me, his classic handsome man's up-and-down ogle accompanied by a facial expression conveying are-you-shitting-me bemusement. "No thanks, Gramps." He took a step toward me, flicked one of the extended corners of my mustache the way one might flick away an insect.

My mustache? He dared flick my meticulously trimmed and patiently waxed white mustache, a symbol of my very virility and manliness? An element of grooming so distinct as to render me visible among a sea of otherwise invisible men of a certain age? He then made the backhanded shoo-away gesture one might fling at a naughty child, adding, "Why don't you hobble off and find the AARP crowd. Or better yet, go cruise a cemetery where you can dig up a peer." He smirked, that nasty little shit, turned his back on me, spoke to several of his fellows, jabbed his thumb in my direction. All eyes turned to me, and most in the group snickered.

Yes, my jawline sagged with a second chin, but my love handles remained relatively small, and my pecs still held firm under my gray t-shirt emblazoned with navy blue "Provincetown." My head was no balder than those of many a younger man in the crowd who shaved for stylishness.

In centuries past, gentlemanly etiquette would have justified—nay, demanded—my tugging off a white glove and slapping it across this offender's face. The next morning we would have engaged in a duel—now by sword, now by pistol—and although his youthful reflexes would have proved keener than my aged ones, my decades of superior experience would have won out. My dignity would have been avenged.

However, this was not centuries past.

I felt an urge to bite and tear off a hunk of lean bicep exposed by the arrogant blond bastard's purple tank top, to thumb-pummel his kidneys, to flatten him with a right hook to the jaw, then to stomp on his prostrate body and grind the heel of my black Skechers Sparta 2.0 (extra wide) sport shoes onto his nose to mash it into pulp, to plunge a pocket knife I did not hold into his cold, miserable heart repeatedly until he fountained blood. Had we been alone in an alley, I might have shown him the strength possessed by a man of merely sixty.

Stepping off to the side, away from my "fellow" North Americans but within sight of them, I stared at this arrogant Byronic Onegin and his fellows, memorized each face and torso silhouette without any immediate intention of fanning the flames of my ignited inner burn. I would bide my time.

As temporary balm, I acknowledged in my moment of humiliation that two among them had not snickered. The Japanese fellow (not flat enough a face to be Korean; not round and soft enough a face to be Chinese unless northern Hakka, which was a possibility, but no…he struck me as Goldilocks just-right Japanese) had looked down at the ground in empathetic embarrassment. Nor had the muscular Black fellow joined in the sniggering. Rather, he seemed to make a point of meeting my ordinary brown eyes with his remarkable kelly green ones and holding my gaze before raising a golden can of Pilsner in my direction and then to his lips for a guzzle. These two were undoubtedly sensitive young men, no strangers to the slings and arrows of entitled White men. I would remember them, too.

I left the festival, took three deep breaths, forced my mind onto the fascinating surroundings.

Several blocks away, on a quiet street between a bookstore and a café, across the street from a dress shop named, so inventively in English, "Dress Shop," several older men sat at sidewalk tables drinking beer. I joined. Well, not actually joined—I did not impose by inserting myself at an occupied table. Rather, I sat at an empty one among them. Charming to see men my age and older in twos and threes, chatting and occasionally flirting with back-of-the-hand pats and forearm squeezes. I caught an occasional glance of interest from passersby—*younger* passersby.

A cheerful young blond waiter brought a menu. And a smile. I had considered staying here at Freundschaft, a gay hotel-restaurant-sauna complex, but feared noise from disco queens thumping throughout sleepless nights. Given the sedate quality of Freundschaft's early, outdoor supper crowd, I wondered if I had misjudged.

A meal of piquant yet not overly acidic tomato cream soup followed by a curry-ginger house sausage ("the longest 'willy'," according to the witty menu). How I loved the sensation of slipping an oversized hunk between my front teeth, biting down and piercing the sausage sheath as it spurted liquified fat, the spongy meaty chew. So satisfying, especially in that spicy sauce and accompanied by thick steak fries, all capped, of course, by a cappuccino, which I was just setting down on its saucer post-sip when I heard youthful banter in English.

Turning my head to the hotel's entrance I saw them, the entire gaggle of disdainful boys, including the fat bald chaperone and the arrogant mandibular blond. Although I had expected them here for the FuckFest, I had not anticipated such early arrival.

They walked right past my table without so much as a hello. Either they did not notice me, did not recognize me, or did not care. Now was my chance to hunt down the arrogant blond with the mandibular prognathism and make certain he would remember me forever. Or if not me, then the day.

You see, Mr. Hahnemann, having inadvertently caused the death of the little blond in Copenhagen, I had now begun to contemplate the ease with which one could, as a general matter, inflict death or, at least, significant physical damage. Especially if sensual pleasure were to be one's reward for the effort. I asked myself: could a similar experience here replicate the intense arousal I'd enjoyed at Buddies in Copenhagen?

My brief reverie was broken by the kind young muscleman among the group of boys entering Freundschaft, the one who'd seemingly raised his Pilsner in toast: he hesitated at the hotel entrance, met my gaze with those kelly green eyes of his, offered a gentle smile—one of neither apology nor pity, but of simple greeting and respectful acknowledgment. I returned the smile. We shared a nod. I wished to meet this young man and properly thank him for affording me a modicum of dignity. Might he possibly be attracted to older men such as myself? Might his smile even have been intended as flirtation? Might we later share a tender embrace? Perhaps unlikely, but nevertheless another incentive to enter the sauna.

Even had the boys not been visiting Freundschaft this evening, I would have made a point, sometime, of exploring Munich's largest sauna. It's not that men are necessarily more exciting in one country than another (except, perhaps, in Turkey—recall the great Ella Fitzgerald's, "Oh, those Turks!"), but that saunas truly make for sources of cultural insights, revealing active, living social interactions including the (dis)courtesies and (a)romantic inclinations of a people. An essential component of any travel itinerary.

I left on the table sufficient cash to cover the bill and tip for the handsome young waiter who more than once had smiled at me—cash, mind you, so as not to leave any credit card identification trace. One was on one's toes.

I entered the hotel and followed signage down the entrance hallway to a wood-paneled corner with sauna reception desk "manned," so to speak, by a woman in maroon polo shirt uniform and cascading thick black hair. The first time to be welcomed to a sauna by a woman. (What does this hiring policy suggest about German embrace of equality of employment, as well as their lack of puritanical squeamishness over homosexual promiscuity?) Of course she made no request for ID. She buzzed me in through a paneled entrance door, stepped inside behind a counter, handed over a beige towel and asked if I wished a locker. Her face betrayed surprise when I requested the more expensive *kabine*, small room. Perhaps tourists tended not to splurge on privacy? Not that I expected to use the *kabine* for other than moments of rest and regeneration between periods of Grand Sex Tour-boy observation and my own hoped-for bouts of energetic dissolution and, if lucky, a moment of revenge.

Although I withdrew my wallet, she explained that payment would be required only upon departure. How odd.

Following her instructions, I walked through the adjoining locker room and headed downstairs. The signs were of modest help, so I fumbled a bit through a maze of hallways until stumbling upon my *kabine* 33, a meticulously clean, faux-marble tiled small room replete with red-gym-matted raised bed reflected in its entirety in a floor-to-ceiling wall mirror. The admittedly gaudy stylishness suggested at least an attempt at self-respect, as opposed to the self-disdain implied by the ratty mattresses with torn sheets and patched walls so typical of dingy U.S. bathhouse rooms.

After stripping and donning my beige towel, I wound my way through the enormous establishment in search of your Grand Sex Tour boys, Mr. Hahnemann. I chose to start on the top floor and work my way down. The top floor turned out to be a tiled and humid "wet floor"—a foyer with hot tub, steam room entrance door, and showerheads lining the wall out in the open so that everyone could ogle as everyone else showered and thus select one's preferred (un)cut of meat. At the far side of the hot tub, a husky middle-aged couple were locked in noisy amorous embrace. Feeling the need to enjoy a moment of sensuality, I hung my beige towel on a wall hook beside the steam room door, crossed with ginger steps so as not to slip on the wet tile, and entered the tub's frothy jacuzzi warmth at a modest distance from the couple, thereby implying availability for orgiastic complicity but not intrusively so. The shaven-headed one appeared to be semi-seated on the other's lap with legs wrapped round torso. Intense passionate kissing, not much groping, very few waves in the tub, but many groans and lip-smacking sounds. As I watched (i.e., stared with envy), a swarthy, hairy-chested, dark-eyed fellow—thinning hair, but a good ten years my junior—slipped into the tub beside me. I turned to look at him, as one does at such moments. He did not offer a smile—the usual signal of incipient interest—so I re-focused on the passionate pair.

A few seconds later, a hand caressed my thigh beneath the water. So as not to break the spell of forbidden touching, I did not look at the caresser. Rather, I kept eyes directed toward the Innamorati and reached out beneath water to find the swarthy cruiser's thigh, which I reciprocally caressed. His hand slid to my inner thigh; my hand slid to his. His hand grabbed my excitement; my hand grabbed his much larger one. Having now greeted one another with proper sauna handshake, we turned to look into one another's eyes. He spoke something in German; I asked, "English?"

This excited him—a linguist, perhaps?—and he pulled me toward him, reached both hands beneath my buttocks, buoyed me up close to the surface, took me deeply into his mouth. I moaned delight until he pulled back his head. I leaned down to kiss, but he shook his head. "No. Not homosexual."

Ah, one of those who would do the deed but "dare not speak its name."

He asked, "You homosexual?"

"Most definitely."

He hoisted himself up to the tub's edge, sported his circumcised erection proudly. I demonstrated my own skill at speaking in tongues. His groaning and breathing intensified until he pulled my head off him. "Stop. I fuck you now." Rather presumptuous of him, but he had not misread my desires.

Desires. Yes, desires of various kinds were now surging through me, so unlike my torpid reactions during bathhouse forays of the past. It was as though the erotic charge I had experienced with the little blond had flung me open to all manner of sexual joy, as if some clogged libido artery had been angioplastied by the taste of blood and feel of dead flesh so that now, even bloodless and life-affirming frivolity could serve as source of joy.

"You have *kabine*?" asked the endowed would-be fucker.

"Yes," I replied.

Stepping out of the hot tub and starting to towel off, he asked where I was from. Hearing "America," he gave a wistful smile. "My son studies in America to become doctor."

A bell rang in my head, but I could not yet hear the chime clearly. I asked where he was originally from.

"Turkmenistan."

And so. How many Turkomans could there possibly be in Munich? Had not Fatima, the hotel's breakfast waitress, said this morning that her son was studying to be a doctor in Florida? If she and this cocksucker weren't husband and wife, I was in an Ionesco play.

Had I realized earlier what a despicable cheat this Turkoman was, I'd have chomped down hard on his mouth-watering erection in the hot tub and left bloody teeth marks. He'd have had quite the time explaining to poor Fatima how some stray neighborhood pit bull had mangled his cock without so much as piercing his trousers.

"You don't happen to be an anesthesiologist from Ashgabat," I asked, "do you?"

I'd never before seen as startled an expression as his. He stared in stunned disbelief.

"And your son in America," I continued, "he's studying medicine in Florida, correct?"

The man's eyes expanded silver-dollar wide, his face taking on an overall cast of horror.

"And your wife, Fatima, serves breakfast at a local hotel."

"You…you secret police?" he paled, fell back against the tile wall as if about to faint.

I shook a scolding finger in his face. "How dare you cheat on that lovely woman. How dare you risk bringing heaven-knows-which diseases into your marital bed."

He put up his hands as if fending off attack. "I legal resident. I have papers. No deport."

"Then don't ever let me catch you here again!"

He shook his head repeatedly, darted to the stairs and, presumably, fled the sauna. The amorous couple in the hot tub were now staring at me. "Lovers' quarrel," I tossed out in explanation.

I bear no tolerance for cheaters like the worst of my many foster fathers. How many nights had my last foster mother cried herself to sleep on her New York City fire escape while that bum was out carousing with heaven-knows-how-many Times Square whores? At sixteen, I confronted him. He back-slapped me across the face before ordering me to "mind your own goddamn business, you little faggot."

How had he known?

(The following morning at breakfast, I would ask Fatima how she and her husband had spent their Saturday. She responded that he'd gone to work in the afternoon as he typically did on Saturdays to catch up on paperwork, but then returned home surprisingly early, "and with the most beautiful flowers, and then, teehee, he showed me more romance than for many years."

It not being my place to destroy illusions, I revealed nothing of her husband's sauna philanderings.

"I do not speak of such privacy to another man," she continued, a slightly puzzled look on her face. "But to you is acceptable. You are a special man."

"Not special, just homosexual."

She gasped and covered her mouth with fingers finely manicured and nails painted pearlescent pink. "I have seen on German television and also on the street two men holding hands in a romantic way. But never before do I speak to one."

I chose my words carefully. "I'm certain that you have spoken to one, my dear, but simply were unaware at the time. We homos lurk everywhere. Perhaps even beneath your own bed."

She laughed at the absurdity of my suggestion.)

Pleased by my virtuous righting of a marital wrong, yet at the same time frustrated at having lost out on what would likely have been a hearty and once-in-a-lifetime Turkoman fuck, I lay back in the now-empty hot tub just as I heard that familiar gaggle of American voices. Yes, the street festival's insulting boys—*your* boys, Mr. Hahnemann—were coming up off the stairs. They, with their aren't-we-fashionable red-white-and-blue headbands. And that tall, arrogant, I-resemble-Spanish-royalty jawed blond was among them, his thick nipples protruding and nearly begging for a good chew. Or severance from torso. 'Imagine yourself his employer granting him the ultimate severance package,' I thought to myself, snickering at the pun.

The group looked around, assessed, seemed not even to notice me. My bile rose to a tropical storm pitch of humiliation anger. It was then that the kind muscleman offered me a kelly green wink that I returned with a smile. Hope springs eternal. He opened the glass door and stepped into the steam room.

I thought to follow, but first wished to see if the mandibular blond might enter the hot tub. Daddy's little rich boy, no doubt, fed cream of wheat on a silver spoon, raised by doting nannies, popular in his private schools with his cute little navy blue sailor suit uniforms and caps, top grades because he paid other boys to do his homework and take his exams, the high school star athlete and Prom King who fucked—raped?—every girl in school while secretly sucking half the football team under the bleachers. He attended some Ivy League college—Princeton?—a legacy student admitted because of Daddy's multi-million donation of an endowed chair in whichever department Pretty Boy chose as major for the unearned degree he'd be granted. Probably took a private limo into Manhattan every weekend to shop at Brooks Brothers and slum about in a Chelsea bathhouse, ever the hot center of attention because of his model-like good looks, getting as much cock and ass as he pleased. How I wished to teach him a lesson he'd never forget.

Two of the group—the Latino and Japanese fellows—slipped into the hot tub without so much as a glance in my direction. Actually, that is not true. The Japanese fellow glanced quickly at me but instantly lowered his gaze, as if to spare me a meeting of the eyes that might remind of my earlier public humiliation at the festival.

The others, however, including the mandibular blond asshole, tracked the green-eyed muscleman into the steam room. I counted five seconds, stepped out of the hot tub, then grabbed my towel and followed suit.

Inside the dimly lit room, billows of steam clouded my vision. I groped for the slippery tile wall, slowly felt my way around the room's perimeter, followed soft grunts audible beneath the periodic hiss of released steam. I discerned a shadow cluster oddly undulating *Othello*-like—a classic beast with multiple backs. A cluster suck.

I sidled closer until within groping range. I slid my hand along one slick back and another, up onto various sweaty shoulders, now to wet curly hair, now to kinky hair, now to long straight and fine hair sticking to skin. Absorbed in their collective sucking and lapping, unable to distinguish faces in the steam, no one stopped me. Here, all hands, dicks, nips, and mouths were welcome.

I felt along this cheek and that, this jawline and that until—yes! Here was that distinctive protruding jaw. I slid my hand down to pincer his thick nips, but two men's heads blocked my approach with their furious nip-sucking. I stepped aside and reached behind him—his towel was off.

Carpe diem.

I grabbed his muscular buttocks, slid my finger ever-so-gently between them so as to tickle this asshole's asshole. No resistance—in fact, he slightly arched his back to grant easier access. Had I been able to throw an erection as spontaneously as in my youth, I'd have thrust into him mercilessly and torn up his insides then and there, but another option popped into my modestly aging head. So, I maneuvered beside one of the nip-suckers, reached around to feel a thick-haired head bouncing up and down on the phallus as enormous as I recalled it to have been during my observation in Copenhagen. I felt below and grabbed humongous full balls hanging low in the steam room's heat.

Adhering to orgy etiquette, I dropped to my knees, craned my neck, extended my tongue, and awaited permission to join. Without unfilling his mouth, the cocksucker shifted just enough to the side to grant me shared access, and I proceeded to lick those musky hairless balls. I licked and licked, biding time and awaiting my opportunity, listening as the asshole groaned with pleasure. I felt his forearm brush against the back of my neck as he reached to grab the cocksucker's head and shove him further down. The sucker gagged, pulled off that horse cock, coughed and backed away.

My moment!

I lunged to replace the sucker and deep-throated the cock to the base, decades of experience having trained me in gag reflex suppression. I allowed the asshole to grip the back of my head and facefuck me. Up-down fast, up-down fast, faster faster masturbation in my mouth. Just as his hand-shoves and hip-thrusts revealed imminence of explosion, I clamped my front teeth down onto the base mightily. I bit as I had my supper sausage, pierced through skin and attempted to gorge on as great a mouthful as my rage-hunger could contain, all while frustrating his near orgasm.

An instant of stilled shock, then an agony howl. He thrust out his hands to claw at my head and pummel. As he writhed, the nip-suckers groaned and clamped tighter onto his chest, their shifting shoulders inadvertently shielding me from the worst of my victim's attempted blows. Resolute pit bull that I'd become, I chomped down even harder, swallowed wet gushes as I brought my gnashing molars into play and shredded as much flesh as possible. The spew of his blood did not in the least offend me the way the spew of semen would have. On the contrary, I relished the hot coppery taste even more now than I had the little blond's in Copenhagen.

In the heavy fog of poorly lit steam, others around couldn't possibly perceive what was happening, must have thought him in the throes of ecstasy. He shrieked and shrieked, flailed at me to no avail. As I gulped his heady red liquor, feverish arousal spurred me passionately on to gnaw furiously halfway through his cock until a landed blow between my shoulder blades brought me to my senses. I gave a good final strafing of teeth along the now-raw shaft, reared back, and crawled quickly away amid a growing commotion.

Before exiting the steam room, I yanked off my towel, stuffed a corner into my mouth to absorb whatever evidence remained, wiped lips, mustache, chin, and chest of spurted blood, hurled the towel into a corner. Stepping calmly out into the wet foyer's relatively cool air and bright illumination, I casually stood beneath one of the showerheads and quickly washed face, neck, and chest while keeping an eye on the steam room door.

I did not have long to wait.

In mere moments, my victim flung the door open while grabbing his crotch and screaming in agonizing curdles, "My dick! My dick!" The group's Nubian wrapped arms around him from behind, supporting him while desperately asking, "What the fuck happened?"

"My dick! My dick!" He removed his hands to display the carnage. What amazing butchery! His softened-but-still-enormous dick dangled half-severed. Blood gushing. The Nubian grabbed a towel from a wall hook and pressed it to the man's crotch in obvious attempt to stanch the flow. "Cute tampon, big boy!" I wanted to hurl in effeminizing humiliation, but restrained myself so as not to attract attention. He collapsed onto the wet foyer floor.

The Latino and Japanese boys in the hot tub yanked themselves free from the embraces of apparent locals, jumped out and joined their compatriots who were rushing from the steam room. In admirable display of group cohesion, they carried my victim—my conquest—to the stairs and down.

I re-immersed myself into the frothing hot tub, dunked my head for a quick underwater gargle. Ever-so-faint traces of incriminatory pink bubbled around me, then quickly dissipated among the roiling jacuzzi swirls. I leaned back in the hot tub where the remaining locals sat and frantically gossiped. I shut my eyes, rested back of head on hot tub rim, softly sighed as all tension drained from arms and legs.

However, my throbbing erection refused to subside. I thought to release myself right there in the public hot tub, but the notion struck me as inexcusably vulgar. So I suffered while secretly proud of my pubescent vigor. If only others would take notice!

. . .

You cringe, Mr. Hahnemann, and cross your legs tightly in the face of my explicitness. In fact, your pallor has acquired a hint of green. I shall ignore your squeamish reaction, but permit me to point out that my reflexive arousal at encounters with death and gore is not all that dissimilar from your reflexive distress at hearing me tell of it. Reflexive responses both. Are we not relatively similar beings, then? Both victims of bodily reflexes? Should I be condemned for my reflexive physical responses whereas you are to be pitied for yours?

The instantaneous arousal in Copenhagen sparked by the dead little blond's cold clammy skin and tasty bloody towel were one thing. But now, my remarkable physiological response to the partial ingestion of bloody penile sponge and residual savory taste confirmed that it was not only actual death that could excite me. No, my erotic impulses were proving to be of considerably broader range, as they had been in the fantasies of my youth. The taste of blood, the life source itself, was sufficient to arouse. Life, not death. Rather, life as well as death. Did that make me bi-existential?

And, of course, I realized—one is not, after all, un-self-aware—I realized that both encounters involved the exercise of power to inflict devastation onto a considerably younger and allegedly more virile male. Intoxicating aphrodisiacal power. The power of ecstasy and agony, life and death, lay within me. I was lion, hear me roar.

My Memories: Munich—Post FuckFest

What the fuck! First we lost Little Frenchie in Copenhagen and then Dean got attacked in Munich? What a fucked-up coincidence. The Pope and other celibates'd say it was punishment for our sins.

Shitfuckpiss!

So here's what I saw, how I realized, and what I did: I was sitting in the van down the block from Freundschaft. I was watching the screens of the boys' and Burt's livestream video feeds from inside the sauna. I saw the boys climb the stairs to the wet area—stepping *carefully* on the stairs so they wouldn't pull a Little Frenchie—and watched 'em file into the steam room. Really thick steam. Fuzzy in there like in the steam room at Buddies.

Note to Self: in order to cover up video limitations, say in next season's prospectus that we'll show some action in haze or shadows **on purpose**, *leaving it to the viewers' imagination. Call it a nod to good taste discretion and that sort of bullshit.*

At least I could hear all kinds of grunts and slurps from the steam room's audio feeds. And I could see outlines of the boys groping, locals feeling 'em up, and everybody doing what's normal. Half the boys dropped to their knees—I couldn't make out faces, but I could more or less guess who was who based on body shape and movement. Lotsa shadows of locals snaking around 'em and giving/getting head. All normal.

Then a tall one with long hair and thick nips—had to be Dean—made himself the center of an orgy mob. A kneeling sucker—I couldn't make out anything in the steam except he was average to husky, definitely not thin— took Dean's monster cock deep while twisting his head right and left. I figured he was some gag-the-fag guy who loved being cock-choked. I thought, "Wow, way hot." Then Dean wolf-howled in a weird way, pounded his fists on the cocksucker, or tried to. His fists couldn't reach because a coupla nip-suckers got in the way, so Dean was more like flailing than pummeling.

Dean wolf-howled more and more. His arms went wild. He shrieked like some wounded beast in the forest. Something was wrong. Burt—I could tell it was him from his sexy dad bod—rushed in close and yanked those guys off Dean's nips. All the boys' video feeds went haywire in all directions and I couldn't see the cocksucker anymore, just random steamy ceiling and tile floor shots and close close close-ups of Dean's face. Even through the steam, Dean's face looked twisted like those old European paintings of men being dragged down to Hell. What the fuck?

I jumped outta the van and raced to the sauna. By the time I got inside, the boys and Burt had already gotten Dean to the front desk where the panicky woman manager was calling Munich's 911, from what I could make out. Burt had squeezed a towel around Dean's dick, but blood kept soaking through.

Paramedics showed up fast, gurneyed Dean to an ambulance. "His dick! Hold his dick!" yelled Burt. He yanked the locker key wristbands and headband cams off himself and Dean, tossed 'em to me, and jumped into the ambulance to leave with Dean.

The boys were freaking out. Yuki and Freddy stood frozen, in obvious shock. Femmy Tommy clutched bearish Sam like that'd make himself safe. Manny stomped around, cursing *"coño!"* and other Spanish shit, made throttling hand gestures like he'd choke the goddamn son-of-a-bitch who did this. Big Bill elbow-leaned on the entry counter with tears streaming down his cheeks—you just knew he was mourning Little Frenchie all over again.

My God, poor Dean. And the other boys, so terrified.

What the fuck should I do to help calm 'em down? Be sensitive? Be firm? It was my job as coach to take charge.

Then I realized: holy shit—the boys were all still wearing their headbands, so that meant that *the boys' live-streaming cameras were still filming.* That meant our subscribers had seen the attack online, the blood-gushing, the paramedics, and were now watching the boys' reactions at the front desk.

I had to think quick—maybe I should shut tonight's FuckFest down right now because everyone was so freaked out? Maybe cancel the whole Tour? But, if I did that, we'd lose the pot of gold at the end of the rainbow. And if we didn't at least return investors' front money, they'd go apeshit on my ass. Italian Mafia, Russian Mafia (i.e., ex-KGB), drug cartels, bloodthirsty jihadis, and nuclear Kim Fucking Jung Un.

No, I couldn't disband the show now. The FuckFest had to continue. But would the attack on Dean turn viewers off? It was one thing to watch fucking, but another to watch mutilation, although a few pervs might get into it. Would the majority abandon us?

Or maybe…maybe I should film the boys' reactions on purpose? Yeah. Yeah, that was it. Brilliant, Paulie, brilliant! Just show the boys as they are, I realized. Show 'em upset. That'll make 'em relatable to viewers and make 'em sympathetic and real, more than just sexy fuck machines. The fear. The shock. Even Bill's tears. Especially Bill's tears.

So, I slipped Dean's headband camera around my neck, facing front, and yanked Burt's onto my head.

With the woman manager's permission, I huddled the boys in a corner of the locker room while a dozen patrons nervously rushed to dress and leave. How many understood what had just happened?

I let the boys vent for a while, then, "Boys," I said, scanning 'em with my cameras, "look at me. Direct your cams to my face." My time on camera. My time in the spotlight. A make-or-break moment.

"Boys, we've had a shock. A terrible, hideous shock. As producer, I'm the first to say we all know that Dean can be an asshole. Maybe he pissed some guy off? Maybe he turned somebody down with that hotter-than-you attitude he had."

"Don't you go blaming the victim," sputtered Manny. "Dean's an asshole, but he didn't deserve this."

"You're right," I said. "I apologize."

Apologies shift power to the one who gets the apology. Manny puffed up his chest. "Besides," Manny continued, "we'd practically just arrived. We were all walking around in a group. Dean didn't have time to treat anybody like shit before we went into the steam room."

"You're making good sense, Manny," I said, focusing my cameras on his face, "maintaining objectivity. The attack on Dean makes you angry, doesn't it?"

"You bet." He pounded fist into palm.

The line between rage and lust is sometimes thin—I wanted to help the boys cross it so their anger would sex-juice 'em up. "Let's see your macho power, Manny. You're lean, but you're a hurricane."

"If I ever find the *cabrón* who did this, I'll smash his face." Again Manny punched fist into palm.

"Manny, our protector."

"You know it."

"Bill?" I stroked the back of Big Bill's sweaty head while keeping the cameras focused on him. He looked up—those sad Beagle eyes would tug viewers' heartstrings for sure. I patted his massive shoulders. "I know you're reacting to Little Frenchie's death in Copenhagen, too. You two really had a connection, didn't you?"

He spoke softly. "What's going on, Paulie? What kind of psycho attack was that? Nearly ripping a dick off during an orgy suck? A week after Little Frenchie slipped and—? I've been going to the baths for years and never saw anybody get hurt. Well, maybe somebody'd slip in the shower, or an old man'd get a heart attack from too many poppers, but that was it. Nothing like getting your dick chewed off. Or falling down a flight of steps and breaking your neck. What's going on?"

"Maybe it is Europe," said Yuki in a dry voice. "Europe is more free than U.S., but freedom costs. In U.S. bathhouses they always ask for ID, but not here. So, crazy people are feeling free to misbehave."

"That wouldn't explain Little Frenchie's accident," said Bill.

With his arm protectively around Femmy Tommy's shoulders, bearish Sam said, "The manager called the paramedics, but not the police. The monster could still be roaming around in here. Paulie, tell the manager to call the police."

Like hell I would. The manager was a savvy businesswoman who probably didn't want the police shutting her place down, spreading the word to newspapers, causing her to lose business forever. Did I want her to call the cops? Fuck no. The last thing I needed was German cops asking questions. Especially if one of the boys spilled something about Little Frenchie dying in Copenhagen. Two horrors at saunas when Paulie's boys were in town?—like Bill, the cops would connect the incidents and maybe get suspicious even though we're totally innocent. We could all end up in a concentration camp.

"Sam," I said, "we're guests in this country. They have their own ways of doing things, and we shouldn't interfere."

"But—"

"Look, the maniac knows that everyone here's on the lookout now, so why would he stay and risk getting caught? He probably already left. The cops'd never find him."

"Or he could still be hiding in a *kabine*."

"Come on, he's a coward who attacked during a group session. He was hiding under cover of steam. People like that never attack out in the open. So, to be on the safe side, just stay away from the steam room."

"Stay away from——?" asked Femmy Tommy. "You don't expect us——"

"——to keep screwing around tonight, do you?" Sam finished Tommy's question like they were one mind.

"Yes," I said while wondering if maybe I was going too far. "I do expect you to keep screwing around."

Tommy and Sam looked at one another, then Sam said, "Are you out of your fucking mind? You think I'm going to risk getting my dick chewed off?"

"Come on, Sam," I said, knowing I had to do whatever was necessary to save the Tour. For everyone's sake. "You're not gonna let some maniac win, are you?"

"Paulie's right," said Manny. "We can't let that fucker win."

"He's a terrorist," I continued. "A homophobic terrorist. We can't let terrorists win."

"Paulie," said Tommy, "you expect us to risk our lives so you can make money?"

"You think all I care about is money?" I asked. "After all the money I've spent on you boys—booking you nice hotels, arranging interesting outings and restaurants? I care about you fellas, about each and every one of you. I'm heartbroken over Little Frenchie, and sick with worry over Dean. The reason I want you boys to march right back up there and fuck your brains out is for your own self-confidence. The attack on Dean is an attack on each of you. It's like falling off a horse—if you don't get back on right away, you never will. If you boys don't mix it up again right now, your fear will grow and grow over time and you might never feel comfortable playing in a bathhouse again. Hell, you might never feel comfortable even having sex again. Is that what you want?"

"Cut the crap," said Sam. "Tommy's right. All you're thinking about is your show and money."

That pissed me off. "So what if I am thinking about the show in addition to your well-being? What if I am thinking about money? We owe it to all our subscribers, who've paid big bucks to watch you guys." I said this for the subscribers who were watching us live. "And don't forget, it's your money, too, Sam, right? Tommy? Not just the grand prize, but the tens of thousands each and every one of you will get as a cut if the show's a success. You don't all wanna lose that, do you?"

The boys looked from one to another for a few secs, thinking.

"I guess each of us really needs the money, or else we wouldn't be here in the first place," said Tommy as he rubbed a hand along Sam's hairy back the way one husband does to another. "We've all got a stake in this, Sam."

Sam looked down at the linoleum floor. "I guess you're right, Paulie," he said. "Sorry for being such a prick."

"No worries, Sam," I said, "We're all stressed out of our gourds."

Part of me was loving this discussion. Every second was being live-streamed—the boys' fears of getting their dicks mutilated, the talk about terrorists. I couldn't have scripted it better. Talk about reality show drama!

At the same time, I really did wanna help the boys reduce risk: "Listen, fellas," I said, "I need you to stay safe, so keep totally away from the whole floor with the steam room and hot tub. I'm declaring it off-limits. For your safety, on the outside chance the psycho's still here, although I'm sure he's gone. The building's got two other floors. Maybe three, I don't know. Explore. They advertise glory holes and mazes. Find 'em, have sex to get your mind off Dean, and show that Nazi terrorist he can't win. Think about Little Frenchie, a real sex trooper. He was the most gung-ho cocksucker I ever saw. Not afraid of anything. If he were here, I know he'd want us to continue. Don't you think, Bill?"

I crossed my fingers. Thank God, Big Bill slowly nodded. "Paulie's got a point," he said. "Little Frenchie would never back down to anyone. Nobody was more into that first FuckFest than him. We should fuck our brains out for Little Frenchie. Paulie, you'll keep track of Little Frenchie's share of the show's profits like he was still alive, right? And send them to his mother back in Montreal?"

Shit, I hadn't thought about that. But what could I say? "Sure, Bill, sure. I'll keep track of Little Frenchie's cut and will make sure his mom gets it." As if Bill would ever know what I did with Frenchie's share.

"See, guys," said Bill, "Paulie's decent. Let's do this for Little Frenchie, in his honor, okay?"

Slowly, one after another, they nodded.

I waved all the boys into an arm-around-shoulder huddle and said, "For Little Frenchie."

The boys repeated, "For Little Frenchie." It became a chant. "For Little Frenchie. For Little Frenchie. For Little Frenchie!" They sort of pumped themselves up.

I broke the huddle and slapped a few firm asses like a football coach. "Okay, boys, go find your adventures for Little Frenchie."

"For Little Frenchie!" they said in one voice as they left the locker room.

"And for Dean," muttered Manny, turning his head to me just before leaving.

Killer Interview 5

Have you given any thought to my previous intimations from the last time we spoke, Mr. Hahnemann? That you and I share wisps of kindred spirit? Might your interest in my perspective reach beyond typical perverse curiosity and actually extend to a worry about yourself? A fear of what might lurk within?

. . .

There's no call for you to denigrate me with foul names, Mr. Hahnemann.

I have made my point and shall not belabor the issue. Let us return to my narrative of the events of that evening:

After the steam room commotion had moved elsewhere—the FuckFest boys had left the sauna's wet floor and were presumably carrying my disgorged steak tartare to an ambulance—and after my youthful distension finally began to lose rigidity, I stepped from the hot tub, grabbed someone else's damp towel from a wall hook, cinched it around my waist and ever-so-casually departed the floor to explore others. I soon discovered the elegant relaxation room consisting of an upper level with lounge chairs, a lower level covered in red mats, and a spacious middle level sporting an exposed brick wall, subdued lighting from wood-framed windows, and small trees in planters. So soothing an ambiance. Not another soul. Presumably, half the patrons were reacting hysterically to my, shall we say, early evening munchies—'munchies in München,' I rather like that!—while others were continuing to pursue their oblivious or disinterested fornications.

I lay back on one of the ergonomic loungers coated in blue glass mosaic tiles, luxuriated in the warm radiating heat. Draping towel modestly across crotch, I then clasped hands behind head, shut my eyes, smiled gently at the faint, residual, back-of-palate metallic flavor of dickblood. A Francis Bacon quotation jingled through my head: "Revenge is a kind of wild justice." I'd never before considered myself wild, but had always regarded myself as just. A comforting adage. By general appearances, I was—am—an ordinary sort, quiet and soft-spoken without external manifestation of barbarity. But within my core, I possess as much primal scream as any man.

Becalmed by soft music that overlay sounds of rippling water (merely the sound? an actual fountain?), I debated whether I should permit the indulgence of mutilating and/or killing once more for the sheer erotic pleasure of doing so. Most likely, I was sufficiently clever to avoid detection and evade capture.

I did wonder, nevertheless, whether my elimination of contestants might potentially result in a diminution of investment returns. After all, maximization of profit had been my motivation for investing in The Grand Sex Tour in the first place, had it not? Indeed, I'd followed the boys to Europe precisely to keep a close eye on the performance of my venture capital.

I cogitated.

After considerable contemplation, I concluded that as long as an adequate number of boys remained alive and sufficiently intact to revel as planned in the remaining three FuckFests, nothing would be lost because the monetization streams would continue to flow: as word of The Grand Sex Tour continued to spread, subscribers would continue to pay their registration fees, watch and gamble, and you, dear Mr. Hahnemann, would still be able to splice together your subsequent "best of" director's cut film for sale. True, subscribers who had already bet on the deceased little blond or the now penis-disabled Mr. Arrogance, might theoretically skulk away in frustration at having gambled on the wrong contestant. More likely, however, given gamblers' inclination to throw good money after bad, they would bet once again—this time on a surviving contestant—thereby providing us with unanticipated additional revenue.

Inhaling the relaxation room's flowery fragrance—gardenia?—I reasoned further: might not my elimination of those two from competition actually enhance overall public interest in our venture? Inadvertently, had I not injected into The Grand Sex Tour a hitherto absent element of suspenseful danger?: if one boy died and another suffered brutal attack, what sort of other risks lurked in bathhouse shadows? Might viewers gamble not only on which contestant would achieve the greatest number of sexual conquests but also on which one would most likely survive intact? Yes, my actions had not at all hurt our profits; on the contrary, they had likely enhanced them. And so, if at some point in the near future, I were to feel inclined to permit myself another erotic indulgence that might involve a tad of gore or that might result in another boy's—

"Must be a super dream."

I opened my eyes to see the gorgeous red-headed African American muscleman seated on the mosaic lounger beside mine. I detected traces of shower-washed Aramis cologne, that distinct mix of grassy cinnamon notes and woody leather. Estée Lauder's finest. (Apropos of nothing except interest in trivia: Estée Lauder, née Josephine Esther Mentzer, is buried in Block 3 at Beth-El Cemetery, Paramus, New Jersey. Ms. Lauder would, no doubt, appreciate the occasional spritz onto her massive, yet tastefully simple headstone, should you or your readers care to visit.)

"You were smiling," said the fellow while breathing hard, with perspiration dripping, kelly green eyes darting about, hands fidgeting in lap. He'd initiated conversation with me, a resting patron. A desire, finally, to meet? To interact? To play?

I sat up and faced him. "Hello, my boy." As soon as I spoke the words, I realized the potential for misunderstanding, and instantly explained myself. "I don't mean to insult by addressing you as 'my boy.' Nothing racial. I just mean—fatherly, you understand. I would use the same expression for a White young man, a Latino or Asian."

"Understood. But thanks for explaining."

I reached over and placed a hand gently on his muscular forearm. "You showed kindness to me at the gay festival, and again when you noticed me sitting at the café table out front. And your wink beside the hot tub—I am deeply grateful."

"Don't mention it." He neither removed my hand from his forearm nor recoiled at my touch. "Sorry I'm bothering you, but—"

"Nonsense, not a bother at all."

"—I just need to talk to somebody, and I know you speak English, and you seem friendly."

"By all means, my boy." I stroked his forearm. No resistance.

"I shouldn't be in here," he said. "I should be out tricking around."

"But if you're tired, why should you not relax a bit?"

"I'm in a sex competition thing. Have to score lots of tricks to win."

"You look like a winner to me."

"Thanks—really—but right now, I'm freaking out." He massaged his forehead, inadvertently shoving his red-white-and-blue headband askew, like a drunk's tiara.

I reached over and pulled the headband entirely off. "Your sweatband looks uncomfortable," I said, and set it beside him, bulge—camera—facing down. The less I appeared on film, the better.

"Oh, thanks. Yeah, it would be a bummer to lose the camera."

"Camera?" I needed to play dumb.

"For the competition. To prove we're tricking. For the points."

"Sounds complicated."

"Not really, it's just sex. But right now, I…"

"Has something upset you?"

"You didn't see? You were upstairs in the hot tub, right?"

"Yes, I immersed myself for a short while, then left."

"You must've come down here before it happened."

"Before what happened?"

"Some monster attacked Dean, one of the other guys in our group. The blond guy who was an asshole to you at the festival."

"You don't say!" Campy clutching-at-pearls shock gesture worthy of a commedia dell'arte veteran.

"Some guy in the steam room nearly bit Dean's dick off."

"Good Lord!"

"I know, right?"

"Did they catch the perpetrator?"

"No. So much steam, we couldn't see shit."

A suspicion occurred: "What about your camera? I noticed your friends were wearing similar sweatbands. Also cameras? Perhaps someone picked up the monster's face?"

"No. Paulie—he's the guy who watches the camera video feeds—he was watching all our steam room footage while it was happening. He said he couldn't see anything except shapes, a bunch of guys on their knees in front of Dean while others were groping him."

"Typical orgy, a mass of writhing arms and other limbs "

"Yeah."

"What about sound? Perhaps the perpetrator's voice?"

"Just grunts, according to Paulie. Then Dean's screams."

"Typical." So…those headband cameras could transmit sound. I had not considered the possibility. If sound, then…conversation? My current conversation with this fellow?

I reached up and stroked his beautiful jawline.

"Thanks for that," he said. "The tenderness, I mean."

At that moment, the two Germans who'd been frolicking in the hot tub earlier now entered the relax room and sat on two other loungers beside ours. "If you'd like," I volunteered, "I've got a *kabine*, as they say. We could continue our conversation there."

"You sure are nice. But, I don't want to waste your time. You didn't come to the baths to calm some upset guy."

Waste? Would it be a waste of time to take a gorgeous, near-naked young man to my private lair? Where I could offer comfort and inspire emotional intimacy that could lead to who-knows-what fulfillment of deep desires I still had yet to discover? I patted his hand. "There are many satisfying ways to connect with another man. Come, let's go."

He picked up his headband and pressed the camera against his palm in a tight fist, much as the little blond had done before his fateful fall at Buddies. "Paulie doesn't need to see and hear everything," he said.

Perfect.

As we walked downstairs and made our way through a circuitous labyrinth I trembled in excitement at the possibility of making love with this Adonis. In my private *kabine*, I could perhaps give vent to my newly awakened desire for mutilation and murder. How would it feel to close my fingers tightly around his throat as I sat upon him, rocked in prostatory ecstasy? Initially, he would think my throat-grasp an effort to restrict breathing so as to enhance the explosiveness of his own orgasmic release. Only too late would he suspect my true intentions. Would the body expel ejaculate at the precise moment of death? Had university studies been conducted? What joy to be the last to take in this stunning young man's life force before death.

On the other hand, had not White men committed enough harm to Black men over the centuries? Might not my murder of him be misinterpreted as an expression of racial animus? At the moment of realization of my intent to kill, might he himself misperceive my motivation as racial hostility? I was happy to mutilate and/or murder, but I refused either to inflict cruel psychological pain or appear to indulge in barbaric White supremacist cliché. (I leave it to you, Mr. Hahnemann, to determine which I find more offensive: White supremacy or cliché.) No, I would enjoy simple pleasures and spare him pain of any kind. Mercy, I reminded myself, was a quality of the Divine.

"Here we are," I said as we entered my small, faux-marble tiled *kabine* and shut the door.

Looking shyly down at his feet, toying with the headband, yet being careful to keep the camera pressed against his palm, the young man asked in a soft voice, "Would you hold me? It's not a come-on. I just really could use a daddy hug."

Ah, I'd long wondered at the possible pleasures of daddy-boy roleplay wherein each partner offers a relationship needed by the other yet with a sexual component supplementing and intensifying otherwise routine expressions of filial affection and love. A psychological inter-generational "69" one might say, each fulfilling a deep reciprocal need.

"You sweet young fellow," I said, reaching out to him, pulling him close. Again, a faint whiff of somewhat faded cinnamony Aramis cologne. This earnest young man wrapped his arms around me, stooped a bit to rest his head on my shoulder. In the wall mirror, I saw him reach over to the chair and drop the camera band there, face down. He tugged off his towel and tossed it on top. I undid my own towel and tossed it atop his—our conversation would be totally muffled against the camera's microphone.

I felt warm tears on my shoulder and the gentle stirrings of his arousal against my belly. "How's about we lie down," I said softly, "so I can hold you properly, and you can talk to me."

"I'd like that, Daddy."

The appellation suffused me with indefinable warmth, my always having assumed I'd one day die without ever hearing such ordinary, yet profound, address.

We climbed onto the red-matted table-bed and spooned, me behind, holding him. We were now facing away from the wall mirror. Even as I gently pressed against his muscular buttocks, I resisted the urge to reach down and fondle him. All in good time.

He talked and talked about the competition taking place in varying cities. I pretended to be surprised, fascinated, titillated as I stroked first his muscular upper arm, then his shoulder. My fingers stopped when he spoke of another friend's "accidental fall down a staircase at a sauna in Copenhagen." Ahah, so no one suspected the little blond's fall to have been murder.

I then butterfly caressed his neck with my fingertips. He stopped speaking, flipped around to face me, looked straight into my eyes. "You're such a kind man," he whispered. "We just met, but you took me right under your wing to make me feel safe. Like a real daddy would."

"You showed me great kindess today."

"Daddy?" he whispered, toying tenderly with the waxed curled tips of my white mustache.

"Yes…my son?"

He kissed me. Full on the lips. Slipped in his thick tongue that I reflexively sucked as deeply into my mouth as possible. Could such fantasy be real?

He pulled back his head and stared into my eyes with those practically kelly green irridescents of his. "I've always had a thing for daddies," he whispered. "I don't know why. Even before my own father died last month. Back in Austin. Missing him is like carrying a ton of cement on my chest. Should I have pulled out of the competition? I signed up before he died. Am I a bad son for going through with it now?"

I caressed his cheek. "By asserting your maleness in the competition, by displaying the beauty of your father's genetic creation, his legacy, you do him honor."

He again kissed me deeply. "Even before you came over to us at the gay festival, I noticed you and thought you were way cute. And when you did come over, I thought maybe I'd have a chance to talk to you, but then Dean shot off his mouth. And when I saw you at the restaurant outside, I was kind of hoping you'd come into the sauna. And when I spotted you in the hot tub, and we winked, I thought maybe you'd follow me into the steam room. But I couldn't see a thing in there—did you follow me in there, Daddy?"

"No, but I wish I had, my dear boy," I whispered, holding him close, feeling his stiffness press against mine. "I just assumed you gorgeous young fellows would regard me with disdain, so I stayed out of the steam room. I'm not a pushy sort."

"Daddy," he said, kissing my forehead. Then we clutched at one another nearly with desperation, kissed once more. He roamed hands over my hairy back and beneath my towel to clutch the fleshiness of my behind; I ran palms along the muscular armature of his back and buttocks and thighs, gentled my fingers along his soft, dyed-red velcro hair, then far below where I grasped—sigh—remarkable.

He shoved me back, pinned my wrists to the table-mat. This was too good, too amazing, too beautiful and rare. Harm this dear, passionate, beautiful young man who regarded me as a Creator figure? Impossible. Rather, I felt a completely new sensation, an overwhelming desire to please him. Let him take charge, let him do with me as he would. Whatever he wanted. His licks along my neck made me writhe, then his nibbles on my nipples—electric shocks jolting me with pleasure. Just as I wished to please him, so he wished to pleasure me. I'd never known such genuine lovemaking.

He lunged further down and sucked me deep into his mouth. I gasped and moaned, groaned and sighed. He did not rush me, took his sweet time until I shuddered in climax.

He swallowed, climbed back up to kiss me lightly. "Thank you, Daddy. This one was off-camera, totally for me."

"I don't know what to say." This was truth. Never had I been so generously ravished by such a beautiful young man. Never had my body, mind, and heart joined to allow me such deep thrills. I was now experiencing what I had dismissed long ago as romanticized impossibility. Might this possibly be, I wondered, the phenomenon of ever-elusive love?

...

Yes, Mr. Hahnemann, I said "love." Do you think me incapable of this most noble of emotions? I wished to receive more of his tender kisses, to hold him longer in my protective paternal arms, to remain in this man's Herculean presence. Even without tasting his blood.

He stood, picked up his towel and headband (again clutched tightly in his fist). "I feel better now that I've got Daddy inside me. I'm ready to keep going with the contest. Thank you."

"Thank *you*," I said, stepping over to him. "Thank *you* thank *you* thank *you*." I pulled his head gently down and covered his face with kisses.

"By the way," he said, grinning broadly, "my name's Freddy."

"And I'm...Daddy." My ordinary brown eyes met his startling kelly green ones. I daresay he pierced something within me, truly making me feel seen and known. We pooled into one another's gaze for many seconds. Then, "Before you go," I said, hoping not to tarnish the moment by unduly extending it, "would you tell me...you mentioned that your competition will take you to various cities." As if I didn't know. "I'm touring Central Europe myself, and love to enjoy the saunas, so if I happen to be in the same city as you, perhaps I could find you and say a quick hello? Not in expectation of another special encounter like the one we just shared. But it would be lovely to say a hello and, if you have a moment, to share a quick embrace."

"I'd like that, too, Daddy. Vienna's next. But I don't know which sauna, Paulie hasn't said."

"Next Saturday night?"

"Yes. Then Prague, then Berlin. Saturday nights."

"If we do coincide in time and place, I shall stand discreetly off to the side and leave it to you to come over to me. If you're otherwise engaged and circumstances don't permit you to step away from your competitive activities, I'll surely understand."

Freddy kissed my forehead. "I'll always have time for a hug from Daddy." He went to the door, blew a kiss—such a romantic!—and left.

Seated on the red-matted table-bed, I stared at the shut door for a considerable length of time, as if continuing to see my boy's lingering shadow, as if hoping he would knock or burst through the door and declare undying passion. Of course he did not return. Nor would I pursue him again this evening because to do so would surely frighten him off. We had already spoken our *adieus*—no, our *au revoirs*. After all, had we not made another date? For the following Saturday evening? In Vienna, the imperial center, the city of waltzes and refined cuisine, one of the most romantic capitals in the world.

Yes, I would see this man again. Freddy. My Freddy.

And I vowed, whether he grew to return my fondness or not, ever to protect him from harm.

Hidden Camera Transcript: Freddy and Yuki

Both young men are naked on Freddy's single bed—Freddy face down on his stomach, Yuki sitting on Freddy's buttocks, leaning forward and massaging Freddy's shoulders.

"That feels so good," says Freddy.

"You are very tense."

"Aren't you? Dean's an asshole, but still—nobody deserves to have his dick practically chewed off."

"Very difficult to have sex afterwards."

"Bad joke."

"No, I am not meaning difficult for *him* to have sex afterwards." Yuki slaps Freddy's back lightly, covers his own embarrassed giggle. "I am meaning difficult for us to have sex after that attack. To continue with FuckFest. I could not become hard for an hour after. Each time I think about Dean, my dick shrivels in fear."

"Tell me about it. I totally freaked. Couldn't stick my dick through the basement glory holes the rest of the night—I kept thinking, 'what if that lunatic is standing on the other side waiting for me to stick it through so he can bite it off.'"

"I sucked at glory holes, but that is all. Two different men wanted me to go to their *kabine*s, but I followed advice from Paulie to stay in public areas."

"Like that was safe. The steam room was a public area. There was an entire goddamn crowd in there when Dean got chewed up."

"True, but at least we could help him. You should not have gone into *kabine* with that old mustached man."

Still lying on his belly, Freddy turns his head to the side. "You saw? Are you stalking me?"

"Keeping eye on you for protection. We are friends, right?"

Freddy nods.

"What if that old man," says Yuki, "was crazy one who attacked Dean?"

"It couldn't be him, he was too nice. In the relaxation room, I'm the one who went up to him. He wasn't after me. When he saw how upset I was, all he wanted to do was cuddle me. I needed that right then."

Yuki lies down flat on top of Freddy. "I cuddle you. Much safer." Freddy flips over, embraces Yuki tightly, rolls both men onto their sides. The two wrestle playfully for a while, now one allowing himself to be pinned, now the other. Eventually, they return to the side-by-side, face-to-face embrace. And hold one another. And fall asleep.

Hidden Camera Transcript:
Tommy and Sam

Tommy, swinging his leg along the side of his hotel room single bed, scolds, "After the attack on Dean, you became a wild whore."

Perched on the narrow desk's corner, Sam gives him the finger.

"Is that any way to show affection to your ex?" asks Tommy.

"You want it up your pink Irish ass?"

"Like you could get your finger hard enough, Jew boy."

Sam blows him a kiss. "I miss our banter."

Tommy opens his arms. "I'll take you back any time."

"Don't do that to yourself, Toms. You deserve better than to be so easy."

Tommy lowers his arms to his side. "But you still want to take care of me, don't you, Sam?"

"In a different way, but yeah. Always."

Tommy walks over to him, hugs him. Sam hugs him back. "I love you, Sam. I mean that in a family way."

"If you're in the family way, Toms, I'm not the guilty party."

"Asshole," says Tommy, hugging Sam tight.

My Memories: Munich—Final Night

Trying to sound enthusiastic, I said to Burt, "I can't believe our subscriber numbers sky-rocketed while we were still in the fucking sauna locker room."

"The pervs watching must've texted friends to jump online. Gambling picked up, too. Nothing beats a sex-violence combo." He grinned, took a gulp from his stein of lager. He'd promised to have only this one beer, so there was low risk of his turning dangerous. "According to comments on our website," he added, "Manny's Mr. Macho routine was a hit, the way he promised to smash the fucker who did that to Dean. And lotsa viewers loved Bill's Mr. Softy tears over Little Frenchie: hard muscles, soft heart—perfecto."

I took a sip of my own beer, not knowing exactly how to say what I wanted to say.

"And get this—" Burt continued, "at least half a dozen comments asked if something's going on between Tommy and Sam. We've become a soap opera, Paulie. A reality soap opera like Bravo TV's best. Perfect hook to keep the audience coming back and spreading the word."

"Yeah, that sounds really good, Burt."

He set down his stein. "Your words don't match your face. You don't look pumped."

"I was pumped, Burt. At first. Real excited there in the locker room." We were the oldest guys at this sidewalk café in the chi-chi Schwabing neighborhood. Lotsa torn-jean studenty types were sitting around us, and rich fashionista kids in designer slacks and shirts, sandals and sunglasses. "But now, to be honest, now that I really think about it, I'm feeling a little guilty. I couldn't really be sure the attacker had left the sauna, could I? I really was putting the other boys in danger. For the money."

"Of course you were. It's your job to make sure we all get our money, the boys included. It's not like you were forcing 'em, just encouraging 'em, that's all."

"I know, but…I mean, the way I egged the boys to react to the dick chomp on camera, and then pressured 'em to keep going when maybe they were risking getting their own dicks chomped. Didn't I cross some line?"

"All of a sudden you've got a conscience? They're all adults, Paulie. Just like the boys we use in our porn flicks back home. They're in it for the money as much as we are."

"I guess. But this, I don't know, this feels different than our movies. It's not just sex and money now. Someone really got hurt."

"And you bitch about my drinking. You're the one should stop. It's making you wimpy. You were just doing your job, Paulie. Running the competition and maximizing the bucks for everyone—that's your job."

"I know, but still."

"It's not like you arranged the attack." Another slurp, then Burt lowered his voice, added, "You didn't arrange the attack on Dean for the ratings, did you, Paulie?"

"For Chrissake!" I shouted. "Of course not!"

A coupla yuppies at the next table turned and stared.

"Calm down," Burt said. "Just checking, Paulie, just checking. Listen, there's no reason to feel guilty. We can't control what the boys do during a FuckFest. Or what others do. And we can't control what's gonna excite all the internet pervs."

"I guess you're right."

"If you think about it, Paulie, the FuckFest put out a social service message: be careful in the baths because anything can happen. Kids are way too innocent nowadays. By showing how upset the boys were at the attack on Dean, we're helping our younger viewers savvy-up. If you think about it, we're doing good works like nuns do."

I raised an eyebrow like, 'You expect me to swallow that load of sour cum?'

"Fine, don't believe we're doing any good," Burt said. "But we're not doing any bad, either. It happened. Dean got mauled. So why shouldn't we make a few bucks off it? Is that a fucking crime? We'll give Dean his share of the extra money, right?"

"Of course," I said, making sure my face didn't show any hesitation, "no question."

"Alright then. When Dean's outta the coma the docs put him in, we'll send him a big bouquet of roses and a thank-you note for taking a hit for the team."

I took another few sips of beer, hoped Dean wouldn't prick a finger on our roses' thorns.

Vienna

My Memories:
Auf Wiedersehen Bavaria
Hello Vienna

Monday morning, more than a day after the Munich FuckFest, the boys were still in a lousy mood. I was, too, to be honest, but had to hide it for the boys' sakes, and Burt's. I just had to shove the whole thing outta my mind, or how else would I be able to keep up everyone else's mood? The Tour's success depended totally on me.

A good thing Burt booked the boys and me a charter bus tour through the Bavarian Alps while he took the van and headed to Vienna to set things up (i.e., to hide closed-circuit video cams in the boys' rooms). Bavaria's green rolling hills were amazing, all those valleys and lakes.

"I'm filming this outing of ours, boys, so at least pretend to have fun," I said. Most of 'em rallied. After I declared that he won the most orgy points at the Munich FuckFest "according to the computer algorithm," Big Bill began perking up enough for a "wow" here and there. I got some good footage of the boys creeping around Crazy Ludwig's dark and gloomy Neuschwanstein castle with its spires and turrets right out of some evil witch's place in an animated Disney flick. An hour later, all of 'em except Freddy splashed around the garden pool at Linderhof Palace with its center gilt fountain until a gaggle of gray-uniformed dumplings scolded and chased the boys outta there. Even Freddy cracked half a smile when those angry *hausfraus* started hollering and waving their arms.

That was Monday. Early Tuesday, we trained it to Vienna. I wish we could have stopped in *Sound of Music* Salzburg, but there was no time. I made a *Note to Self: for a future FuckFest in Germany/Austria, be sure to book a coupla days in Salzburg and do the Julie Andrews Sound of Music "Doe-a-Deer" routine, but with the boys climbing trees naked. Hokey, but sure to be a subscriber draw. Fags love musicals.*

After our bag drop at the Vienna hotel, I sent the boys with Burt to Schönbrunn, that was supposed to be Vienna's version of Versailles just a few stops away on the subway line. Freddy begged off, said he wanted to sit in his room. Poor guy's been glum from the get-go.

"The Vienna Marriott's nice, Freddy," I said, "but no moping allowed."

"I need to get my head together, Paulie, that's all."

Was the attack on Dean bumming Freddy out that much? "How's about you go to Schönbrunn with the others today, and then tomorrow you can skip the Belvedere and other museums. I wanna be sure Burt gets lotsa film footage at Schönbrunn. The grounds are supposed to be spectacular: giant fountains, super gardens, a fancy-schmancy palace."

"Okay. I'll go today, but tomorrow I'm just going to hang on my own."

"Deal."

After Burt and the boys left, I relaxed in the hotel for the afternoon to help get my own head back in the game. There's no better way of shaking off a blue mood than finding a good hook-up or two or three, so early evening, I hunted down a bar advertising "Hairy Tuesdays." I sat for an hour waiting to get the vibe of the place; turns out it wasn't for fat and hairy guys like me, just for fit/muscular and hairy guys, so I never even took my shirt off.

I left and took U-Bahn U-6 (Burgasse) to a small sauna advertising a Bears Night happening at the same time, just to get a feel for the place. I knew it'd be smaller than Köningshaus, the big fancy bathhouse smack downtown that Burt had scoped out for the next FuckFest. But maybe we'd have less chance running into nutjob attackers in a smaller sauna?

The neighborhood was kind of seedy, so as soon as I spotted the SAUNA sign, I rushed right in. I got free admission because Bear Night is free for tubbies 95 kilos (209 lbs) and over, according to the entrance scale. I saved sixteen euros for being fat—that was a first! The L-shaped bar was packed with a chubby crowd from their thirties to their eighties, all guzzling beer and stuffing themselves with free whipped cream pie. Lotsa blond/red/gray beards but hardly any body hair. Weird for a Bears event. Bummer.

Upstairs in the yellow locker room, I changed into a white towel, then clomped back downstairs to the communal showers where a ruckus was going on because, from what I could figure from hand gestures and yells, some drunk kept grabbing everyone's balls in the showers. Good for him! I tried the pool, but it was fucking freezing. Back upstairs to a red-painted TV room showing lousy porn (kind of like the shit Burt and I used to pump out when we first started) while a coupla crotchety limp dicks played with themselves on a sofa and eyed me. One stuck out his tongue, flicked it up and down fast like a lizard. "Save that for a clit," I mumbled.

A side room had maybe three cubicles, not more. And when I walked into a dark room and sat on a mat-covered platform to wait for my eyes to adjust, some spider lunged and grabbed my head in both hands, begging in English for a blow job because, "I lonely worker from Bosnia here ten years need sucky sucky." Had to elbow him in the gut to get him off me.

By then I knew this place was a waste of time for me and would be for the FuckFest, too, but before leaving, I at least wanted to taste that whipped cream pie, so I went back down to the bar, grabbed a slice on a paper plate and squeezed between two smiling chubs on a bench in a little side lounge. I didn't mind the guys feeling up my shoulder and back hair, especially when one asked if I was American—I guess it showed. Helmut (big sexy nipples, three slices of whipped cream pie), bought me a beer so he could reminisce about touring U.S. national parks in his youth. He introduced me to his obese friend, Hans, who loved showing off his deformed, diabetic toe ("two surgeries"), and complaining about Hungarian, Slovak, and Syrian hustlers ruining Köningshaus, "the most beautiful bathhouse in the world."

My boys were so hot they wouldn't need to pay any hustlers, so I wasn't worried on that score. But at least Hans's description of Köningshaus confirmed Burt's choice for Saturday's FuckFest. No way would I switch it to here, whipped cream pie or not.

Killer Interview 6

Naturally, I spent my first afternoon in Vienna perusing the Kunsthistoriche Museum—did you spend time there, as well, Mr. Hahnemann? Or were you too engaged in commercial pursuits? No need for reply. Raphael, Velazquez, van Dyck, Rubens, Dürer, Breughel, Titian, Caravaggio, Giorgione, Tintoretto, to name a few representative familiars. One hopes you didn't miss the Kunstkammer chock-a-block with incomparable decorative art objects of chalcedony, rock crystal, and silver, to say nothing of carved-ivory statuettes, gem-encrusted gold pitchers, goblets and dishes, particularly from the 16th-17th centuries—endless riches beyond imagination, of the sort I should have been born to enjoy daily (both the riches and the imagination, if you please).

Why is it, do you think, that some are born to luxury yet others to penury? Why could I not have been born, say, a prince, if not a king, in a prior century when birthright equaled merit? To be due something—everything—simply by dint of birth. By implication, others were due nothing, all thereby balancing out for humanity as a whole, collectively. A pie is a pie is a pie, however one divvies up the slices.

And so with longevity, as I have been contemplating since our last conversation, Mr. Hahnemann. Some possess long lives, others short ones, the collective lengths averaging out. If one believes in fate or destiny, then my shortening of a life here implies the lengthening of another somewhere else. Perhaps I am actually fulfilling an undisclosed plan preordained by whichever forces determine universal physics. Had that little blond been destined to die on the date my shove led to his demise at Buddies in Copenhagen? Perhaps I was merely the instrument of his destiny fulfillment, a marionette manipulated by the forces of the universe or by God if one must rely on vulgar metaphor. Likewise, perhaps Mr. Arrogance was destined to have his manhood mutilated on that very day in the Munich sauna; in fact, he might have had no choice but to insult me on that particular day so that I would be sufficiently incensed to perform my role as set of incisors at the disposal of the Three Fates.

True, should I have "chosen" to maim or murder another, I might, in that moment, have believed myself to be exercising free will, but we all know the conceptual fallacy underpinning belief in self-determination. My psychological mood, my passion-of-the-moment, would have been a mere by-product of cosmic forces set in motion millennia before, all of which culminated in each given instant that was the here and now. Had not Marx dispositively proven that we all live subject to historical forces beyond individual control?

Marx, of course, had merely been expounding upon an insight first asserted in the Anglophiliatic world by Shakespeare: "all the world's a stage, and all the men and women merely players." We neither write the script of human destiny, nor choose our roles. Rather, we inhabit the prescribed roles into which we are born...cast...or outcast. The Indians understand the concept of caste better than any. Historical determinism.

Thus, whether contemplated from the perspective of physics, Shakespeare, Marx, or Eastern philosophy, one must conclude that our actions are not of our choosing. Actions not being of our choosing, we bear no responsibility for them. Blame your Deus Ex Machina for my acts of murder and mayhem, blame the Big Bang, blame Galileo (he wouldn't notice a little more condemnation), Einstein or Hawking, but on no account blame me!…

…

Yes, I "gotta be fucking kidding," as you so eloquently say, Mr. Hahnemann. Although no, I am not. Nevertheless, you continue to demand answer to the question of why an ordinary, middle-aged-or-perhaps-older-but-in-any-case-not-yet-ancient man might engage in an out-of-the-ordinary-yet-not-unheard-of enterprise of sequential mayhem and murder, especially accompanied (prompted?) by admittedly unusual erotic impulses? Such a question presupposes a singular articulable answer. There are many "*a* reason," but you request "*the* reason." You seek to understand *the* reason for my actions so as to feel better protected against such a series of attacks happening again, especially to yourself. Terribly sorry to be the bearer of bad tidings, but no such silver bullet of self-protection exists.

Besides, have I not already given explanation, *ad nauseam*, of the origin of my repressed sexual inclinations and their subsequent liberation from psychic confinement? Permit me to add: does a man not possess the right—nay, the duty—to protect his dignity, the health of his very own psyche? To add sparkle to his otherwise dull life? To seek a modicum of joy? To indulge in formerly repressed but now realized sensual delights? To create memories to be cherished in one's eventual decrepitude? Am I to blame for having discovered an alternate self…more precisely, an ever-present yet theretofore hidden side of self…more precisely still, an expanded sense of self, a self possessing a broader range of attributes and abilities, psychological variations as well as emotional expressions and physical prowess than I had previously permitted myself to enjoy? An enhanced self. Yes, I like that: this past spring in Europe, while engaged in acts of mayhem and murder, I discovered and gave expression to *my enhanced self*. Should not such self-actualization be the subject of celebration rather than condemnation?

Now that I have vented a bit, I shall return to my first Vienna day which, whether of my choosing or history's, was delightful: in the Kunsthistoriche Museum's exquisitely marbled Cupola Hall café, I indulged in a rectangular *Esterházy Schnitte*—thin layers of hazelnut meringue bonded together by liqueur-infused buttercream all coated in white fondant icing and flaked almonds. One's mouth, currently coated in the perpetual bitterness of prison slop, drips with memory.

While on the subject of Viennese recommendations, permit me to suggest the Hotel Das Tigra on a quiet side street within walking distance of everything in Vienna worth seeing. Mozart stayed in this building as a child; Beethoven resided next door. And, of course, I stayed there. A Holy Trinity of references.

I spent the following morning at the Belvedere, a delightful palace-turned-museum offering an abundance of the finest Schiele and Klimts, Biedermeier furniture and—

. . .

Fine, Mr. Hahnemann, as you wish. I shall limit myself to the day's "plot," as you call it, although the loss of my travelogue is yours.

As I was exiting the Belvedere, I spotted your boys just entering. My heart leaped and I thought to wave to Freddy, my Freddy, but he was not among the group. Had he lost interest in art? I would have to discuss the matter with him on Saturday night when we would surely find private time at the FuckFest. I must undertake to mentor him in humanity's finery, my dear sweet boy.

Disappointed, I returned to Das Tigra to freshen up. And here we reach what is of greatest relevance to your questions, Mr. Hahnemann. My afternoon destination was Köningshaus, which I presumed to be the venue for the boys' upcoming Saturday night FuckFest. After all, located in the heart of town and bearing the reputation as the grandest bathhouse in the world whose original foundation traced to Roman antiquity, which bathhouse had been erected in the 19th-century as the city's only (legitimate) one, this sauna clearly offered the finest possible pedigree for your competition. Only a fool would pass it by, and I knew that you, Mr. Hahnemann, although many questionable things, were no fool.

My objective was to gain familiarity with the facility during a weekday afternoon when it was sure to be fairly empty, to gain a feel for the layout, which, according to internet commentary, was more of a maze than most. Armed with foreknowledge, I would be able, on Saturday night, to avoid detection by your boys' headband cameras while still lurking and maintaining an eye on my investment. More to the point, I would be able to track Freddy and find him for another, albeit most likely brief, loving tryst.

Freddy. Perfectly proportioned muscular Freddy. Red-haired Freddy. Green-eyed Freddy. Sweet tender Freddy, the perfect combination of physical strength and emotional tenderness, in need of a daddy's love. Mine.

Up until this time in my life, I rationalized myself fortunate not to have sired children. Not that I could have done so with a woman, although artificial means had become a possibility. However, never able to sustain a relationship for more than a few months, not wishing the burdens of single parenthood, and unwilling to permit paternal duty to inhibit my foraging among meat racks at a moment's whim, I denied myself offspring.

Yet I adored the children of co-workers dressed to the nines and shown off at our place of employment, waving their little hands in salutation. I sat for hours at a time in local schoolyards on Saturday afternoons, watching little ones swing and jump rope and hang from monkey bars, all under the suspicious eyes of parents who misinterpreted my interest as predatory. Was it so wrong to seek the momentary surges of joy that only a child's giggle can elicit? One thinks not.

Yet now, having attained an age nearer conclusion than beginning, I have found myself wondering to whom I would leave the millions sure to be won as a result of my investment in your venture, Mr. Hahnemann. And more: would I be remembered beyond the span of this blood-pulsing life? How lovely it would be to have a son, to know that my visage, voice, and wisdom would appear to someone in memory long after I ceased my walk upon this earth. And, before departure, to hear during my remaining years, from an appreciative young man (other than one I might pay), the tender appellation of "daddy."

Freddy had called me "Daddy." Spontaneously.

Would he be surprised to see me at Köningshaus? Surely not—we had made a date, as it were. He must be thinking about me, tossing in bed, unable to quench desire for the me of memory-inspired fantasy. He would gasp in joy upon seeing me Saturday night, would lunge lustfully and abandon all restraint in fulfillment of his desire. I would likely fling to the winds my own good sense of restraint and whisper into his ear my wish to pamper him forever, to reward his love with greater financial gain than the competition could ever provide him, to be his (sugar) daddy. He would resign from the competition, pack his things and join me in Hotel Das Tigra. Vienna would be the city of our honeymoon. We would stuff ourselves on pastries, schnitzels, the finest Austrian Rieslings, and one another.

I apologize, Mr. Hahnemann, for such digressive self-indulgence. Such is the nature of Vienna, sensual seductor that the city is. Such is the nature of love, delusional as it always proves to be.

Composure restored, I now continue my narrative:

Strolling along the cobblestone pedestrian mall past the 18th-century, green-cupolaed, Baroque Roman Catholic Peterskirche and such unlikely culinary spectaculars as Wienerhaus and Benny's Bar and Grill, I reached St. Stephen's Cathedral, the gloomy Gothic mother church of the Roman Catholic Archdiocese of Vienna, worth a quick glimpse.

However, in the plaza outside the Cathedral, I encountered a mass of slain children laid out flat on the cobblestones, bleeding children, shrapnel-pocked children, limb-severed children, all populating dozens upon dozens of photographs. Behind them milled a small crowd of Middle Eastern-looking women and men, the women modestly in long sleeves, skirts and kerchief-covered hair, the men in jeans and t-shirts. Placards, in both English and German, placed around this expansive photograph mosaic declared Putin and Assad to be murderers, butchers, beasts. Other placards begged for protest and intervention.

Had we not all heard, Mr. Hahnemann, of the incessant bombings and chemical attacks carried out upon rebellious civilian populations by Russian forces at the behest of Syria's president, all under the guise of battling jihadi ISIS terrorists? Seeing these horrific photographs obviously taken by bereaved parents, relatives, and friends; witnessing the somber expressions on adults in the Vienna crowd, and noticing the absence of buckets for the collection of funds, one could not help but feel a sincere ache within. How had these people made their way to Vienna? Had they trekked across Turkey, risked lives while drifting on rubber inner tubes to Greece, hiked through the hostile Balkans? Scaled border fences to enter Austria? Were they hunted here now or finally welcomed?

My eyes met those of a handsome young man with oval brown face and prominent nose. The shadow of lean muscles rippled from beneath his red t-shirt, nipples pointed. His calves extending from khaki shorts were covered in seductive thick dark hair. "I'm so sorry," I said, hoping he understood English. "I just need to say that. I'm so very sorry."

His brown eyes peered into mine as he extended his lean muscular hand. We shook. He held my hand, rocked it, and I felt the warmth of his calloused palm and fingers blend into my own. Or was that fanciful thinking? Flustered, I muttered, "May I give a donation?"

He let go of my hand, his expression shifting to puzzlement.

"Money?" I added, reaching into my pocket.

"No money," he said with an accent new to me. So this was Syrian English. He shook his upturned hand as one might shake a head. "No money. Write please. To government. To United Nations. Letters." His hand extended in display over the photographs. "Today, my children. Tomorrow, your children?"

Overcome by emotion, I bit my lower lip, nodded in understanding.

"You will remember?" he asked.

"Yes, I will remember."

He gave a pronounced nod, then turned his attention to another apparent tourist gawking at images of dead Syrian children.

I relate this incident, Mr. Hahnemann, so that you and your readers understand my capacity for empathy and caring. I am not a monster, although I have learned, on occasion, to let loose the monster within myself, the monster within each of us, the monster whose most-of-the-time restraint proves one's overall civilized nature, the monster lurking, perhaps, within you. If we do not admit to possessing impulses we routinely harness, then we are not "civilized," merely dull.

I mourned those suffering and murdered Syrian children even as I chewed chunks of beef sausage accompanied by two slices of rye bread, all purchased from a vendor whose kiosk stood mere feet from the photography display. Sadness has always sparked my appetite.

Wiping mustard from my manicured white mustache, I vowed to write letters of protest upon my return to Boston. I would insist that we bomb Damascus regardless of how many ancillary children might fall victim to our attack because our infliction of death would be executed in order to carry out legitimate vengeance.

After swallowing, I made a right turn, walked a bit, made a left turn onto a narrow street, and strolled past a cigar shop, a jewelry store, some restaurants, and sundry other commercial venues, including a haberdashery displaying in its window Tyrolean jackets, vests, and britches of beige cloth accented with green lapels and buttons. How dapper I would look in such a culturally expressive outfit, but on which occasion to wear it? Hitler's birthday? One would rather not.

Then past an outdoor café on the corner of a small cobbled square facing a stark, gray Franciscan church, in front of which stood a fountain bearing a statue of curly bearded, staff-bearing Moses glowering down at all us mortals. And just beyond the small square, beside a home goods store displaying fancily wrapped soaps, assorted lamps, colorful dishes, wooden kitty bookends, and porcelain doggies, stood my destination— Köningshaus, a *herrensauna*, men's sauna, housed in a building of off-white Baroque façade adorned by a variety of window pediments looking like so many mustaches over gaping mouths.

How perversely apropos for a gay bathhouse to situate itself across the street from a Franciscan church and just beyond the gaze of Moses, the giver of a so-called moral law relegating hedonists to ostracism and social disdain through the ages, condemning us forever to choose among the three ex's: excommunication, exile, execution. As if we have ever been granted a choice. Stoned to death. Burned at the stake. Imprisoned. Hurled from rooftops. Moses and his ilk are among the world's greatest violators of human rights.

Was his fixedness a just-desserts comeuppance punishment for him— condemned to stand in perpetual shocked horror at our golden calf-ish sort of crowd? Or, was Moses's dour presence here a mere coincidence? Or, was I completely misinterpreting: might he perhaps be gazing down in penitential blessing of our promiscuity?

Giving Moses the finger, I crossed the narrow street, walked through the forest green door and entered the Köningshaus foyer, rang the bell, waited to be buzzed in. A pleasant chat with the entrance clerk who, like those European counterparts I'd so far met, did not think to check the guest's identification. To what end do U.S. bathhouse entrance clerks all demand to see government-issued IDs? What do they do with our names and government identifiers? Do they hand them to the bathhouse Mafia owners for purposes of future blackmail? Do they turn our names over to corrupt local police so that those men in blue may know whose door to knock upon in the middle of the night when horny for forced head? Do they pass along lists of us to the Department of Homeland Security so that our fascist-inclining government can determine whom to round up and confine in notorious Manzanar and other abandoned concentration camps once used to corral and warehouse Japanese-American U.S. *citizens*?

After paying the twenty euro fee in exchange for towel and locker key wristband, I was escorted by a young, bearded attendant through a gaudy restaurant-bar devoid of patrons, along a hallway lined with green-doored *kabines*, up a long white marble staircase to the locker room where he courteously taught me how to unlock my locker with my magnetic wristband key, took the trouble to point out the bathroom opposite. Yet he refused the two euro tip I pressed into his soft palm. What dignity, I thought, and pride in his work. Admirable self-respect. My initial impression of Vienna—clean, grand, elegant, welcoming—was enhanced.

Suitably attired in skimpy white towel, I sloughed oh-so-Norma-Desmond down the banistered marble stairs, began wandering the seemingly empty facility, a maze of mazes lined with walk-in-closet sized cubicles, many equipped with a bench and upper wall television displaying fairly decent porn. (Take a lesson, Mr. Hahnemann, take a lesson.) Initially, I walked the labyrinth in circles, puzzled at how I could possibly have arrived at my starting point yet again.

Somehow I took a turn that led me to the wet area, including showers, bathroom, steam room, and small but exquisite Turkish-style pool lined with blue-and-white mosaic tiles. The whole perimeter was ornamented with offwhite Moorish horseshoe arches supported by marble pillars. Luxurious. A quick shower and towel off, then into a large dry sauna lined with two sets of bleacher-like wooden platforms opposite one another. I climbed up onto one side's second level, sat wrapped discreetly in my damp towel, enjoyed as the dry heat evaporated the remaining moisture from my hairy shoulders when suddenly the glass door opened, and in walked a stunningly handsome young man of, I'd say, twenty-five.

He sat on the lower of the platforms opposite. He looked vaguely familiar: brown complexion, jet black hair, handsome oval face, wiry tight-muscled build. Although his chest was hairless, his calves were covered in thick dark hair, as were those parts of his exposed thighs. Satyr-like. He greeted me first by posing a question in German. After I shrugged my shoulders and shook my head in signal of incomprehension, he offered a "Hello how are you?" in accented English—the newly familiar Syrian-accented English.

Yes, he resembled the Syrian young man who, mere moments before, had implored me to remember his dead children and write letters of protest. Had this stunning, towel-clad man, himself, been at the demonstration earlier? Was he a young father? Had he lost a child over there or along the trek here?

Reminding myself that some beautiful young men, like Freddy, were in search of daddies, I responded to this one's hello with as warm a paternal smile as I could muster. At a minimum, his initiation of conversation demonstrated the younger-to-older respect permeating traditional cultures.

Rather matter-of-factly, he then unhitched the towel's corner from his waist, spread his legs, and revealed his thick, relaxed circumcised enormity. "Hot here," he said as if remarking on the sauna's temperature.

I chuckled lightly: it wasn't as though we were two guys on the down-low in a presumably hetero gym, so why the euphemistic game? Would he next inquire as to whether I were a friend of Dorothy or a fan of Judy Garland, the Divine Miss M, Barbra, Cher, or Lady Gaga? Composing myself so as not to offend and lose a potential, highly memorable opportunity, I stared boldly at his cock, licked my lips as salaciously as possible, and replied, "Yes, very hot."

He fingered himself in display. "You like?"

"I don't like," I replied. "I love."

"You want touch?"

I nodded, climbed awkwardly down my set of platforms and crossed to his side. I sat, reached my hand first to his thigh, rubbed. He spread his legs wider. I reached over and seized the thickening cylinder. "Oh," came out of me automatically. "Oh." The joy of squeezing a young man's strength even at semi-rest. The power of touch to soothe not only the touchee, but the toucher as well.

"You want?"

I nodded, inhaling through my widened nostrils the sweet musky scent of recently washed flesh whose oils and sweat were just beginning to assert themselves in the room's dry heat. He hardened in my hand, thickened, lengthened. My hand could not contain him. My eyes were fixated. I leaned over. As I inclined my head toward his lap, he placed a hand flat against my upper chest and shoved me upright.

"Twenty-five euro," he said, "for suck. Fifty for fuck."

"And for kissing?" I blurted so as to grant myself a moment of composure. I was completely startled.

"No kiss. Suck—twenty-five euro. Fuck—fifty euro."

A hustler.

While I'd been conjuring reasons for sympathy, this filthy whore had been defining me as an easy mark apparently so old and desperate as to be willing to pay for young exotic dick. As if I could not (on occasion) obtain young dick, exotic or otherwise, for free. Oh, if only my Freddy were here, I'd show this son of a bitch. I'd wrap my arms around gorgeous muscular Freddy, draw him in close and give him a deeply passionate so-there kiss while the Syrian whore watched and marveled.

I stood and stepped away. "I don't pay." (Not entirely true, but I was making a point.)

"Twenty for suck. Forty for fuck?"

Ah, lowering his price. Haggling for a hookah or magic carpet was one thing, but bargaining down one's own genitals? No self-respect. Disgusting. I'd shown him who was the desperate one.

He shook his huge appendage at me. "Taste good. You like. Fifteen for suck?"

Reducing his price yet again? I had Jewed this Arab down, so to speak. Now who was humiliating whom?...

Yes, Mr. Hahnemann, I recognize the anti-Semitism and anti-Arab racism inherent in my thinking, but is not recognition of such thoughts the first step toward redemptive correction of one's micro-aggressive implicit biases? More to the point, do you not wish me to be brutally honest in my self-expression? Would you prefer that I mask my thoughts?

...

I thought not. So, back to the whore: "Fifteen?" I asked in confirmation.

"Yes, but must swallow all."

I, as paying customer, would decide whether or not to swallow; and swallow I most definitely would not. "Sure," I said, "fifteen for a suck." I knelt, inhaled the mix of washed skin now coated lightly in perspiration; I lunged and indulged myself, filling lips, mouth, and even throat (thank goodness childhood tonsillectomy and adenoidectomy had enlarged gullet capacity). I savored this epitome of maleness, exciting it to the fullest, taking possession of it deep within, losing myself in the fulfillment.

He began to thrust.

Reflexively, I pulled my head back before gagging on the inevitable—some international flavors one wished to sample, others one did not. But he grabbed with both hands, locked my head in place to prevent my withdrawal. He continued to thrust and, before I could even think to bring teeth into play as I had in Munich, I was so flooded and overcome by a gagging-coughing fit, I thought I would drown.

A series of grunts and final thrusts, then a release of his grip. I yanked myself away, my throat stinging and eyes tearing. I spat out what I could, wiped back of hand across lips and chin.

He leaned over, collared the fingers of both hands around my neck, brought his face so close to mine I could smell his breath's mix of cumin and onion. "Pig," he spat directly onto my lips.

One grasped the significance of "pig" for an Arab, presumably a Muslim. "Now to locker," he growled, squeezing those fingers, constricting my throat, "and you pay, yes?"

I nodded quickly in apparent acquiescence and acknowledgment of his superior physical strength.

However, he bore no idea of the strength of my dignity.

Without so much as a moment of formulation, my plan crystalized: what had worked inadvertently in Copenhagen would prove effective intentionally here in Vienna, albeit with a minor tweak to fit logistical distinctions.

"Good pig," he said, releasing me, slapping me lightly across the cheek. "To locker now."

I stood, and we walked side-by-side, he leading the way through the maze until we reached the marble staircase. He pointed up toward the locker room. "Go. I follow." I contemplated the poetry in what was about to ensue, my performance of a leitmotif, a personal signature if you will. As I led the way, he walked so close behind that with each step his knee banged the back of my calf. So close that I could select any moment I chose: at the very top of the stairs, I jabbed my elbow back into his diaphragm, spun round, and as he hunched in belly clench and gasped for the wind I'd knocked out of him, I shoved with all my might.

Flailing, he fell backward down the marble staircase.

Not a single cry. Stunned and out of breath, he rolled, bounced, and crashed his head onto the bottom marble step. Crack.

Blood seeped and pooled.

At the top of the steps, I took a quick moment to smile in triumph before darting into the bathroom, where I quickly wetted several paper towels, and dashed down the stairs, intending thoroughly to wash his genitals of my saliva, thereby removing any traces of my DNA, not that the authorities would have other DNA against which to compare it, not that they would likely investigate the death of a Syrian hustler in a homosexual venue in the first place, however—one must never underestimate the value of well-reasoned precautions.

As the Syrian's blood continued to flow from the back of his head, I dabbed fingertips in the red puddle and brought them to my lips. An intense rush of desire coursed through me, an uncontrollable urge to suck his enormity once more. A victory suck, if you will.

Although soft, the appendage was still more than an ample mouthful. While savoring its roll against tongue and upper palate, I lifted his dead, increasingly clammy hand beneath my towel to my insistent erection. How one had been fantasizing about this sensation ever since the missed opportunity with the deceased little blond in Copenhagen. Finally, to know the feel of such coolness of flesh, the damp hand gripping me as I guided it to the rhythms of my own fast-pulsing blood. Oh, oh, oh, the surge, the surge, the surge!

Utterly thrilling. Proof that my amazing sexual encounter with the dead little blond in Copenhagen had not been a one-off aberration, but a resumption of adolescent fantasy interruptus, a re-discovered source of sexual satisfaction, one that contrasted with—and thereby brought harmonious Zen-like balance to—the love-lust I had experienced with dear Freddy mere days before.

. . .

Pish posh, Mr. Hahnemann, there was nothing predatory in my behavior whatsoever. I had killed for the sole purpose of avenging my honor, not with any intent to create a vehicle for the explosive dead-hand masturbatory orgasm that turned out to be an incidental benefit of the enterprise. Should I not have taken advantage of such a rare opportunity? It was not as if one would likely be encountering newly dead, pre-rigor-mortis hands every day. Should I have let this fresh corpse go to waste?

Now that I think more about that moment, might my behavior not actually be regarded as an act of generosity, granting that young refugee the chance to serve fellow man one final time, thereby engaging in a modest act of soul redemption at precisely the right pre-Paradise moment? Consider the possibility, Mr. Hahnemann. All I ask is that you consider the possibility.

After cleansing myself with one of the wet paper towels, I leaned forward and began my originally intended ministration of washing the Arab clean of my fluids, both his genitals and now his hand. That's when I heard the fateful gasp. I looked around and up.

Freddy. It was my Freddy!

"What the—?" he murmured, a look of utter bewilderment on his face. How beautiful he appeared, the darkness of muscle-sculpted complexion contrasting with the soft whiteness of towel wrapped tightly around waist and emphasizing the thickness of thighs. Those beautiful vibrant green eyes, that whimsical red hair. That familiar whiff of cinnamony Aramis cologne.

"The poor man," I sputtered while dropping the dead hand. "I was at my locker upstairs when I heard a crash. He must have slipped. I fear that he's dead."

"But what are you doing? Washing his hands—and his dick?"

The easiest way to avert suspicion is to admit the obvious while tossing into the mix an incredulity to serve as distraction. "Just confirming the absence of pulse in his wrist and crotch while cleansing him. It is my calling."

"What?"

"I thought I could show him respect by confirming his demise and cleansing his body quickly for the sake of privacy and dignity. What if he's married? He's obviously Arab, and they tend to be closeted and to marry young. What if the coroner does DNA testing and finds saliva—or worse— on his privates, and reports that to the fellow's widow? I was trying to spare him the shame, and his widow—the humiliation. Without evidence to the contrary, she might live with the delusion that he thought this an ordinary steam bath, a Turkish hammam, if you will, one of those public baths so popular throughout the former Ottoman Empire."

Freddy brought hand to forehead and massaged as if physically trying to find the means of absorbing my absurd explanation.

"I'm a mortician," I lied. "I don't generally mention this because most people find the profession disturbing. But it's my calling, my way of showing caring to humanity."

Freddy's eyes took on a cast of suspicion. "In Munich, you were in the hot tub outside the steam room right before Dean got his dick chomped. I saw you."

"Freddy, surely you're not suggesting—" I reached out to him, but he recoiled. I tried to soothe: "Did I not offer you comfort in Munich after the attack on your friend? I held you. We made sweet love. Was I not a tender lover? Your daddy? How could I possibly have displayed such tenderness mere moments after maiming a man as horribly as you describe your friend to have been mutilated?"

Freddy looked down at the Syrian, up at me. "But you were there when that happened, and now you're here when this happened."

"As are you, are you not? Should I now suspect you of the attack on your friend there and on this innocent victim here?"

The Syrian's blood continued to pool. Freddy took a step backward. "I know I didn't do it."

"And I know that I didn't do it. An accident is the only conclusion. A slip on the steps."

"A slip on the steps," Freddy murmured. His eyes took on a sudden, harder edge. "That's how Little Frenchie died in Copenhagen. He slipped on the steps and fell."

"Little Frenchie?" I played innocent, but knew this was bad.

"My friend who died. I told you about him when we met in Munich. Frenchie died at the baths in Copenhagen. He fell down the stairs."

"Are you suggesting that I had something to do with his fall? But I wasn't at Buddies that night. I wasn't even in—"

Freddy's face turned ferocious, his fists clenched. "What did you say?"

"That I wasn't at Buddies the night your friend—what was his name, Frenchie?—slipped down the stairs there. I wasn't—"

Freddy practically leaped over the Syrian and grabbed me by the shoulders. "All I said was that Frenchie fell down the stairs at *the baths in Copenhagen.* I never said he died at *Buddies.*"

I struggled to free myself from the clamp of his grip, blurted, "Everyone knows the main bathhouse there is Buddies."

He dropped his hands, looked at them in wonder as if they were not part of him. "So, you weren't in Copenhagen a couple weeks ago?" he asked.

"No. A couple years ago I was there, and visited Buddies. But not this trip. I flew from Boston to Paris to Munich. That's where I met you."

"Paris, not Copenhagen." Freddy's face was a swirl of confusion. How difficult the contradiction between empirically implied fact and ego's denial that one's trust has been misplaced or betrayed. I reached up and caressed his sweat-dampened face. "Daddy understands—you're in shock. As am I." I looked down at the Syrian. "We must inform the entrance clerk."

"I'll go," Freddy said, turning.

I grabbed his bicep. (God, how thick and hard and delicious.) "Not yet. We should dress first, in preparation for leaving immediately after informing the entrance clerk. Assuming that he won't choose to cover up the incident in avoidance of adverse publicity, he might attempt to detain us for the police. I, for one, do not wish to be interrogated, or otherwise forced to participate in whichever sort of inquest they perform in this country."

"But—"

"Do you wish to explain to the Austrian police the reason for your visit to Vienna? Surely they would then interrogate the others in your party. Are you certain your group's sex competition is legal here? What if the authorities were to shut you down? Do you wish to risk losing everything you boys have been working so hard for? To risk arrest?"

"No, but—"

"Look, you didn't see him slip and fall, nor did I. So we could not offer witness testimony. Nor is there anything we can now do for this poor Syrian."

"How do you know he's Syrian?"

"An assumption, that's all. There was a group of them demonstrating on the main plaza. Perhaps you passed them yourself."

He nodded. "But the police will ask the entrance clerk who found him, and he'll—"

"He'll say two English-speaking tourists whose identifications he never checked. Two good Samaritans who reported the tragedy before departing. Had we been guilty of something, we simply would have fled without reporting the accident, correct?"

"I guess. But I've got to come back for the FuckFest."

So, I'd been right—the FuckFest would be here.

He continued, "What if the same entrance clerk's here then and recognizes me? It's not like thousands of Black men come here. He could call the police when he sees me on Saturday, couldn't he, so they could come interrogate me then?"

"Quite true. Good head on your shoulders, my boy. So, here's what we'll do: you dress and leave without saying a word about the accident. After you've gone, I'll go inform the entrance clerk of the death. No association with you whatsoever."

"You'd do that for me? But what if you want to come back here some time? The clerk might recognize you and call the police on you."

"I'm just another frumpy middle-aged White tourist. Unlikely he'd remember me distinctly at all."

"I guess."

"Come. Dress quickly. You exit first and meet me by Moses."

"Where?"

"The statue in the little square up the block. In front of the church."

We dressed quickly in the locker room. With forced casualness, Freddy meandered to the entrance, returned his towel and locker key without so much as a word or acknowledgment from the clerk, then stepped outside while I spied from a distance. After waiting several minutes, I followed.

Of course I said nothing to the entrance clerk about the dead Syrian—as Freddy had cautioned: why would I risk the clerk associating me with the death, and remembering me if he were here upon my return for the FuckFest?

"I'm freaking out," Freddy said as I took his elbow and hustled him away from pedestaled Moses in his perpetual holier-than-thou pose.

"Of course you are," I said, "decent fellow that you are. May I invite you to dinner? And offer you private comfort in my hotel room afterwards? Daddy's been known to provide great comfort to his sweet boy."

Giving a questioning, can-you-be-fucking-serious squint, he replied, "Thanks, but I've got to hustle to the hotel before Paulie and the guys get back from their sightseeing."

Did I detect a shudder across Freddy's shoulders? Had I failed to show appropriate sensitivity and distress at the "discovery" of the dead Syrian? "I don't feel much like eating, either," I said. "I just didn't want you to be alone right now, you're so traumatized. As am I. I'll let you return to your hotel and rest."

"Yeah, that's the best thing."

"Just so you know, I was indeed planning on visiting Köningshaus again this coming Saturday night. If your group will be there then, perhaps we'll bump into one another?"

He said not a word, just penetrated my eyes with his kelly green ones. Searching for a flicker as proof of fabrication?

I offered a soft smile.

"Sure," he finally said, "maybe I'll see you there."

I extended a hand, he shook it limply, then asked, "Just one thing: you're sure you weren't in Copenhagen two weeks ago?"

As if in reply, I shook my head, but actually I was attempting to dispel from thought the sad realization: suspicion is the death knell of infatuation.

Hidden Camera Transcript: Freddy and Yuki

"If Paulie find out, you in trouble," says Yuki, dipping tea bags into each of two paper cups of boiled water.

"Okay, it was wrong to go to the sauna yesterday," says Freddy. He piles four white pillows up against the wooden headboard behind his bed, leans back against them. "I just wanted to get away from all the guys for a while."

"Liar—you wish to check out sauna while rest of us being in museums. You seeking unfair advantage. I am disappointed."

"Fine, I'm a real shit and you can hate me. But that's not important now. What if I'm right about that guy?"

"You sure he same old man as in Munich?"

"Of course I'm sure. We had a whole conversation there. We cuddled there. I sucked him off there."

Yuki lifts the tea bags from the cups, drops them into the waste can, hands one cup to Freddy. "You feel better after tea. Relaxing."

Freddy takes a sip, then sets his cup onto the faux walnut dresser between their beds. "He was in the Munich sauna when Dean was attacked."

"Yes, I saw him go into steam room with all of you, but—"

"You saw him go into the steam room with us?" asked Freddy. "But back in Munich he told me he hadn't followed us in there. I asked him and he said he hadn't gone in because he figured none of us would want an older guy like him. You sure it was him you saw?"

"Yes."

"And Dean had been really nasty to him at the gay festival, so…so maybe he followed Dean into the steam room to get even, and then lied to me about it to cover up."

"He is old man. Maybe he forget. Or maybe you misunderstand."

"And now he's here in the Vienna sauna when this Arab guy died…or was murdered."

"Maybe it was coincidence in Munich. And maybe here old man was right and Arab slipped on stairs and fell."

"The same way Little Frenchie did in Copenhagen? You don't think that's too big a coincidence?"

"But old man said he was in Paris, not Copenhagen."

"Like he'd really admit it. Frenchie and the Arab are dead. Dean was mutilated. How can I just sit and do nothing?"

"Like what? You tell Paulie you see old man with dead Arab at Köningshaus when you are alone there breaking Paulie rules? Or will you go to Vienna police and tell them you did not report dead man in sauna, but they should arrest old man you sucked in Munich with name you do not know, now staying in Vienna somewhere you do not know, because you think maybe he told lies about being in Copenhagen not Paris?"

"Because if I'm right, he was in all three saunas when something nasty happened."

"Same as you?"

"He said something like that, too. But—"

Yuki holds up a hand, sits down on his bed, sips his tea with a loud slurp. "Old man said he will be at Köningshaus FuckFest, yes?"

"Yes. I'm sure he wants to have sex with me again. But I don't even want to see him, let alone touch him."

"Yes you do. You and I both know what he look like. We stay together and search. When we find him, you have sex with him while I filming you both with my head camera. Then we have proof he is here. Then we tell Paulie this man was at Munich gay festival and at Munich sauna. Maybe he is stalker who wants to hurt our show?"

"I see what you're getting at: if we make Paulie suspicious, then he'll check out the Copenhagen sauna film footage."

"Exactly. And you do not need to tell Paulie about Arab, or you being at Köningshaus before rest of us."

"If the old man shows up in the Copenhagen footage then—"

"Then he was in Copenhagen not Paris. Then we know he is liar. Innocent man does not lie. Maybe at sauna you can find out his name and hotel? Then Paulie could show all film to police and they could find him and investigate."

"You really think Paulie'd do that?"

Yuki sips. "To protect us and whole show, yes, I think."

"Paulie'd never risk the police shutting us down. But maybe after we return home. Then he could send our film to the police in Vienna and Munich and Copenhagen. Anonymously with a note about his suspicion. And the old man's name if I can get it, and where he stayed at which hotel—Interpol could trace him and catch him."

"If he is guilty."

"If he's innocent and it really is a bunch of coincidences, then he'll go free. I like your plan, Yuki, and there's no real danger for me—he had his chance to off me in Munich, but he didn't. I'll be safe with him, although he gives me the creeps now."

"Many much creeps at FuckFests," Yuki says with a sigh and a slurp.

Killer Interview 7

Indeed I remember that sad Saturday. I awoke massaging an anxiety lump in the pit of my stomach. 'I should linger in bed,' I thought, reaching up to my forehead in the hopes of detecting non-existent fever. No cough, no sniffles, no intestinal distress. No justifiable reason at all to forego the day's sightseeing plan, nor the unfortunate task preordained for that upcoming evening.

Over my spare hotel buffet breakfast of three slices of smoked salmon, two poached eggs, one seeded roll, a cappuccino, and assorted pastries, I wracked my brain in a final attempt to excavate some logic I might present to Freddy later at Köningshaus so as to allay all suspicions while not seeming, alas, to protest too much.

I feared that my Freddy might have grown sufficiently suspicious to urge your examination, Mr. Hahnemann, of the raw film footage taken during the Buddies sauna FuckFest in Copenhagen. Although you would not have seen me actually shove the little blond down the stairs—the young man had removed his headband camera by then, and his fellow contestants had departed the venue—your cameras might well have caught a fleeting glimpse of my presence at Buddies, in which case Freddy would know I had lied about having been in Paris that week rather than Copenhagen. Freddy would then urge you to review his own film footage of me during our initial conversation in Freundschaft's relaxation room, irrefutable proof of my presence in two attack locales. The evidence against me would mount. Too great a risk for me.

Resigning myself to the unavoidable, I felt genuinely saddened because I'd so enjoyed our lovemaking in Munich, Freddy's and mine, had fantasized about future copulatory unions and so much more, as I have already shared. Alas, self-preservation takes precedence over self-indulgence.

I did worry whether my murder of him might appear racist, but I took immediate comfort in the notion that I'd already murdered one White contestant and mutilated another. In addition, I had murdered an Arab of brown complexion. If you reflect for a moment, Mr. Hahnemann, were I to spare Freddy, might some regard my inaction to be a form of racism by omission, as if he were not worthy of my blood-lust intentions the way White and Brown men had been? No, I was an equal opportunity attacker. (On the other hand, this back-and-forth about Freddy's race does put race at issue in a way that it was not with regard to my previous, non-Black victims. An Escher-like conundrum.)

In an effort to encourage positive thinking, I reminded myself of the surge of pleasure experienced upon termination of the Syrian's life—might not my disposal of Freddy likewise inspire lustful fulfillment? Even more so since he meant so very much to me?

. . .

So, I disgust you, Mr. Hahnemann, do I? *Quelle surprise.* How self-righteous you are in deeming me a "pervert." I ask why you feel entitled to privilege certain sources of orgasmic ecstasy more than others? Each person enjoys achievement of orgasm in his or her idiosyncratic way, so why condemn mine? Do you not yourself experience greater joy when using another person as source of sexual fulfillment rather than just your own hand? Why put me on the defensive for recognizing the pleasure another can afford? We are not so different, you and I.

. . .

Spare me your meaningless protestations.

After dabbing cloth breakfast napkin against the perfectly curled, waxed ends of my white mustache to remove any stray dribbles of coffee or yoke, I rose from the breakfast table, stood with shoulders back and stomach in, strode with purpose to the elevator. I would not waste my Saturday, as deserving a day of the week as any other. Of what value was moping?

So, on to the Museum Quartier and the Leopold Museum. How interesting that the museum ticket taker required me to leave my driver's license as collatoral for an audioguide, whereas the entrance clerk at Köningshaus had not requested to see identification of any kind. Quite a commentary as to the relative value of museum audioguides and paintings on the one hand, versus towels, locker keys, and the dispensable lives of sex-starved homosexuals on the other.

I spent a good deal of time among the fourth-floor Klimts, lingered before his enormous "Life and Death," which depicts a Grim Reaper grinning at a cluster of future human victims. I looked, too, at the Kokoshkas, then discovered Gerstl, a talented self-portraitist who apparently killed himself after his mistress ended their affair and returned to her husband, the composer, Schönberg. Gerstl's insistence upon his own entitlement to kill himself because another man's wife rejected him, strikes me as the epitome of narcissistic self-indulgence. The third floor was all Schiele, whose renderings of twisted torsos I'd longed to see here, as I may already have mentioned. Delightful in composition, color, and conceptualization, although generally inferior to those on display at the Belvedere. Have you studied Schiele, Mr. Hahnemann? Do you appreciate him as I do? So sad that this artist succumbed to the Spanish flu at a young age. How frequently death finds the least deserving.

Oh, Freddy.

A couple hours strolling along part of the magnificent Ringstrasse in an effort to buoy my spirits, stopping to gaze at the vast neo-Gothic city hall known as the Rathaus, which sounds remarkably unflattering to the ear of an English speaker, do you not think so? Then on to the neo-Baroque Burgtheater and back to my hotel for a nap so as to recover my strength. An early dinner in a cute little courtyard: sweet Austrian Riesling, *Leberknödelsuppe*, then *Wienerschnitzel*, which was served, as anticipated, with a serrated steak knife that I pocketed after dining. Apple strudel and a café au lait.

Artistically and gastronomically sated, I took a slow stroll in the direction of Köningshaus, lingered before the Baroque Roman Catholic Peterskirche from which strains of Mozart piano sonatas emanated, luring me like so many Sirens of old. Although tempted, I resisted what would have amounted to another effort at procrastination. The boys must have arrived at Köningshaus by now. I had to go.

My poor Freddy.

A clerk I did not recognize now manned the Köningshaus entrance. Having passed through the empty restaurant (unescorted this time), I reached the foot of the staircase leading up to the locker room. I looked askance at the marble floor, discovered no trace of the Syrian's blood. How reassuring to know they kept the sauna spotlessly clean.

Before ascending, I listened for the familiar banter of the FuckFest boys—Freddy's voice, in particular. No sound other than the occasional clang of a locker door. I walked up, looked around, found my locker, changed into my white towel and, after double-checking that no one was observing, wrapped the *Wienerschnitzel* knife horizontally into my towel's waistfold.

I would need to perambulate around the facility with care to avoid the boys' various cameras. A quick scurry past showerheads opposite the gorgeous, tiled Turkish swimming pool, wet sauna, showers, and rows of damp towels on hooks. I walked along a bridgeway overlooking a skylit, exposed brick-walled room; below, among rubber plants, ficus, calla lillies, and palms, I spotted one of the FuckFest boys, the bodybuilder lying in a lounge chair. He must have been here long enough to tire himself out, which meant that I might well catch Freddy during a post-climax breather when his guard was down. I hastened beyond, lest the bodybuilder look up and direct his forehead camera in my direction.

After mingling among other paunchy middle-agers circling the perimeter of a room centered with a cluster of glory hole closets, I moved along a short corridor lined in cubicles and poked my head discreetly into a large porn video room filled with bleachers where your FuckFest bear-presumed-Jew was sucking a humongous Aryan. Had he no shame? I reached for my knife, but reminded myself that it was not my mission to wreak vengeance on another tribe's race traitor.

As I withdrew my head from the bleacher room, I spotted him: Freddy. Together with his Japanese friend, who had also shown me respect in Munich. They were walking ahead of me and up a half-flight of stairs into what appeared from a distance to be a dark room.

How my heart skipped a beat at the sight of Freddy. For a moment, I thought to rush and embrace him from behind. But, of course I did not. Instead, I calmed myself.

I counted to three so as to make certain Freddy did not quickly descend. As I was about to move to the stairs, Mr. Hahnemann, I spotted your portly cameraman, watched him clump up those very stairs. Damn! I held back as he entered the dark room. Fortunately, he quickly spun round and descended, mumbling, "Too dark for cameras."

Perfect.

After he stepped around a corner in pursuit of other fornicators to film, I crept up the stairs. Yes, a completely dark room heavy with the delicious aroma of male musk. Pitch black except for dim shadowy doorway light that barely penetrated the depths. How find Freddy in this murk?

"Yuki, there's space over here." That was Freddy's whisper from the far back of the room. With outstretched hand, I made my way around a group of standing men and their kneeling suckers, discovered a hip-high, mat-covered platform from which many pairs of feet protruded. Sounds of snoring, sounds of grunting. I cocked an ear—"I'm here," whispered Freddy, as if to me, but not. The sound of a body squeaking its way onto a mat.

I followed the sound, narrowed my quarry to two sets of side-by-side feet barely detectable in the thick shadow.

I pinched a toe. "Do not!" No, not Freddy's voice. That must be his Japanese friend.

I pinched the toe of another foot. "Cut it out, asshole," said Freddy with a kick. "What's with these European bathhouse freaks?"

I lay down on the mat, sidled up alongside him in the pitch dark, a sufficient number of inches away so as not to intrude on his space, yet close enough to sniff confirmation: yes, Freddy's sweat-faded, cinnamony Aramis cologne. I studied his breathing that grew increasingly rhythmic and soft. Post-coital nap-breathing. My eyes had now sufficiently accustomed themselves to the filtered darkness so that I could make out the general shape of Freddy's head mere inches from mine, and his torso as he lay on his back, one knee raised.

How I longed to lean over and kiss him, to scoot down and swallow his sweet thickness. But a more bitter task demanded my attention.

On my other side, a couple was making the standard soft wet thwurpy sounds of worm-like sixty-nine copulation. I marked time until their thwurps quickened, enhanced by muffled groans. I sat up, careful not to creak the mat and waken Freddy, reached up and undid my towel's tautly folded waistband, gripped the *Wienerschnitzel* knife. Awaiting the inevitable sound cover, I raised my arm and placed it in careful position, hovered.

The couple's grunts grew louder and louder, and at the precise moment they simultaneously blurted the universal plaintive moans of climax, I clamped one hand down onto Freddy's mouth, and drew the other across his throat. A quick and clean serrated slit worthy of the finest butcher.

Freddy undulated and croaked a series of hoarse burbles. Hearing them, and inhaling deeply the rich aroma of his spurting blood, I uttered uncontrollable whimpers of delight as I spontaneously ejaculated onto the mat at his side. Without even having touched myself. Oh my goodness. I shuddered and trembled as if experiencing a youth's sexual initiation. How very much Freddy had excited me! So much more satisfying than the thrill upon murdering the Syrian. I'd always maintained that sex with the object of love is of greater intensity than sex with a mere object of beauty. Here was empirical proof.

An unsolvable mystery, Mr. Hahnemann—the personal nature of desire, arousal, fulfillment. Were I able to define for myself the why's, I would readily share them. But, alas, I am as in the dark about the psychological source of my erotic impulses as are you. I am left merely to accept or reject them. Given that they are part of self, I embrace them fully.

"What?" I heard from Freddy's Japanese friend there in the dark room, "Freddy, what you doing so wet? You peeing?"

I slid off the platform, quickly groped my way toward the room's exit.

"Freddy?… Freddy?… Your chest all wet. Did you pee yourself?… Freddy? Answer me. Wake up. Freddy?…Your throat!… Oh my God, nooooo!"

I raced down the short stairway, flinched at the piercing screams reverberating from the dark room above and behind. A remarkably harmonious chorus of various-pitched shrieks. Hmm, a new joke: how many drama queens in a dark room does it take to—?

…

Never mind, Mr. Hahnemann.

Feeling wetness on my own hands, I examined them in the dimness of a corridor, wiped them quickly on my towel, which I then removed, folded inside out, wrapped around the *Wienerschnitzel* knife, and tossed into an open cubicle.

As I rushed from the screams, a good dozen men ran toward them. Good Samaritan first responders or perverted disaster oglers?

One who brushed past was that formerly dozing bodybuilder. Had he recognized his friend's voice? Had he spotted me? Had one of his cameras picked me up as I ran by? Cameras were of much greater threat than DNA.

I dashed to the wet area, jumped into the empty pool—brrrr, so cold— to wash off any visually incriminating traces of blood that might have been clinging—then emerged pristine. Born again thanks to Judeo-Christian ritual bath/baptismal cleansing.

To cover my nakedness, I grabbed a damp towel from the wall rack beside the showers. Let some other reveler walk around baring his shame.

A dash to the locker room where I quickly changed before elbowing my way down the marble steps through a crowd of frantic half-naked men now stampeding their way up, presumably to dress and flee.

At the bottom of the marble stairs, I turned to make my leave.

"You?" I heard from behind. "You Freddy's old man from Munich!"

The voice of Freddy's Japanese friend. He'd spotted me. And recognized me from Munich.

Damn my unforgettably distinct dapper white mustache.

I knew enough not to turn so that even if his headband camera were filming me from behind at that moment, it would reveal only the back of my head. Just another overly thick middle-aged man with a bald spot.

I hurried casually through the empty restaurant toward the Köningshaus front entrance, tossed towel and key at the entrance clerk and darted out. I literally ran up the street—this time not daring to look up at scowling pedestaled Moses in the square—and attempted to lose myself in Saturday evening tourist crowds. Breathless with dry mouth, I slowed down lest I draw attention. In Stephanplatz, I stopped at a *Café-Konditerei* practically beside the cathedral, found a free table, ordered a *Früchtekuchen* and cappuccino, then purposely engaged the plump young waitress in conversation, telling her that "your *Früchtekuchen* was Mommy's favorite pastry," at which point I launched into a feigned sobbing jag, asking her for a handkerchief. She handed me a wad of paper napkins. I seized her hand, kissed it, looked at my watch and wept that it was 9:27, the precise minute of Mommy's death from heart attack—too much whipped cream over the years, you understand?—exactly one week ago right here in Vienna where she'd asked to spend her final days, so would the waitress please become my new Mommy? The young waitress opened both mascaraed eyes so wide I thought they would pop from their sockets. She scurried away for the manager, an older woman with hairnetted bun who walked slowly over, patted my head, said what a good son I must have been, so please enjoy the *Früchtekuchen* for free then wouldn't you like to go light a candle for your *Mutter* in the cathedral next door? I "forced" myself to eat the plumb cake, left and indeed sat in Stephansdom for a good hour, satisfied at having created a memorable alibi with the café staff should my evening's whereabouts ever be in question.

I felt rather frustrated: here I'd gone to the trouble of killing Freddy so as to eliminate a potential witness against me only for that very act to have created another potential witness—Freddy's Japanese friend. So what had been the point of killing poor Freddy? His friend had undercut the very meaning and purpose I'd intended to impart to Freddy's death, and had now foisted yet another burdensome task upon me. How dare he.

. . .

You label me, Mr. Hahnemann, a serial killer? Nonsense. Up to this point, I had killed a White little blond, had maimed a tall WASP, and had murdered a Syrian and a Black American. Now I'm telling you of my plan to execute a son of the Land of the Rising Sun. How much more different could my victims have been from one another? I see and respect human individuality. There is nothing "serial" about my behavior. "Sequential," perhaps, but not the base and common "serial." Furthermore, as the evidence has shown, I possessed neither a single *modus operandi* nor a uniform motivation for attack. Rather, I have responded to various stimuli as they arose, and through a variety of means. You must, then, reconsider your definitions.

Seated in one of the cathedral's wooden side pews, shivering from the cavernous chill and alternately looking down at the brown-and-white tile floor, up at the remarkable rib-vaulted ceiling, the various side chapels and altars, carvings, stained glass windows all shadowy in the night, barely illuminated by an insufficient number of candles and a few stray bulbs, I wondered if so-called God liked to lurk in shadows as much as I now did. Out of a sense of shame, perhaps? After all, should He not have protected Freddy from the likes of me? If God were all-powerful, why would He permit me to murder an innocent? Simply because Freddy loved to engage in sex, that God-given desire? If He exists, what a cruel taunter God must be— granting desire only to then punish those who seek its fulfillment. How did such sadism differ from, say, the offer of poisoned Halloween candy to a child—want it, sweetie? If you dare to indulge, this yummy candy might just kill you.

Is it any wonder the angels rebelled?

My Memories: Vienna: Post-FuckFest

Horror.
Horror. Horror.
Horror. Horror. Horror.

From the van a coupla blocks away, I heard screams from Yuki's and Freddy's cameras and then the others'. My shock grew as I pieced it all together. Freddy! That great kid. Some monster had cut his throat! No!!!

I saw Burt quickly take charge, so I resisted running in like I'd done back in Munich. I didn't wanna make things crazier. Instead, I forced myself to sit tight. Fuck—I was sitting right there in the van and watching 'em all. I knew that everything was being live-streamed from the boys' and Burt's headband cams like in Munich. Burt remembered that, too, obviously—he specifically ordered the boys to keep wearing the headband cams because subscribers had the right to see everything, good and bad.

Burt instructed Big Bill and Yuki to carry Freddy's body from the dark room over to the bottom of the front marble staircase. Yuki was balling his eyes out and shaking hard. At the foot of the staircase, Yuki stopped, trained his camera on the hairy back of some old guy, and hollered something at him I couldn't make out.

Then Burt told 'em all to shower off and get their asses outta there pronto. While the boys dressed, Burt grabbed the wallet and hotel key outta Freddy's locker so the cops couldn't know he was American the way they'd identified Little Frenchie in Copenhagen. The less chance of connecting him to us, the better. To the cops, Freddy'd be just another dead faggot, which pissed me off because I really cared about that kid, but we had to protect the other boys. And ourselves.

Through the van's window, I saw a coupla cop cars and an ambulance pull up, and I warned Burt through his micro ear receiver.

Lucky for us, it turned out there was a second, back staircase down from the locker room. So, as the cops headed up the main staircase, Burt hustled all the boys down the other. The entrance clerk was on his cell phone babbling hysterically in German, so he didn't notice our boys rush out with lotsa other guys who couldn't get outta there fast enough.

It was only after Burt and the boys fled that I ran outta the van and into Köningshaus to see what the cops were up to, what the paramedics would do with Freddy, and if they had any idea who he was. By then, half a dozen fully dressed looky-loos were milling around, so I didn't stand out. I saw an ambulance gurney covered in a sheet near the bottom of the marble stairs. A coupla cops kept lifting the sheet, gawking and pointing at *"grosser schwarzer Schwanz."* I knew enough German to understand: "big black dick." Racist motherfuckers. Freddy was such a good guy, sophisticated, compassionate, totally decent. But all those motherfuckers saw was—why was I surprised?

The paramedics took Freddy away. Poor Freddy, that sweet, sad kid.

The clerk argued in German and gesticulated with the cops a lot, looked all frustrated. After the cops left, I asked the clerk about his conversation with 'em. He was practically screaming as he told me in English that they weren't gonna investigate shit. "They say it is another case of spontaneous suicide."

"What?" I asked.

He explained that years back, something happened to an American who fled Köningshaus hysterically one night, naked but for a towel. According to the cops, he ran for blocks and blocks, then jumped into the Danube Canal and drowned. They called it "spontaneous suicide." The cops never even bothered to dredge the canal. The victim's mother, a police officer herself, flew over from the U.S. because she didn't believe those blatant lies and was suspicious about the circumstances of her son's death. They never found the body.

"What?" I couldn't believe it. "Local police didn't investigate?"

"Bullshit, of course," said the clerk. "Dead gay man in sauna—who cares? Especially if he is foreign."

By the time I got back to our hotel room, I'd gotten all worked up. "How can we count on the cops to send Freddy's body home, Burt? They don't have his ID, so they don't know who he is."

"You saying I did something wrong, Paulie?" On our room's cream-colored chaise, Burt was chugging one of the dozen beers he'd filched from our executive floor's lounge. His fifth if the empties on the round little coffee table signaled anything. "Are you blaming me for taking his wallet?" Burt's a mean drunk, so I had to be careful. "You criticizing me for the millionth time, Paulie? You think I'm not fucking tired of cleaning up your shit?"

"Burtie-boy, whatcha saying? Of course I'm not criticizing you. You were fucking brilliant to take Freddy's wallet and hotel key in order to protect all of us."

"Damn straight. Fucking genius."

"I'm just thinking about Freddy, that's all. I wanna do right by him. I wanna make sure his mom gets to bury him her way. How do we get his body and send it home? If we don't, those racist homophobic cops might just dump him in a canal or something and make him disappear."

"What choice do we have? You go to the cops and whaddaya think they'll do? Just hand him over? You think they won't ask a shitload of questions? Maybe detain us here for who knows how long? Shut down the whole goddamn Tour? Are you fucking nuts?"

"You make a really good point, Burtie-boy, you sure do. And this isn't an accident like Little Frenchie's in Copenhagen or a dick chomping like in Munich. This is cold-blooded murder, so the cops'd take it seriously, for sure. But can we just abandon him?"

"Stop taking care of the dead and start taking care of the living, for God's sake."

"You've got a point there, Burt." He really did. I don't know how he could think so clearly after all that beer, but wasn't he making a shitload of sense? I felt so confused.

I fell back onto our king-size bed.

"The third one, Paulie," Burt said. "Our third boy to get hurt or killed. This is no coincidence."

"Third? Dean's attack in Munich and now Freddy. That's two."

"I'm beginning to think Little Frenchie's fall in Copenhagen was no accident." Burt polished off that fifth bottle, started in on a sixth.

"You think someone's—you really think someone's after us?"

"That's exactly what I think."

"But why, Burt? Who?"

"No fucking clue."

"A pissed investor? Burt, I told you we should have stuck with small investors. I told you we shouldn't go after money from Al-Qaida and drug cartels. But you insisted—"

Burt hurled his beer bottle straight at my head. I ducked. The bottle hit the wall, dribbled beer down the dark gray wallpaper behind the wooden headboard. "Don't you go goddamn blaming me. You wanted me to get the financing for this project, so I did. Yeah, we got a bunch of individual douchebag investors, but the big bucks came from organizations that wanted to launder their dough in a porn/sex business. You knew that. Don't you go saying this is all my fault."

His nostrils were flaring, and he was breathing hard. A bad sign. If he wanted to, he could beat the crap outta me with one hand tied behind his back, the way he'd done a few times over the years. But only when he was shit-faced. He never hit me when sober. Burt's always loved me. "You're right, Burt. I apologize. My fault. It's all my fault. But why the hell would an investor come after us? We're not late on any payments yet."

"Or maybe it's not an investor," Burt said, wobbling his way to the bathroom, grabbing a white face towel, stumbling back to the bed and climbing over me so's he could wipe the beer off the wall. He smeared it around more than he cleaned it up. "Maybe it's some cunt competitor wants to put us outta business."

"You mean, trying to scare us off?"

"Trying to take us down so he can launch his own copy-cat sex competition show like some drug dealer muscling in on another's turf. Or maybe it's a competitor and investor both: maybe the whole reason investors gave us money was to figure out how we did everything so they could muscle in."

"Fuck that shit!" I yelled. "This contest was *my* idea and *my* hard work. No asshole's gonna dick-chew it away from me!"

Burt grabbed a beer from the mini-bar, plopped back onto the chaise. "Or maybe it's just some garden variety lunatic homophobic stalker."

"So what do we do? We can't just sit back and let the other boys get mauled or killed, Burt. I mean, c'mmon, they're our responsibility."

"Good papa."

"I hate to even say this, but you think maybe we should cut our losses and hightail it home?"

Burt bolted upright at that, lunged across the room at me, jumped onto the bed and grabbed me by the throat with one hand while still holding his beer with the other. "You outta your fucking skull? How we gonna pay back the investors if we cut the Tour short? Yeah, we got a giant cumload of cash shooting in so far, but it's not enough yet to pay everything we owe. You think somebody's after us now? Just wait 'til we don't pay up."

I pried his thumb back 'til he let go. I wanted to hit him, but knew better. I crawled back into a ball against the wooden headboard, peeped, "Maybe if we explain about the murders, the investors'll understand?"

He lumbered back to the chaise. "Some of the individual investors—okay, I'll give you that possibility—those old queers trying to up their nest eggs might understand. But our anchor organization investors? You telling me the Mexican drug cartel bosses'll understand? The Russian Mafia? You wanna get hung headless from a bridge somewhere or be served poison Novichok tea in some coffee shop?"

"I know, Burt, I know, but—"

"Besides, why the fuck should we give up our one-and-only chance to land on easy street? If you think I'm going back to shooting your lousy porn films for crap pay, you're outta your fucking gourd."

"So, we just keep risking the boys' lives?"

"They're risking their own lives, Paulie, nobody's forcing 'em. We're making 'em fucking superstars, right? And remember, tens of thousands of jerk-offs didn't start watching us *despite* the attacks, they're watching *because of* the attacks. According to the analytics, in the hours after Freddy's murder tonight, our subscriber and betting numbers nearly doubled. Doubled! The public wants to see our boys get mutilated and snuffed. If anybody's guilty, it's them—the public—not us. We're just giving the public what it wants. I bet the audience can't wait to find out—is it a coincidence or a stalker? Paulie, we've got a real-time, honest-to-God murder mystery reality show on our hands. First in history. Cheers."

Was that really what was drawing people in now—the gore and suspense about whether another kid'd get mauled or killed? What kind of audience were we tapping into? What were we doing? "But Burt," I asked gently, so as not to piss him off, "just because maybe the murder mystery is what the public wants, does that mean we gotta give it to 'em? Risk the rest of the boys?"

"It's not like we're hiding the attacks from the boys. They know what's going on. They wanna call it quits, let 'em. They just have to pay us the penalty fee for quitting early."

"It's a steep penalty fee, Burt."

"Don't we have a right to cover our bank account and our asses, Paulie?" He finished his beer, came over and collapsed on the bed beside me, passed right out.

I covered him with the white blanket, kissed his forehead. I knew it was the beers made him a grouch. He'd be his good ol' self by morning.

Not knowing what else to do, I went to the mini-fridge for a few beers of my own—my throat was kind of sore from Burt's squeezing—all the while wondering what the right thing to do was. The right thing for Burt. The right thing for the boys. The right thing for Freddy.

The right thing for me.

My Memories: Vienna—Post-FuckFest (cont'd)

I woke up that AM with a dry, pasty hangover mouth and a piss belly about to burst. Checked the clock—shit, no time to shower. Where the fuck was Burt? Splash of water on my face, then down to the breakfast room. I joined the boys—the surviving boys—and Burt at a large round table. Bear Sam and Manny were nibbling around the edges of a roll each, but slowly, like novocained bunnies. Big Bill took a few stabs at a tiny sausage. Femmy Tommy kept dipping a spoon into a bowl of yogurt, lifting it, licking just the back of it. Yuki sipped weak tea, but wasn't eating anything, just wiping tears from the corners of his eyes.

But Burt looked all showered and perky, no sign of a hangover. He was gobbling a plate heaped with pastries. "Yuki says he saw the guy."

"What guy?" I asked, putting sugar in the coffee the waitress brought me.

"The guy he thinks killed Freddy. Yuki says he pointed his head cam at the guy as he was leaving Köningshaus."

"Yuki, what're you talking about?" Then I remembered seeing Yuki at the bottom of the marble staircase, yelling at some old guy with a hairy back.

Yuki spoke deliberately. "I saw old man with white mustache."

"You saw this guy kill Freddy? You filmed it?"

"No, I did not see him killing, but I saw him leaving Köningshaus after. He same man in Munich sauna with Freddy."

"You saw that same old guy in Munich? In the sauna?"

"Yes."

"Did you see him in the steam room there? Did you see him attack Dean?"

"No, but Dean insulted him at gay festival. And I saw this same old man go into steam room right before attack on Dean. Then Freddy went with this old man to *kabine*."

I thought for a minute. "But nothing happened to Freddy in Munich. If this guy was after him, why didn't he kill Freddy in Munich when he had him alone? Why would he come all the way to Vienna and wait to sneak around in a crowded dark room to kill him here?"

"I do not know. Maybe because few days ago, Freddy saw this same old white mustache man at Köningshaus over body of dead Arab."

"Dead Arab? What dead Arab? Yuki, what are you talking about? And what do you mean, 'few days ago'? When?"

"Does not matter if I tell you now, I think. Freddy went to Köningshaus another day. Before FuckFest, to gain advantage."

"Freddy was cheating?" I couldn't believe it. "Damn it, how could he do that to me?"

"Does not matter now."

Yuki was right. Pissed as I was, what difference did it make now?

Yuki explained more, "At sauna, before, Freddy saw same old man with body of dead Arab. Then I saw this old man leaving Köningshaus after Freddy was killed. I pointed my head cam at him. You find him on film and we can show police."

No way I'd get those asshole Vienna cops involved. But, all the other boys were watching with hopeful poodle eyes. I had to soothe them and Yuki. "Sure, we can do that, Yuki. We can look on film for the old guy, but it'll take a while. We've got a fuckload of film—each boy's headband footage goes on for hours. Burt's too."

"The only cam feed we need to go through from last night is Yuki's," said Burt, giving me a look like maybe Yuki was on to something.

Fine, I'd play along, although I knew Burt didn't wanna get the police involved any more than I did. "Okay, Yuki," I said. "We'll go through your film from last night and look for a guy with a white 'stache."

Yuki nodded in excitement. "You will recognize him. Everybody was seeing him at Munich street festival when Dean insulted him."

"Burt, you remember that guy?"

He shook his head.

"Boys?" I asked. "An old white-'stached guy in Munich?"

"We fuck so many old faggots nowadays," said Femmy Tommy, "they all blur together into one saggy, wrinkly mass."

Everyone around the table nodded and shrugged.

"Okay, Burt and I'll show Yuki any guy we find on film with a white 'stache."

Yuki gave a solid nod at that.

"Meanwhile," I added, "I'll search for smaller saunas in Prague and Berlin, safer ones with no dark rooms where somebody can thug you out in secret. I already started looking into that here, actually, checked one out our first day in Vienna, but it was the pits. Prague and Berlin have a lot more saunas to choose from. In a small one, Burt'll be able to keep his eye on everybody at the same time. While I watch your live streams in the van."

"So you get a front row seat while somebody off's us," said Manny, "just like you did last night. That's great, Paulie, really great. Even in the smallest sauna, there are dark corners and cubicles. Dean got his dick chomped right in the steam room when we were all around, remember? The only way to be safe is to ditch the rest of the Tour and go home."

"Re-read your contract," said Burt calmly. "If you miss a FuckFest session, you owe a fifty grand penalty. If you miss both Prague and Berlin—you'll owe Paulie a hundred grand. Plus, you'll lose out on any profits."

Manny glared at me.

"I gotta pay back our investors," I said sheepishly, "or they'll take it outta my hide."

"Or yours," Burt said to Manny. "Some of our investors play rough, Manny. If they don't get what they want in cash, they'll take it out in blood. Paulie's, mine, or maybe yours, too. Maybe that's what the attacks have been about—a warning for us to keep going. No shit."

That was a new idea to me. But, why would an investor knock some of the boys outta the competition as a warning to the others to stay in the competition? I kept my doubts to myself and my face blank.

Manny looked from Burt to me. "Your *investors* would come after us? *Coño*, who the fuck are they?"

"Boys," said Burt like a dad trying to teach his kids, "you're in the big leagues now. Sure we got money from run-of-the-mill small fry investors, a few old queers. But Paulie and I, we got big ideas for The Grand Sex Tour. We want it to be a huge fucking deal. For you and your careers as well as ours. That means we had to hit up organizations with big bucks behind 'em. Think it through: what kind of big buck investor would front a sex/gambling competition? Who's got that kind of dough and is willing to take the legal risk?"

"You mean," asked Sam, "like, the Mafia?"

Burt just shrugged.

Tommy's eyes reddened. "I can't believe this," he said. "I just can't believe this."

"By the way, Tommy," I said, trying to calm him, "the computer algorithm put you in the lead last night."

"Like that'll keep me alive, right?" He covered his eyes.

Burt and I sat and watched while the reality sank in.

"Tommy and I are from Brooklyn," said Sam. "We know better than to mess with the Mafia."

Tommy nodded slowly. The other boys just stared until Big Bill broke the silence. "A more important issue for this morning: what about Freddy's body? At least you'll go to the police to make sure he gets shipped back to the States for a proper burial, right?"

"Already taken care of," Burt lied. "I went to the police station at dawn this morning, said I was his tour guide and got suspicious when he didn't return to the hotel last night, that I checked around and heard he went to Köningshaus and heard about the murder of a Black guy and figured it must've been him. I made all the arrangements."

Big Bill nodded. Then he and the others, looking a little dazed and as if on cue, stood and left the breakfast room.

"You're a cold bastard, Burt," I said.

"And I'm all yours, so that makes you a *lucky* bastard." He blew me a kiss.

Hidden Camera Transcript:
Tommy and Sam

Both are fully clothed in jeans and white t-shirts. Black socks.

On his bed, Tommy turns his head to Sam, who's lying on the other bed, Tommy asks in a mousy voice. "Would you hold me? Not in a romantic way, just in a safe way."

Sam opens his arms.

Tommy springs up and snuggles beside him, back to front.

"I gotcha, baby," says Sam

Tommy sighs. "Now I feel better."

They spoon.

"The Mafia," whispers Tommy. "I guess we should have known. Or maybe we just didn't want to think it through. The Mafia. You won't let anything bad happen to me, will you, Sam?"

Sam squeezes. "You're safe while I'm around, Toms."

"My hero."

Prague

Killer Interview 8

I found the Karlův Most—the Charles Bridge—that traverses the Vltava River, to be a rather hyperbolized tourist destination. By no means does the flat span rival Rome's Ponte Sant'Angelo—Bridge of Angels—over the Tiber, which, if you've strolled across, you'll recall to be much shorter but of eminently greater dramatic impact because Rome's ten statues are clean white marble whereas Prague's thirty statues and statuary groupings are mostly carved from now-gray sandstone and, consequently, stand as a monument to little more than the grime of passé Communism.

No other tourists were about at that warm, pre-dawn hour. Lurking within arch shadows of the Old Town Tower, I watched as, illuminated by full moon, the boys unzipped and tossed shoes, jeans, and t-shirts into an irreverent pile at the foot of the Madonna and Saint Bernard. Apparently, in an effort to distract them from sadness and worry, you, Mr. Hahnemann, had brought them here for a *Walpurgisnacht*-ish frenzy: "Come on, boys, fantasy time while Uncle Burt films you. Pretend the statues are the hottest sex partners you've ever humped."

Your appreciation for figurative art, Mr. Hahnemann, warms me, and reinforces my sense of our kinship, our similarity of sensibilities and values despite your protestations to the contrary. We are, in so many ways, of one mind.

Initially there on the bridge, the boys fidgeted and looked at one another, displaying a shyness that surprised given their lack of self-consciousness in bathhouses.

"Come on, boys," you urged, yourself now unrobed in display of your hirsute pastiness modestly akin to my own, although I maintain myself in considerably better shape overall (pre-breakfast push-ups and stomach crunches). "It'll do you good. I gotta get you boys outta your funk. I know we're all bummed, but we've gotta be good soldiers and carry on. Force yourselves. It'll make super footage and get us lotsa subscribers. You wanna end the Tour with a bang, right? For Freddy's sake, so we can send lotsa money to his mom. Come on! And get this," you continued, "I found a super safe sauna for us. Small but not too small. Still interesting. Dionysus Sauna. Usually they sponsor foam nights on Fridays, and mask nights on Saturdays, but this Saturday, it'll be both foam and mask night. Very special. Only the best for you boys."

Ah, the Dionysus Sauna. I had read online of their "foam parties," which I couldn't quite picture. Intriguing.

"In order to get us all back in the mood," you elaborated, Mr. Hahnemann, "tonight's a chance to let loose and get your kink on. Have fun and randy it up—just don't cum! Remember, we don't wanna waste it, boys. Save your juices for Saturday night."

Your hefty cameraman raised his video camera, announced that filming had now commenced. In Pavlovian response, the boys slowly cast shyness aside. Inhaling deeply, exhaling, and rubbing his flat tummy, the naked wiry Latino boosted you atop a pedestal and joined you, practically crawling up beneath the robes of Saints Cyril and Methodius. The huge muscleman took to stroking the lean sinews of first one male figure then another supporting the statue of St. Xavier. Not in the least lascivious. Rather boring, to be perfectly frank.

Then, as if not wishing to be outdone—these boys were competitors, after all—your effeminate Irishman launched into action: he climbed onto enrobed St. John the Baptist, gained an awkward footing on the pedestal's edge, balanced so as to insert the holy man's exposed big toe into the boy's shapely backside. To the muted yet supportive cheers of all, he rode the saintly toe for all he was worth, most likely shredding hemorrhoids. His brilliant improvisation was that much more impressive when one considers his preference for enjoying others' bottoms rather than serving up his own for delectation (as I recalled having observed at the Copenhagen FuckFest). What confident self-awareness he demonstrated by publicly undulating his posterior in unmistakable imitation of Marilyn Monroe's distinctive sway, thereby admirably asserting that one man's beefcake can transubstantiate into another man's cheesecake. Or vice versa. As if he were giving the finger to black-and-white biblical designations of gender immutability and, by extension, implying the Bible to be little more than myth or fairytale unworthy of the parchment it's written upon. Take them Eden apples and shove 'em up your bum, so to speak.

Turning my attention away from him, I noticed that the bearish Jew, having disrobed and witnessed the others' shenanigans, quietly re-dressed in contravention of your instructions, now sat cross-legged below St. Francis of Assisi. A Jew refusing to defile monuments to Christian honoraries, demonstrating sensitive respect for Christian history and creed? A gentlemanly Jew striving to redeem his fellows? Perhaps intentionally following in the footsteps of that most famous of historical good-neighborly Jews, was he? Interesting.

My gaze shifted to the Japanese, who had begun gently rubbing his erection against the draperies of sandstone St. Augustine of Hippo. After a few half-hearted thrusts, his erection flagged. A reaction to the rough texture of cold stone? To the philosophy of St. Augustine and his notions of original sin? Or had the young fellow been overtaken by grievous thoughts of his late friend and mine, dear Freddy? Yes, the young man's face actually took on a melancholy cast. No—a sullen one. Obviously still grieving the loss of poor Freddy, departed merely days before. Who would have thought a contestant in a commercial sex competition capable of such profound compassion and suffering? A young man of character. Most unfortunate that I would have to eliminate him. Yet fortunate that he seemed to be in an emotionally frail state—how much easier it would be to catch him unawares and snap him like a twig of wilted cherry blossoms.

Yet, how could I regard him—or your Jewish fellow, for that matter—as anything other than good boys with conscience and respect for others? In fact, I recall thinking that had I ever sired sons, I would have liked them to be very much like that Japanese and that Jew. Should my sons have been like Freddy? No no no. I was attracted to Freddy physically and even, I admit, emotionally. As much as I had reveled in our daddy-son sauna mascarade, it would be wrong of me to wish for an actual son to whom I might grow attracted. I am a civilized being who adheres to natural law.

...

Oh, come now, Mr. Hahnemann. You must admit that murder is a natural, God-given right. In fact, it was practiced by biblical figures with greater regularity than incest.

...

Very well, we shall agree to disagree.

Back to the Charles Bridge that first Prague night: having achieved my objective for the evening—overhearing mention of which sauna would serve as our next venue—I could depart. Turning, I absent-mindedly reached fingers to upper lip to tug at my dapper white mustache as I was sometimes known to do. I'd been considering shaving it off so as to make myself less recognizable to the Japanese fellow. But now I had no need for erasure of those white, testosterone-inspired secretions, that brushy expression of my maleness, my distinctiveness, my refinement, my dignity: wearing a mask at Dionysus on mask and foam night, I would pass undetected before him. Thank you for your venue selection, Mr. Hahnemann. You facilitated my next murder, you certainly did. One might even label you complicit.

. . .

There there, Mr. Hahnemann. There there. One merely jests. Almost.

I strolled back to my small but comfortable hotel room on Haštalská, a mere fifteen-minute walk from the bridge through the deserted, enormous Old Town Square with its sand-and-gray-colored Gothic-Renaissance Old Town Hall displaying, on one side, the famous 15th-century Astronomical Clock with moving Apostle statuettes and a skeleton, the figure of ever-present Death. Perhaps placed there just for my inspiration and amusement?

I passed, mid-square, the Jan Hus Monument, a massive black bronze group sculpture devoted to the religious reformer burnt at the stake as heretic in 1415. Would a statue be erected one day in my memory? Of me and those boys whose lives Fate had demanded me to end? But in which city should such a memorial be placed? Here in Prague's Old Town Square? Beside Moses in Vienna? Doubtful because homosexual achievements are rarely lauded. The many manifestations of homophobia.

In the cool pre-dawn moonlight gray, I continued for blocks along sidewalks of small cobblestones in artistic patterns: diamonds, diagonals, stripes and squares, some even set in the shape of a cross before a church entrance. I passed five-story apartment buildings sporting Rococo curlicue design ornamentations as if the entire town had just spent the day at a beauty parlor. Into my art deco hotel, up a gentle elevator to a small but charmingly appointed room of polished, minimalist furniture. I slept the exhausted sleep of the dead, so to speak.

Hidden Camera Transcript:
Bill, Yuki, Tommy, Sam, and Manny

Big Bill, wearing a pale blue t-shirt and black jogging shorts, is seated on the single, yellow polka-dot armchair in his and Yuki's hotel room. Yuki, in a forest green sweatsuit, is curled up on Bill's lap, whimpering, his head resting on Bill's shoulder.

"You're missing Freddy," Big Bill says softly.

"He was my friend. I laying beside him when…his throat…c-c-cut." Yuki shudders.

Bill squeezes him tight. "We all feel like shit."

"Freddy was a good guy," says Tommy. In navy blue bikini briefs and white undershirt, he's seated cross-legged on Bill's bed by the window. "Freddy's muscles weren't as big as yours, Bill, but he was sculpted like a statue."

"That is why I could not have sex with statues on Charles Bridge," says Yuki.

Bill gives Yuki a peck on the cheek. "Sweet fella."

Manny, sitting upright on the edge of Yuki's single bed draped in a yellow spread, massages his own stomach through his black t-shirt. "I have to admit, the statue kink got me out of myself a little, but now my belly's back in knots."

"Let's get real, guys," says Tommy. "As upset as we are about Freddy, that's not the only thing. I'm scared shitless. I'd be willing to bail on the contest if all that meant was owing Paulie a fortune. What could he do if I didn't pay—sue me in court because I refused to fuck in a bathhouse? But then there's this Mafia investor bullshit. Like I really want to wake up in bed next to a bloody horse's head."

Sam imitates Marlon Brando's godfather throatiness, "What's a matter with you? You don't think you'd look good in cement overshoes?"

Tommy gives him the finger.

"Maybe," says Sam, "we're exaggerating the sauna danger. It could all be a goddamn awful coincidence, couldn't it? Maybe this kind of shit is normal for Europe, who knows? You didn't actually see that old mustached dude do anything to Freddy, did you, Yuki?"

"No. I was just seeing him leaving Köningshaus. I cannot prove—Paulie says no white mustache man showed on my Köningshaus film—only back of white-haired man's head when leaving."

"See?" says Sam. "Maybe we're blaming that old guy for nothing."

"Nothing? Really?" says Manny, his voice pretzeled in annoyance. "Dean got mutilated in Munich, Freddy was murdered in Vienna, and Yuki saw the same old guy in both those places. And he tells us the old guy had something going on with Freddy. You really believe this is just 'shit-happens' coincidence? How dumb can you be?"

Sam slowly rises to his feet, thrusts out his bearded chin, clenches his fists.

"Hey!" barks Big Bill while still clutching Yuki. "Cut it out."

Manny and Sam glare at one another.

"Back to your corners!" orders Bill. "Now!"

Manny hesitates, stares at Bill, stares at Sam, drops his head, mumbles, "Sorry, Sam. It's not you pissing me off." He leans against the pale blue bathroom door frame.

Sam sits back down. "Yeah, I guess it's wishful thinking to call it coincidence. But why would some old guy be after us?"

"To whittle down the competition," says Manny. "Maybe he's betting big on one of us and wants to be sure his favorite wins."

"If true," says Yuki, "then one of us here in room—I do not wish to be favorite of murderer."

"Or maybe he's a Jack the Ripper type," says Tommy, "wanting to off guys he thinks are immoral."

"Serial killers got different logic than normal people," says Bill. "Did he look weird to you, Yuki?"

Yuki shrugged. "Many White men are looking weird to me."

"At least," says Sam, "Burt and Paulie promised to go through all our film from Vienna, and from the Munich FuckFest, too."

"So they say," says Manny.

"You do not believe?" asks Yuki.

Manny just stares at him.

"That's a shitload of film," says Bill. "All our headband cams and Burt's. They probably won't finish before Saturday night's FuckFest."

"At least," says Sam, "we can protect ourselves by steering clear of any old guy with a white mustache."

"Better than nothing," says Manny.

"I'm so scared," says Tommy, "I don't know how I'll get it up on Saturday night. This whole thing gives new meaning to the phrase 'reality show elimination challenge.'"

"Good one, Toms," says Sam. "If I weren't so depressed, I'd laugh."

Killer Interview 9

After waking mid-morning, I took the metro (smells of stale train exhaust and human body odor barely masked by cheap cologne) north across the river to the drab neighborhood housing the Czech National Gallery of modern art. A wonderful Klimt (the "Virgin"—a cloisonnéd-ish woman surrounded by others in a naked pile), some Kokoshka landscapes, lesser Schieles. Most interesting was the first-floor exhibit of Mucha's "Slav Epic," a series of nineteen humongous murals rendering various aspects of Slavic history and culture. A national fairy tale treasure. In general, I found Czech art to be—

...

Oh?

...

Oh, really?

...

Well, I beg your pardon once again, Mr. Hahnemann, for permitting oneself to be carried away. I thought that, given our shared interest in art, you might care to hear my impressions. Do not think I fail to see what you are doing—suddenly feigning disinterest in art so as to establish a distance between us, to negate the obvious psychological parallels between us, all so as to deny the *me* in you and your guilt by association.

One additional thought on the matter, Mr. Hahnemann: is your primary goal through these interviews to gain understanding of me, or of yourself? Might you perceive yourself in me? We are both rather self-oriented, don't you think? After all, we both used those lovely boys to achieve our respective personal ends, did we not? The both of us? Sacrificing them to our desires and needs? I am being honest about my motivations; are you being as honest about your own?

...

Of course you refuse to acknowledge any similarities between us. Who wishes to gaze into a mirror only to see one's Dorian Gray portrait reflected back?

. . .

Of course, of course. My having touched too close to the heart of matters, you wish me to confine my remarks to details of actions rather than speculations. Very well.

I will summarize the rest of my sightseeing week rather than render it in fascinating detail: the Clemintinum—either you know what it is or you do not; assorted synagogues and a cemetery in the Jewish Quarter; the Castle, of Kafka fame; the Strahov Monastery and Library—

. . .

Yes, Mr. Hahnemann, I am getting to the FuckFest. Come to think of it, perhaps I have been misreading your growing disinterest in my sightseeing. Perhaps you've grown increasingly prurient during the course of these interviews, urging me on to "the good parts," as it were.

. . .

No, I am most certainly not being antagonistic, Mr. Hahnemann, nor combative. I have simply been attempting to provide context for the events to come. One does not behave in a vacuum, but on a continuum. Admittedly both key words bear the unusual double "u" in their final syllables, but—

. . . .

Fine! I shall cease my elaborations, but I insist upon setting the record straight in one critical regard: my sightseeing was not simply for mere amusement nor biding of time. I engaged in sightseeing to distract myself from myself and from my impending task.

True, part of me sparkled at the prospect of again knowing the "thrill of kill," as I'd come to think of it. That electrifying rush at the moment of execution, as if a young man's life force were not so much extinguished as...transferred into my own self. Such an invigorating sensation presumably akin to that experienced by other men my age when—yes, here's the proper analogy: an invigorating rush akin to that experienced by an older man upon ingestion of a younger man's hot ejaculate.

However, another part of me—the profoundly empathetic aspect of character inherent in all men of culture—regretted what was to come. Both lovely Freddy and now the sensitive Japanese fellow—Yuki, yes, you have told me his name—both young men had committed no offense other than to perceive what I had done to others. Hardly actions meriting death, but one must preserve self, after all. A duty imposed by natural law. I resigned myself to my duty while, I acknowledge, feeling a twinge of anticipatory wonderment as to my sexual response to the upcoming murder. Which carnal reaction might dead Yuki inspire from deep within my manly soul?

…

Disgusting? Again you deem my honest expression of desire disgusting. How dare you. I have suffered more than sufficient disparagement from you. I shan't continue these interviews, Mr. Hahnemann. I shall stop here. Kindly turn off the tape recorder and remove yourself from this prison interview room.

…

Oh, really? You threaten denial of profits due from my investment? What if I threaten to sue upon my eventual release from isolation in this German prison?

…

You doubt that they shall release me early for good behavior?

…

Do not laugh at me, Mr. Hahnemann. I caution you not to laugh. I have been known to react badly to humiliation and mockery. My wrists and ankles may be shackled, but my teeth remain sharp as ever. As is my tongue. You cannot withhold my profits simply because I refuse to complete these interviews!

…

That's better. Apology accepted, although one now feels rather deflated. One cannot guarantee that one shall cooperate with the same vim and vigor as in prior interviews. However, one shall try. Next time.

My Memories: Prague—FuckFest Prep

Burt and I managed to go through the rest of the boys' Vienna FuckFest film footage during the week, and saw half a dozen older guys with white 'staches. We showed those film clips to Yuki—none of 'em were his man. Was Yuki thinking clearly? Could he really recognize that guy? Did all White guys look alike to him? I mean, I might not be able to tell the difference between half a dozen old Japanese guys, so why should I expect Yuki to be able to do that with old White guys?

Saturday evening, in the van a coupla blocks away from Prague's Dionysus Sauna, I kept scanning all the headband cam live-feed screens at the same time, back and forth, over and over. I stuck with it even though I was getting dizzy. Come hell or high water, I'd keep a closer watch on the screens than ever to protect my boys. That was the least I could do. I swore that if anybody looked suspicious, I'd race into the sauna and warn the boys.

And in case Yuki was right, I kept looking especially for white 'staches. A bunch of guys were wearing just eye masks, but they were all clean-shaven. Everyone else wore full face masks or hoods. How the hell could I see a 'stache under 'em?

The only part of Dionysus I couldn't see onscreen was the foam room: foam kept covering the headband cams. Burt figured it out real quick and tried wiping foam off his headband cam, but every time he moved, more foam floated up to block everything again, so I told him through his micro ear receiver to stay outta the foam room altogether because what was the point?

So much for my bright idea of foam and mask night.

Killer Interview 10

During the roughly twenty-minute walk to Dionysus, I stopped at a sex shop, purchased a black cloth hood perfect for the "mask" aspect of "foam and mask night." Slipping the hood on even before entering, and adjusting with care so that it left mouth and lower lip exposed while covering upper lip and mustache, I paid my entry fee and stripped in the locker room lined with red, yellow, and blue square lockers. (Even here, there was an attempt at artistic design. Those Czechs!)

Clothed in black hood and white towel, I sauntered through an elliptical bar area where assorted patrons in towels, having removed masks and hoods, indulged in tall glasses of beer while watching pathetic porn films (yours, perhaps, Mr. Hahnemann?) on the wall's television. The loud rhythmic blare of the sauna's disco music drowned out the film stars' canned grunts and groans. Just as well.

Leaving the bar, I turned right, walked past a side shower room to a tiled foyer with lounge chairs, and opened a glass door to what appeared to be a steam room. Yes—a floor-to-ceiling tiled steam room maze. Warm and humid zigzaggy tiled corridors. At the far end, I encountered another glass door, opened it, and walked smack into a wall of fluffy foam. A child's delight! Wading through and batting the citrusy-orange bubbles from before my face, I reached a far corner and stood back-to-wall to assess the large room in its entirety. Up by the ceiling in the opposite corner, a machine resembling a square metal heating duct spewed out billow upon billow of white foam until the suds practically reached the ceiling.

The machine then ceased its discharge.

Giving vent to the little boy inside, I batted foam wads up and about, watched them sluggishly ascend, drift, descend. No bubble bath had ever been such fun! From across the room, just above the foam, I could see the steam room door's upper edge opening several times, admitting various manly forms into the bubbly mass, forms that burrowed cautiously like gophers through earth. I jumped at a crotch grope seemingly from nowhere, then I returned the favor, unable to see my hidden playmate until several minutes passed and the foam melted just enough to reveal blond hair and eye mask.

At some point, the machine resumed its spewing until foam once again rose above our heads. I swatted at it and blew it away so as to breathe more comfortably. Experimenting, I waded through the citrusy billows, reaching out in all directions and encountering a slick soapy erection here, another there. So very easy to slide erections within one's soapy hand, a delicious sensation. I practically tripped over a harness-wearing couple fucking, muttered my apology, and continued around the room until my eyes began to burn from soap sting.

Stepping out through the door and back into the adjoining steam room, I plodded with care through the maze filled with drifting foam tumbleweeds until I spotted in a corner that huge bodybuilder of yours, Mr. Hahnemann. In eye mask and red-white-and-blue camera headband. Being sucked by one masked man while two others munched his pointy nipples. So, the boys had arrived. And all with mere eye masks, of course, so that their cameras could reveal faces for your live-stream audience who wished to monitor their favorite contestants. Very savvy of you, Mr. Hahnemann.

My task was at hand. I felt a mix of anticipatory excitement and regret.

Your muscleman wore leather armbands on each of his biceps, accentuating their magnificent girth. Since I was wearing a hood and his headband camera could not detect my true identity, I approached, gently lifted his gargantuan left arm and indulged by lapping his armpit. Sweet, freshly showered, with the barest hint of musk. He moaned at that—how powerful I felt in eliciting the response.

Then I stepped out of the steam room with others half-covered in foam, each of us looking like so many lumps of poorly breaded chicken. I washed off in the shower room, then passed through the foyer where your Latino in leather jockstrap was kneeling on a lounge chair while some hooded man thrust into and out of him from behind. Adorable. I descended a dark circular staircase amid exposed brick walls, discovered on the basement level several orange-painted *kabines* standing empty except for one where your effeminate Irishman aggressively filled the backside of another while the Jewish bear observed. Where was Yuki? Might I be able to lure him into one of those empty *kabines*, shut the door, cover his mouth with one hand and break his neck with the other, all while the disco music muffled any utterance of distress?

My shoulders hunched at the prospect. Yuki was an innocent caught in the web of circumstance, and I the spider, bound by instinct to seek out and destroy my prey. Necessary, but nonetheless distasteful. Did black widows regret being impelled toward mate-o-cide and—one shivers at the thought—cannibalism? As I believe I mentioned in our first interview, I had long fantasized retiring to Japan where older age has long been venerated. Under other circumstances, might Yuki not have served to fulfill my veneration fantasy right here in the U.S.? Alas, fantasies rarely come to pass.

I moved on.

There he was: on a vinyl sofa, wearing the slimmest of eye masks and the telltale headband camera, sat Yuki. He was jerking off a man on either side, but with an odd detachment—his hands pumped in frenzy, yet his face stared directly ahead, completely devoid of expression, as if hands and face were controlled by two separate minds, or as if the hands were pistoning automatically without any engagement of soul. Obviously still traumatized by the loss of dear Freddy. So as to test whether he could recognize my torso, I removed my towel and stood directly in front of him, semi-hard. Without so much as looking up at my chest or hooded face, he leaned forward and took me in, all the while maintaining his jerking rhythm on each side. Robot-like, with eyes shut tight and saliva dripping from his mouth, his head bobbed in sync with the rhythms of his pumping hands as if to the tick-tocks of an inner metronome. Simultaneously engaged and disengaged.

Not wishing to spew my own "foam" before having completed my task, I withdrew from his mouth, leaned down and kissed him full on the lips, slipped in my tongue that he neither sucked nor spat out. I cupped his face while offering silent penance for this kiss of death. I whispered into his ear, "later, I'll want more, you darling boy."

He stared at my hooded face, said nothing.

I would bide my time, both to grant him a few more moments of life, and to wait for the most opportune of circumstances.

Upstairs, I rested in the main floor's foyer, from where I could see everyone's comings and goings. After a good fifteen minutes of repose, I spotted Yuki approaching from the top of the circular basement staircase.

With the air of a somnambulist, he walked past me into the steam room. This was my opportunity. Much better than having to lure him into a *kabine*.

I stood, followed through the maze to the adjoining foam room. The huge muscleman was in there now, mobbed just inside the foam room's door, although one could not make out the particulars of his orgiastic activities. Yuki practically disappeared in foam higher than he was tall, then made his way slowly to mid-room as if through a snowdrift. I followed, moved close to him, sidled up behind and reached around, pressed my crotch against his butt. "I've come for you, darling boy," I whispered, "it is my turn now."

Unceremoniously, Yuki bent over and flipped up his towel. Listless.

I straightened him up, spun him around, brought his face close to mine in the foam, and spoke into his ear, "I apologize to you."

"Apologize?" he said in a flat voice. "What for?"

"For causing you distress in the past."

"What past? We have met?"

"In a way, but, well, and also I apologize for taking advantage of your innocence right now."

"I am not innocent," he muttered, and his head tilted up toward the ceiling or, I like to think, heavenward. "I am guilty," he mumbled. "I just laying there beside him." As if I, a stranger, could possibly fathom his reference, as if he needed to atone to any and every stranger, to the universe. This poor fellow, suffering so. Clearly I would be performing a mercy now, putting Yuki out of his misery.

Suddenly I wanted him to know it was me so that he would know, before death, that Freddy's daddy now cared for him, too.

"I am your friend," I said, slipping off his headband, dropping it to the floor, covering it with my foot, and quickly positioning my hands on either side of his head before he could react. I filled my face with as much compassion as I could.

"My headband," he said listlessly, attempting to bend and retrieve it.

"In a moment," I replied, as I held him upright. "First, peel off my hood."

Shrugging, he did so there in the foam, then gazed into my face for a full moment before revealing recognition in his eyes. His body stiffened. He gasped an intake of breath.

Before he could let that breath out in what might likely have been a blood-curdling scream, I twist-jerked his head to the side, broke his neck with the unmistakable crisp crackly-crunch sound specific to fracturing spinal vertebrae. I caught him as he slumped forward, lowered him gently through the foam to the floor, and uttered exaggerated grunts as if he and I were engaged in the throes of passion, just in case anyone were near enough to overhear us despite the sauna's disco music blare. Hidden beneath the mass of foam, I dragged Yuki to the room's farthest corner where I had stood earlier in the evening.

Totally aroused, as you might well understand by now, and recognizing the newly familiar opportunity to revel in the clamminess of a freshly deceased even without the aphrodisiac of blood, I lay Yuki onto his belly, lifted his towel and mine, set myself atop him, and thrust between his firm cheeks, so slick from the sudsy foam—not inside him, mind you, because one knows how to respect the dead—just between his cheeks. An inimitable sensation. As I thrust and thrust between those slick and cooling cheeks, I repeatedly whispered my gratitude for his having respected my age and dignity back in Munich. As I uttered a loud animalistic grunt, I heard others snicker nearby in amusement at our coupling.

To finish: I wiped Yuki's buttocks clean of myself with soapy foam and his towel. Curling him into a comfortable fetal position, I left him there to rest, pulled my wet and foamy hood back onto my face, grabbed his towel, drifted casually across the room past the muscleman who remained fully engaged, then slipped out the door into the steam room maze and out. Quick shower. In the locker room, I tossed both Yuki's towel and mine into the laundry bin chock full of towels—even were some fanatic investigator to examine every towel, he would never know which towel had touched which body, especially since all were now mixing and sharing shreds of DNA. At the very moment I was exiting the building, I heard behind me the anticipated series of screams.

My Memories: Prague—FuckFest

Watching the fuzzy feed from Bill's and Yuki's cams, I saw 'em walk through the steam room into the foam room, then disappear like skiers into a blizzard. I heard slurps and other sex sounds from Bill's audio feed, then a weird conversation from Yuki's, some guy apologizing for something even Yuki didn't seem to understand, and then Yuki kind of saying he felt guilty. For Freddy's death, obviously. Poor kid. I couldn't see shit for the foam, but from the grunts it sounded like Yuki and this guy were getting it on. Nothing unusual until a few minutes later when some other guy screamed something in Czech. From Bill's foam-covered head cam, I could vaguely make out that someone was shoving Bill and his playmates outta the foam room and through the steam room maze. By the time Bill reached the front bar, all the foam had dissolved off his head cam so I could see better: lotsa guys frantic and babbling in Czech. Bill asked in English what was going on. A redhead explained that somebody "tripped over a body in the foam room. Dead, we think. Too much drugs maybe."

The disco music shut off. That really freaked me out.

More men piled into the bar area like rats crowding onto the overturned hull of a sinking ship. Bill focused his eyes and cam on Burt, Manny, Sam, and Tommy as they ran in, but no Yuki. Bill kept turning his head this way and that, but still no Yuki. Not on any of the other head cams, either.

Bill yanked off his eye mask, ran back toward the steam room maze, but just as he was about to open the door, a coupla employees stepped out carrying Yuki like a sack of potatoes. Our Yuki! They set him on a lounge chair. Bill knelt beside him, yelled for Burt and the other boys, who shoved their way through the crowd to surround 'em, their head cams filming Yuki.

When Yuki's dead face showed up like that on all the van's livefeed screens except his own, I screamed "noooo!" And the tears just shot out of my eyes in a flood. "Nooooo!" My heart started pounding like a hammer. What the fuck had I done?

I flew outta the van and ran the two blocks to Dionysus, rushed in and told the fat greasy entrance clerk I was "the victim's father." He asked how I knew something had happened, but I just screamed at him to buzz me in, so he did.

By the time I found the lounge area, Bill was cradling Yuki in his lap the way Mary holds dead Jesus in every painting and sculpture you ever saw. Manny, Sam, and Tommy, arms around one another's shoulders, were standing in a semi-circle behind 'em, tears running down their cheeks. Grieving angels.

Burt was directing his head cam at 'em, gave me a wink. My jaw just hung open and my own tears flowed. I was crying for all the boys, I guess. I couldn't stop the tears, just felt my chest heaving and heard myself sobbing. What the fuck was going on? I'd set up The Grand Sex Tour to do something good—but now these boys were dead because of me. My boys were being picked off one by one and I was collecting revenues like I was selling Girl Scout cookies.

What the fuck was wrong with me?

All Burt's bullshit about money—my own bullshit—what did it matter? And the risk of pissing off investors—who the fuck cared! "Why Yuki?" I cried out loud. "He was such a sweet kid."

Burt leaned over and whispered, "The tears are great. Keep it up. Too bad I wasn't there in the foam room to film it. But, at least we're still live-streaming now. Another death—the viewership'll spike again."

That's when I hauled back and hurled a punch to slug him smack in the jaw.

But, Bill hooked my arm with his own before I could land the blow.

I'll never forget that look of shock on Burt's face. "Thirty years together and now you wanna clobber me?" He burst into tears. Just like that, he started bawling in front of everybody. I'd never seen him do that before.

"Burtie-boy, I'm so sorry," I said, hugging him.

He clutched me, sobbed. "I'm sorry too," he said. "I don't know what came over me. Those beers. Dollar signs. I can't believe I grabbed your throat in Vienna, Paulie. Can you ever forgive me?"

"Of course."

"And our boys!" he sobbed in my arms. "Our beautiful boys!"

Finally, I had the Burt I always knew was there.

Next thing I knew, two blond cops in blue uniforms with "*Policie*" in big white letters on their jackets showed up and started asking questions in Czech. The fat greasy entrance clerk said something and pointed at me.

While one cop examined Yuki—checked the pulse at his wrist and neck, put a shiny badge under his nose, placed an ear against Yuki's chest—the other spoke to me in English: "You say you are this man's father?"

"Yeah, well, I said that, I know. To get in. I'm not really his father. I mean, look at us. I wish I was his father. Sweet kid. He'd make any father proud."

"You travel with him?"

Standing behind the cop, Burt was giving that don't-say-anything kind of wave with his hands. He was afraid I'd get us in trouble. Like I needed him to remind me.

"Yeah, a group of boys are taking my tour. I'm the tour leader. The organizer, actually. A tour for young men from America. Young gay men, if you wanna know the truth. There's nothing wrong with that, right?"

"How long do you stay in Prague?"

"Tomorrow's our last day. We leave Monday."

"For America?"

"No, for Berlin."

"You will stay in Prague, please. We will interview your fellows now, and other visitors in sauna, too."

"But our trip. We've got tickets, reservations, plans—"

"Your plans are changed. You will give us your passports now."

I thought I'd shit my pants. Burt and I looked at one another. But, to be honest, scared as I was, I thought—maybe it's finally time to bring the cops into this, whatever that meant.

I explained that we always left passports locked in our hotel, so he settled for my driver's license and let the boys go to their lockers to get theirs. "An officer will accompany you back to your hotel to retrieve your passports. Then he will return your licenses."

Meanwhile an ambulance showed up. They wheeled poor Yuki—covered in a white sheet—out on a gurney. We watched the ambulance drive off.

The cops blocked the entrance—nobody in or out. The boys and Burt all got dressed, same as the other patrons, but were still wearing their headbands. The cops herded everyone into the bar area for questioning one by one.

The six of us huddled in a corner.

"Boys," I said, "I don't know what to tell you." Except—yes I did: "Take off your headbands and hold the cam bulges against your palms. Right away!" If we had a stalker, he might be getting his kicks watching our website's live feed showing us running around like chickens with our heads cut off now that he'd snuffed Yuki. I didn't wanna give him the satisfaction. At least I could stop one tiny bit of his fucked-up fun. But more important, I sure as shit didn't want the stalker to hear what we had to say to the cops, especially in case any of the boys said we were looking for a guy with a white 'stache. What if that'd spook him to shaving it off?

The boys took off their headbands immediately. But Burt hesitated, looked at me until I raised an eyebrow. Then, without a word, he took off his headband, too.

"Why would anyone want to kill Yuki?" asked Bill, stone-faced. His voice wasn't challenging, just in shock. "He was the nicest guy."

"This is bullshit!" spat Manny, massaging his gut, "total bullshit!"

"Agatha Christie," muttered Tommy. "*And Then There Were None.* Or the movie version, *Ten Little Indians.* One after another, everyone gets knocked off."

"I won't let him get you, Toms," said Sam. "I don't care how he tries, he won't get you."

"He and whoever he's working for won't get any of us because we're stopping now," said Manny. "No more FuckFests. Period." He stepped over to me and shoved his face into mine. "You and Burt can go fuck yourselves in Berlin if you want. But we're not going. Tommy, Sam, Bill and I are flying home as soon as we get our passports back from the police. And you're paying for our return tickets. And none of us are paying your fucked-up drop-out penalty. And you're going to hire security back home to protect us from your shit-eating pissed investors if they even exist in the first place. You hear me?"

"Calm down," I said. "If that's what you want, fine. I won't stop you. And of course I'll arrange security."

Burt nodded, shutting his eyes. We both knew I was stalling for time, hoping for an idea.

"Your position's legit, Manny," Burt said. "We respect it. But listen, we're all in shock right now. Let's get a good night's sleep if we can—a coupla good nights' sleep. There's no rush. The cops won't let us go to Berlin right now anyway. Paulie and I'll respect whatever you boys decide."

I nodded.

At that point, the cops came over and took each of my boys to be interviewed in the lounge area. One at a time.

"Pervs," Sam said after his interview. "They wanted to know exactly what I was doing with which guy while Yuki was getting offed."

Finally, the cops let us go…with a police escort to the hotel to confiscate our passports. We walked back in silence.

Later, Burt and I held each other in bed like I don't know when the last time was. He rested his head on my bare chest the way he used to in the good old days. "If the boys wanna go, Burt, we gotta let 'em. And hope nobody'll go after 'em back home. You and I, Burt, we created this shit storm. If anybody's gotta face the music it's us, not the boys."

Burt twirled a few of my gray chest hairs. "While you were in the bathroom flossing, I did a quick number crunch."

"No analytics talk tonight, Burt. Out of respect for Yuki." Hadn't Burt just moved past this sort of money-grubbing crap?

"I know, but listen: subscriber numbers and gambling spiked like a cumwad geyser tonight. We didn't make it happen, it just did."

I rolled onto my side, away from him.

He kept talking. "If we pull off the Berlin FuckFest finale and the numbers keep going, we'll clean up. We can pay back investors with profits, give the boys their profit share like I said. Plus you and I'll walk away with a mint so we can retire and never have to do this again. That's not even counting money from the director's cut film we're gonna make."

Suddenly all I felt for Burt was disappointment. "But how can we put the boys through another one? The risk." Was it hopeless to think Burt could change?

"We won't strong-arm 'em. If they wanna leave, we'll let 'em without penalty, okay? I don't think whoever's been after the boys'll bother tracking 'em down back all over the place in America, that'd be too much trouble, and we're the ones owing the money, so the boys'd be safe enough. But here's another argument we can give 'em to stick with us: if they don't follow through and finish up the whole Tour, then the dead boys would have died for nothing. Do they wanna tell Dean he lost the use of his dick for nothing?"

"You sound like one of our sicko politicians: we don't want that our dead soldiers died in vain, right, so we should keep fighting a losing war and risk losing even more soldiers."

"Don't we owe it to the dead boys, Paulie? To their families? We'll have enough dough to really give 'em their full share. Maybe even more."

He had a point. And I liked that idea. But still—"I just don't know."

"And speaking of profits, I got an idea about the director's cut film."

"C'mmon, Burt, stop. Please stop. I know you're trying to help, but not now." My stomach was feeling hinky.

"Just another second, Paulie, hear me out. We could go with the original director's cut idea, a film with FuckFest highlights and clips of the boys sightseeing and dining and shit, and some of the hidden video stuff from their hotel rooms."

"That's what we decided."

"Or—and here's the new idea—I could edit the whole thing to slant it into a murder mystery. That's what the Tour's become anyway, right? Suspense: here are all these great guys frolicking around Europe when all of a sudden they start getting picked off one by one. Who'll get killed next? And how? Pure Agatha Christie, like Tommy said."

I leaped out of bed, hauled ass into the bathroom, dropped to my knees, and puked into the toilet. "I can't take anymore, Burt," I croaked out between hurls.

He reached around from behind, held my sweaty forehead as I mumbled, "You gotta stop. I can't take another—" And just at that second when I reached the end of my rope, an idea sprang into my head. "The Copenhagen and Munich film footage, Burt. We gotta go through it right now."

My Memories: Prague—Klíma

It took us all night to watch all the Munich film footage, but we did. Then I called the cops.

After that, we joined the boys in the breakfast room, where they'd shoved three small tables together, leaving empty seats for Burt and me. Nobody could eat, we just chugged a coupla pots of coffee. I told the boys that the computer algorithm showed Yuki was the winner.

"A lot of good that'll do him," said Manny.

Soon as we stepped outta the breakfast room, the cops were there in the small lobby waiting—the two blond cops I recognized from Dionysus, and a guy in a black suit and narrow black tie. His stringy, dog shit-colored hair kept falling over his brown eyes. Wide cheeks, crooked eye teeth that stood out when he smiled. Creepy. "Inspector Klíma of Europol." He shook our hands, thanked me for calling the police this morning, and wanted to know what I had to share.

"You really called the cops?" asked Sam.

"I gotta save you boys," I said.

Sam hugged me tight and kissed my cheek. Each of the other boys did the same. They'd never done that before. My boys. It was all I could do to keep from bawling.

Burt and I took Klíma to our room. Soon as the door shut, I blurted everything—the Tour, the competition, the filming, the attacks in other cities. I rushed to tell him we'd watched all the Dionysus footage, "but couldn't find anything showing poor Yuki's last minutes because of the foam. We did have a quick image from Yuki's Vienna footage—the back of an old guy's head. Yuki suspected him, but didn't capture his face. But then, on the Munich—"

Klíma interrupted me: "I am gratified that you have chosen to reveal all. This is in the best interests of the investigation and yourself. You see, I have already been tracing your travels through your credit cards. So easy, nowadays." Damn, his English was good. They must've sent a real expert. I felt a wave of relief and motioned Klíma to sit on the plastic desk chair. He kept standing. All three of us did. Klíma continued, "I contacted Europol and local police in Copenhagen, Munich, and Vienna, and learned all about the unfortunate American death in a Copenhagen sauna. And about the attack on an American in a Munich sauna. And about the murder of a Syrian refugee in a Vienna sauna—maybe he interfered somehow with the killer, or discovered his plans. And I also learned about the murder of an unidentified Black man in that same Vienna sauna…might you know of his identity?"

"Freddy," I admitted.

"Also one of yours?"

I nodded, looking down at the floor.

"Interesting."

"Listen, Inspector, the old guy Yuki suspected had a white 'stache. We found someone like that in the Munich sauna film footage. In the hot tub before the attack on Dean, just like Yuki said we would. Bingo. And later in the relaxation room talking to Freddy. Double bingo. Even caught his conversation—sounded like a prissy nose-in-the-air asshole—before he reached up and pulled the headband cam off Freddy *like he knew it was a camera.* And Burt sort of vaguely remembers him from a Munich street festival before the FuckFest. According to Yuki, Freddy saw this same white-'stached guy at Köningshaus, too. Seems clear he's been stalking us. We still have to go through the Copenhagen film footage, but if we can find him there—"

"You are zeroing in on a suspect. Very good detective work," said Klíma. "I was considering bringing sex trafficking charges against you gentlemen. Or illegal pimping charges. Or both. Anything to inspire your cooperation to provide more details and assist in apprehending the murderer. However, perhaps your voluntary efforts and confession now eliminate the need for pressure on my part."

"Sex trafficking?" exclaimed Burt. "Illegal pimping? Wait just a minute. Those boys are with us of their own free will. And there's no way—"

"Burt, shut up," I said. He scrunched his eyes and opened his mouth like he was gonna blast me, then just pivoted and walked over to the window and looked out. To Klíma, I said, "Of course you don't need to pressure us. We wanna help you catch the asshole who did all this. That's why I called. I've actually got a plan. If the white-'stached guy shows up on our Copenhagen film footage, that's really too much of a coincidence. It means he'll probably be following us to Berlin. So,…"

While I explained, Klíma nodded, even smiled here and there. "Very clever," he said. "That could work if your boys will cooperate. You will please take me to them so that I might convince their participation."

I took him to the boys' room—all four were sleeping in one room now because they were so scared. I left 'em alone, went back to our room, pulled out Burt's laptop so we could watch the conversation from the hidden camera Burt had secretly placed in their hotel room like usual.

Note to Self: hidden cameras are amazing, but after we get home, make sure Burt doesn't stick any around the house.

Hidden Camera Transcript:
Bill, Tommy, Sam, Manny, and Klíma

The boys are sitting in a row on one of the four single beds, each covered in a yellow bedspread. Inspector Klíma sits on the gray plastic desk chair, opposite.

"So you're Europol," says Sam.

"Yes. Not local authority. Europol."

"You're going to catch the killer?"

"We certainly hope so. I have read the local police notes of your interviews with them. None of you gentlemen saw your friend's murder in the foam room?"

"I was in there at the same time," says Big Bill. "But didn't see a fucking thing because of the foam. Goddamnit, if only I'd noticed, I'd have strangled the fucker."

Tommy, on one side of him, pats Bill's jean-covered knee. Manny, on the other side, rubs Bill's back.

Klíma smiles at Bill, remains silent. One beat. Two. Three.

"Honest," says Bill, "I didn't see a thing."

"Have I expressed doubt?" asks Klíma.

Bill squeezes his eyes shut tight. Manny massages his back more firmly.

"You feel guilty for the death of your friend."

Bill pinches the bridge of his nose.

"I wish to establish honesty among us, so I will tell you: as soon as the police realized you four to be the victim's traveling companions, you became the prime suspects."

"Shit!" says Manny. "We loved Yuki. He was a sweetheart. None of us would—"

"The police could not know that, could they? During the course of their interviews with you and other patrons, they made careful efforts to specify the location of each of you at the time of the murder. You were very popular visitors to the sauna—patrons explained the particular locale and sexual activity in which you were engaged at the time in question. Reports were all consistent with your own statements."

"You mean we're cleared?" says Manny.

"Precisely."

"See, guys," says Tommy, forcing a smile, "it pays to be a whore."

"You are, I presume, making a joke. However, this brings me to another, less cheerful issue. Although you are not suspected of murder, you are suspected of…. How shall I be delicate?… Do you gentlemen believe that prostitution is legal in Europe?"

"Prostitution?" says Manny. "We don't charge for sex."

"But you receive money for sex."

"Not from the people we have sex with," says Sam. "Only from Paulie. And he doesn't get money from the people we fuck, either, so don't go calling him a pimp."

"Clever distinctions."

Sam continues, "We're contestants in a competition, and porn stars—we charge others to watch. Is that against the law?"

"Not at all. And neither is prostitution, by the way."

"So, why are you fucking with us?"

"To measure your reactions."

Manny shakes his head.

Klíma continues, "You men are in Europe voluntarily?"

They all nod.

"No forced sex trafficking?"

"Hot fantasy," says Tommy, his arm now linked with Bill's, "but the answer's no. We have sex with whoever we want, however we want, and we get points. It's a competition. Top scorer wins the grand prize. We even do our own filming. Yeah, Burt walks around filming us at the saunas, but we film ourselves, too. With our headband cameras. Nobody's forcing us."

"And you obtain written consent from every man you film having sex?"

The boys all look at one another. "Um, sure," says Tommy. "Just as we're about to stick our dicks into somebody's ass, we whip out a permission slip and ask him to piss on the dotted line."

"I understand that as a no."

"Clever man," says Tommy.

Klíma arches his left eyebrow and gives an aha-gotcha smirk. "Gentlemen, filming sex partners without their consent, and for commercial gain? Hmm, European privacy laws are quite strict. Violation of them, well, there are penalties."

"Are you shitting us? Like we haven't been through enough already?" asks Sam.

"Of course, we could overlook these potential infractions if you were to cooperate."

"Cooperate?" asks Manny.

"In finding your friend's killer. Your several friends' killer, assuming one and the same man perpetrated the attacks in the other cities you have visited."

Softening his voice, Manny says, "You think you need to threaten us to get our cooperation?"

"You think because we're fags we can't love our friends?" asks Bill.

"You think we don't have any loyalty?" asks Sam.

"Or soul?" asks Tommy, sitting up straight, his usually pale, freckled cheeks now burning crimson.

The smirk slips from Klíma's face. "Americans do not have the deepest of ethical reputations in Europe." He looks from one to another. "I underestimated you gentlemen. And so I apologize."

Killer Interview 11

Sprawled on my old-fashioned four-poster bed, propped up on four fluffy pillows with a steamy cup of chamomile tea on the night table and Macbook Air on my lap, I checked The Grand Sex Tour website for any reactions to my prior night's bubble bath adventure. I had not thought before to check the website for subscriber comments. A foolish oversight on my part—these comments offered great amusement: tender eulogies for Yuki, worried urgings that the surviving boys should refrain from attending other FuckFests, curses directed at me—well, not at me by name, but at the "serial" killer, the shared assumption being that one man had been responsible for Yuki's death and Freddy's as well as the maiming of Mr. Arrogant, which several commenters erroneously characterized as a failed attempt at murder by infliction of groinal hemorrhage. No comments appeared about the little blond in Copenhagen, the stupid public demonstrating utter lack of capacity to put two and two together.

While I was reading, a bright red alert message popped onto the screen stating that, so as to display proper respect to Yuki and the other "victims," the Tour organizers had decided to delay the FuckFest finale by one week. The boys would spend this coming week in quiet retreat in Prague.

Très considerate, I thought. Tasteful even.

The alert message went on to say that, to compensate subscribers for the delay in the chance to reap gambling winnings, the competition organizers would announce, four hours prior to commencement of the Berlin FuckFest finale, the name of its venue, thereby giving any viewers who happened to be in Berlin sufficient time to join the festivities. Quite a clever ruse: on the surface, the measure seemed a gracious departure from past practice of keeping forthcoming FuckFest venues secret; but actually—how many subscribers would likely be able to drop everything and whisk off last minute? Hardly meaningful compensation.

However, I thought at the time, what good fortune for me! I would not have to maneuver so as to learn the next FuckFest venue. No matter where I chose to hotel in Berlin, I could learn the venue with sufficient advance notice and reach it by anonymous public transportation. Especially since it was likely to be in a more-or-less predictably central locale. Yes, I certainly was planning to attend the FuckFest finale although, at least consciously, I had not yet determined whether to eliminate or maim another contestant or simply enjoy one or more of them in a more traditional cum-dump sort of way.

Of course, Mr. Hahnemann, I fully recognize, in retrospect, that the alert message had been designed precisely to catch *my* attention. Yes, a set-up. At the time, I did not remotely consider the possibility of entrapment. After all, how could anyone possibly have expected to outmaneuver cunning me? I am secure enough to pose the ironic question—whom should we deem Mr. Arrogant now?

Kudos, Mr. Hahnemann. I tap fingertips together in applause at your perspicacity and cleverness. In general, I have been most impressed by your repeated display of inventiveness modestly akin to my own. Although we certainly are distinct human beings of different classes, bearing, and manner, one continues to notice similarities of ambition, mental acuity and, dare I say, willingness to impose risk upon those we regard as somehow of lesser importance than ourselves. My assessment should be of no great surprise— I have implied, if not stated, such observations throughout our interviews.

The precise way you are now pursing your thin lips reveals my having struck a chord.

No need to respond, Mr. Hahnemann.

Where was I? Oh yes, on my four-poster bed.

As I sipped my cup's cooling bittersweet chamomile dregs, I determined not to remain an extra week in Prague, but to fly to Berlin the following day as planned so as to spend the hiatus there. After all, as charming and quaint as Prague is, it cannot hold a candle to cosmopolitan Berlin chock-o-block with museums displaying Germany's international plunder.

Berlin

Killer Interview 12

How remarkable Berlin's memorial monuments to Nazi sadism—well, not to sadism per se, but to the shame of sadism. Lest we forget, rinse, and repeat. You would never personally engage in sadism of any kind, would you, Mr. Hahnemann? Although one suspects that you might direct and film it for the right price.

...

Tut tut, Mr. Hahnemann, tish tosh. Save your objections for your own interpolations in the book among scribbles of your own design. These are *my* concluding interviews, my last opportunities to shine.

After admiring the historic Reichstag Building on my first Berlin afternoon, I came upon an unexpected memorial enclave to the murdered Sinti and Roma Gypsies—a forest glade containing a small pond surrounded by odd-shaped flat gray stones, many engraved with the names of concentration camps. Mournful viola music soughed through the trees. Outside the glade, a sign summarized the deaths of the roughly half-million remembered there.

I am not a monster, Mr. Hahnemann. My heart bears the capacity to be moved by the thought of so many innocent souls lost.

Crossing the avenue, I peered up at the Brandenburg Gate, then down the avenue to the Memorial to the Murdered Jews of Europe where I wandered among the maze bearing more than two thousand concrete coffin-like stelae, and recalled the many films of suffering I'd seen during my sixty years. I literally jumped when startled by the gewgaw of a racing ambulance's siren shrieking along bordering Hannah-Arendt-Strasse. The U.S. Embassy peered down over my shoulder, casting a shadow over the entire complex. To calm myself, and adjoin my very being to the memorial, I sat upon one of the concrete coffin blocks just as a group of French tourist teens raced around me, playing hide-and-seek among these symbols of racist genocidal torture and murder. So much for contemplative melancholy.

Back across the avenue, a bit into the Tiergarten woods, I encountered the memorial to persecuted homosexuals: a massive gray concrete cuboid bearing no writing whatsoever, just a small window on one side into which I peered and watched an endlessly repeating film of two young men kissing tenderly, the blond now whispering something into the brunette's ear, now cupping his face. As if I'd stumbled upon a hidden privacy, intruded upon a secluded love nest. Oh, to be young again, and hope for innocent love.

Stepping away from the intimacy, I considered the irony of German high cultural esthetics so tastefully memorializing the very same culture's barbarity. I shuddered as if from the Devil's chill, felt a sudden, unarticulated resonance before continuing on my way in search of the Tiergarten's monument to Goethe.

With what joy I occupied those days in Berlin awaiting the FuckFest finale. To list my repeated forays to Museum Island, the Berlin Cathedral, Humboldt University, and Unter den Linden's War Memorial temple holding that heart-piercing bronze everywoman pietà by Käthe Kollwitz, would be to try your patience for no relevant purpose. Although, as I think of it, such a listing might demonstrate, yet again, the extent of my cultured civility, which I offer up as mitigating circumstance so that you and your readers may better understand.

My Memories: Berlin—Planning the Sting

The rest of our stay in Prague, I let those traumatized boys do whatever the fuck they wanted. They mostly walked around, ate sausages, and drank beer. Burt and I spent hours scanning the Copenhagen film footage—finally, we spotted the white-'stached guy prowling around. We didn't catch him doing anything, but he was there in some of the shadows at Buddies. Yuki'd said he suspected the guy lied to Freddy, saying he wasn't at Buddies when the boys were. Shit, Little Frenchie didn't just fall down those stairs, did he? We agreed not to say anything about it to the boys—why make 'em more nervous than they already were?

We got enough film of the guy in Copenhagen and Munich to match his torso (chest with pointy nips and a little white fuzz in the middle, love handles above a cinched towel) to one of the hood-masked men in Prague's Dionysus. Who the fuck was this asshole? And why was he after our boys?

Burt drove the van on ahead to Berlin. The next day, I took the boys there by train.

The day after that, Klíma met us in our room so we could make good on my plan. He was carrying an attaché case. After he watched the film footage, he gave a thumbs-up and handed over the document Burt had asked for: a guarantee of immunity. But it included a statement we hadn't figured on: immunity will become null and void if we *ever* shoot any other film of any kind anywhere in Europe.

Fine, it's not like I ever wanted to film another Tour in Europe after all this shit.

Hidden Camera Transcript: Bill, Tommy, Sam, and Manny

"We'll be watching each others' backs," says Manny as he massages his stomach in front of the floor-to-ceiling glass wall overlooking Oranienburgerstrasse. The hidden room camera does not reveal what he sees, but shows him gazing down in the direction of the German, Cuban, Thai, Singaporean, Indian, and Turkish restaurants lining the street with outdoor seating. He continues, "We'll have to fuck around to make it look authentic, but we'll keep an eye on one another and look for that asshole with the white mustache. This finale won't be about scoring points."

"Right," says Bill, planted in a chair at the expansive room's round white table. "It's about revenge."

"Thanks to the Munich film footage, we know what that asshole looks like," says Manny. "We'll be able to spot him for sure."

"Am I the only one scared shitless?" calls Tommy from one of the two king-size beds.

Sam spoons him tighter.

Killer Interview 13

Brandie's Sauna—so named for its proximity to the Brandenburg Gate—has since been closed, or so I am told. Was the FuckFest finale the sauna's finale, too? Had that been the intention? Or was the facility forced, by circumstance, to shut down in consequence of my foray there? The thought inspires such a feeling of specialness.

Speaking of specialness, Mr. Hahnemann, I remind you of the need to sequester my investor profits until my eventual release from incarceration, should that day ever arrive. I am completing all the requested interviews so you have no specious grounds for withholding a penny. Actually, I petition for a bonus because my exploits unquestionably contributed to a dramatic expansion of viewership-subscribers-gambling. I recognize no *legal* basis why I am due an additional percentage of The Grand Sex Tour's profit, but should you not take *ethics* into account? Have you abandoned all notions of fair play?

Be that as it may: as I strolled toward Brandie's Sauna, I erroneously regarded the locale as a good omen—so near the various memorials to souls murdered in the War, as if enticing me to commit a murder in their vicinity, to become part of history, to leave behind actions producing an impact on the world's psyche. All of which led me to consider: might geography have played a role in my discovery of the joy of mauling and killing? After all, these impulses were unleashed in Central Europe, not exactly the lion-lying-with-lamb capital of the world. Might something about the atmosphere be conducive to one's relishing infliction of devastating harm? Hitler and all that. Human beings are part of nature, are we not? So if one changes one's natural environment, as I was doing, then it stands to reason that something within oneself might shift, as well. Don't you think? If so…which variations in human personality and desire might be triggered by global warming, eh? Just think about that.

I acknowledged on my approach to Brandie's Sauna no particular reason to kill any of the other boys. None of them, I believed at that point, could identify me as having associated with my prior victims. Nor did I otherwise bear any of them malice. Would the thrill be as great were I to attack a victim whom I bore neither animus nor fear? So many unknowns to explore about my new sexuality. This finale would serve as further opportunity to experiment.

I decided to murder one of them without any motivation other than the pure sake of doing so. A pure murder. Purity in the heart of the society that fetishized Aryan purity. Appropriate, was it not? But which boy? Having killed White, Black, Arab, and Asian, I was well on my way toward completing a personal rainbow flag of accomplishment. Perhaps I should choose the arguably non-White bearish Jew? No, to kill a Jew in Berlin might send the wrong signal, to say nothing of constituting outdated cliché.

That left the wiry Latino for completion of my color wheel. Yes, the Latino. Certainly, he was spare enough so that I could perhaps start off pretending to engage in kinky breath play, then "accidentally" go too far. Or I could sit on his face, pin his arms and hands with my knees, and while he'd be giving me a deep rim job, losing himself in the sweetness of my scent, I could ass-smother him. Or I could simply catch him off guard with an unexpected punch, knock him out, strangle him then or, if worse came to worst, one could always repeat oneself and break his neck. The moment itself would provide necessary inspiration. I needed to find a secluded spot. How large was this sauna?

Inside, I requested a private *kabine*, but the entrance clerk explained, in halting English, that all were occupied. The locker room's smallness cued me as to this venue's petiteness. An odd choice for a finale, although I rationalized that you, Mr. Hahnemann, were seeking intimacy in view of the fact that only four boys remained. Little did I suspect your venue-selection motive to be the ease of cornering and capturing yours truly.

Wrapped in de rigueur white towel, I proceeded into the wet area only to remove and hang the towel before climbing up and into the enormous and deep hot tub reminiscent of backyard, above-ground swimming pools from my various suburban childhood foster homes. Three considerably older men were massaging one another's wet chicken-skin shoulders. Another, with an inflated liver-spotted appendage, floated while being sucked. Two others drifted in deep-kissing embrace.

Sliding into the warm froth, I rested my head back on the tub's concrete edge. Soothing. No need to hide my face the way I had in Prague because only the disposed-of Yuki had observed me at Köningshaus. The worst that could happen would be that one of the remaining boys might remember me from Munich. So what if an American had traveled from Munich to Berlin? Was that a crime? Was it odd for an American to tour Germany? Were they not doing the very same?

Suddenly, the hot tub massagers whispered feverishly in German and pointed at a group walking in—my boys with their headband cameras. And the heavyset cameraman. My internet celebrities that these fellow hot-tubbers had presumably observed online and were now here to enjoy in-person.

The boys perused the wet area—nervously, it seemed to me. As the Latino bounced his glance from one hot tub face to another, his gaze latched onto mine for just a tad. Our eyes met. He turned slightly pale. I remember wondering: did he recognize me? And if so, why would he pale at the sight of me? Did he have some sixth sense alerting him to the potential threat I posed? Or was this all my own over-excited imagination? Perhaps he found me rather dashing.

He crossed the wet area, opened the steam room's glass door and entered. As did his fellows. As did several of the older hot tub soggies, surely Grand Sex Tour superfans all.

I followed, thinking to explore the steam room's crannies, and noticed that three muscular blond men had just entered the wet area, each wearing those telltale red-white-and-blue headband cameras. I could even detect earpieces. I wondered, Mr. Hahnemann, whether you had hired extra participants for the finale, or perhaps supplemental cameramen whom you could direct. Bravo for Mr. Hahnemann, I thought.

Two of them followed me into the steam room, sauntered past me. A bit blinded by the heavy steam, I stumbled over some figure on his knees and lost my balance, but I did not fall to the tiled floor. Extending my arm, I found the wall, groped along and made a left at the back of the L-shaped room into a darker section. Sucking sounds, moans, heavy breathing. No one had wasted any time. The predictable ease of male libidinous expression within the unaccountability of darkness.

A hand lifted my towel, a mouth fastened onto me. Such simple pleasure, more enjoyable now than in years past before my sexuality had been liberated here in Europe. After providing several blissful minutes, my pleasurer stood, embraced me, kissed me. I shoved him aside—such foul saurkraut breath! No sense of decency. No sense of community. No awareness beyond the selfish self.

Unable to distinguish the Latino in the murk, I groped my way out of the steam room. A quick shower and towel off. Time to explore further and select the right spot for my upcoming tryst.

I discovered, downstairs, a short corridor of perhaps half a dozen *kabines*. And a deep, unlit alcove containing an enormous elevated platform covered in mats upon which a number of men rolled around in shadow. Definitely a destination meriting return later, or some other day.

Down another short corridor and to the right, I came upon a row of doors. Opening one, I saw a walk-in-closet-sized space containing a narrow floor mat. Unlike the *kabines*, these were not subject to rental, merely to first-come-first-served squatter's rights. I stepped inside, shut the door. All I need do was lure the Latino in here, a presumably simple task given that his primary objective was to score points with whomever. I trembled in giddiness at the prospect of this, my own personal "finale."

My Memories: Berlin—Prepping the Sting

Europol said three decoys were enough for a sauna that small. (How did they know how small the sauna was? Did they hang out there all the time?) I gave the decoys the headband cams that Dean, Freddy, and Yuki used to wear. Klíma fitted the decoys with micro ear receivers like Burt wore for me. When Klíma sat in the van with me and watched the live-feed screens, he could direct his decoys to follow the asshole suspect.

"Perfect," mumbled Klíma.

Soon as I saw the white-'stached guy on the live feed, I nearly crapped my pants. *Note to Self: be sure to carry Pepto Bismol tablets when doing James Bond shit.*

We watched the boys closely, but we couldn't see anything in the steam room except for shapes. That made me nervous. Klíma sent two decoys in there pronto. But the 'stached guy left the steam room pretty quickly—not enough action in there for him?

Klíma directed one of the decoys to follow him downstairs. The other two decoys brought the boys down after, had 'em stand near the matted alcove where a dozen camp followers kept trying to grab hold of the boys' dicks. You could even see 'em angling to get their mugs in front of the head cams, some even giving big grins. That was the downside of advertising on our website where the finale would be—obviously, a dozen locals or tourists already in Berlin had seen the notice on our website and hightailed it to the sauna to join in. Or maybe to get on camera. Everyone was a glam queen.

Finally, the killer showed up from a little hallway and noticed our boys. They all glanced at him, but you could see in their faces they remembered Klíma's instructions not to stare. That's when they let gropers and suckers have at 'em like during a normal FuckFest.

When the killer sidled up to Manny and started sucking one of his nips, Manny's jaw and fists clenched like he wanted to sock the bastard but was holding back. Why'd he pick Manny? Because he was small? That wacko had no idea what a firecracker Manny could be.

Some young guy dropped to his knees and sucked Manny's cock that got so hard I thought it'd shoot flames of fury.

Killer Interview 14

I whispered invitation into the Latino's ear—"anything you wish, *amigo*, anything. I will be yours to command. But only in private. I have found a spot." In retrospect, I should have paid attention to his momentary sidelong glance at the Irishman a mere yard away, the beading of sweat on both boys' brows. Surely signs of recognition and complicity. Cautionary signs I missed in my over-confidence.

I shoved the Latino's kneeling sucker aside, took the Latino by his hot hand, led him down the short corridor. I held open a cubicle's door, and as he entered, I reached up and yanked off his headband camera. He grabbed at it, but I tossed it aside. "I want you completely naked, even of ornamentation. Lie down and let me service you."

His gulp of hesitation—another sign I missed. Why, you might ask, did I erroneously believe this experienced sex star to be suddenly shy with me? In answer, I admit: how overwhelming is the arrogance of an older man wishing to believe himself capable of the sexual allure of years past.

I pointed to the mat on the floor. He lay down. I lay atop him. With both hands, I caressed the sides of his head, slipped my hands to his neck. I was anticipating a struggle, and certainly did feel his body knot in tension, but he did not reach up to remove my hands, another signal I missed.

Noticing the clench of his fists, I finally began to question. At the precise moment my clasp around his throat tightened without encountering any resistance whatsoever, I realized his complete awareness of my intentions, and I flashed puzzlement: did he wish death?

My Memories: Berlin—The Sting

I get chills just thinking about it. The minute the killer led Manny toward that cubicle, Klíma barked orders in German. The decoys heard 'em on their micro ear receivers and followed. Sam shoved his way ahead of 'em. Manny's cam feed went blank for a few secs, then kept shooting from a weird angle, like from the floor corner by Manny's head. Shit, we could see the killer's hands on Manny's face, then down toward his neck. "C'mmon!" I screamed at Klíma. "What the fuck are you waiting for?!"

Klíma machine-gun sprayed more orders in German, including "*eins zwei drei—!*"

Hidden Camera Transcript:
Bill, Tommy, Sam, and Manny

Back in the boys' Berlin hotel room, Manny, naked but for his blue boxers, paces back and forth, punches fist against palm. "I wanted to pummel that *cabrón. Pendejo sucio!*"

"You did great," says Sam, clapping Manny's shoulder each time he passes. Bill and Tommy nod and murmur echoes of the sentiment.

"Khkhkh—shit, my throat still—I know we had to catch him in the act," says Manny, "but just—khkhkh—lying there, waiting for the decoys to burst in…oh, God…letting him grab my neck and squeeze—it felt like forever. At one point, I thought I was going to die. Until you burst in and saved me, Tommy." Manny reaches out and grabs Tommy, yanks him in for a full-body hug.

"You were amazing, Toms," Sam says. "A true hero."

"I couldn't let him get another of us. I just couldn't."

"You just ripped the asshole off me like he was a feather," says Manny, his eyes tearing up.

"The decoys said they couldn't have done it better," says Sam, "the way you hurled him out of the cubicle, Toms, right into the decoys' waiting arms. You proved you can take care of yourself and anybody else." Tommy reaches over to Sam and they embrace.

"You waited long enough before bursting in?" asks Manny. "You got him on film?"

"Sure did," says Tommy. "When I yanked the door open, he turned and looked straight at me—at my head cam."

"I got him, too," says Sam. "I was right behind Toms. We caught him on film, for sure. Smack in the middle of the act, with his hands around your throat. He'll fry."

Big Bill kisses the top of Manny's sweaty hair and then Tommy's. "You guys avenged Little Frenchie and—"

"So he's really the one got Little Frenchie, too?" asks Manny.

"Yeah," says Big Bill, his voice dropping to a whisper. "After we left the sauna tonight, Paulie took me aside and told me he found that mustached asshole on a bunch of film from Buddies in Copenhagen. The old prick was there, goddamn it, even though he told Freddy he wasn't." Bill's voice cracks. "Must've shoved Frenchie down the stairs."

"Poor little guy never had a chance," says Manny.

"You guys avenged Little Frenchie and Freddy and Yuki," says Bill. "All of 'em."

"And," adds Manny, "let's not forget Dean."

Last Words
From The Asshole
And Me Both

Killer Interview 15

Our final interview, Mr. Hahnemann. An opportunity to share conclusions:

Although I am not likely, given my age, orientation, and incarceration, to replicate God's skill at creating life, I have learned, during our shared sojourn in Europe, that I bear within me the God-like power of destroying it. I can pluck a fruit from the human tree of life once planted by (your) God Himself. I possess the wherewithal to cut Fate's thread. Insignificant unknown being that I otherwise am, I have achieved par with mythological supernatural beings. Satan incarnate. If there is a greater aphrodisiac on the planet, I have yet to encounter it.

...

Unnatural, you say once again? Unnatural to mutilate and/or murder a lover? To enjoy another's flesh even if cold? Because it is cold? Did not (your) God create me in His image just as He created you, and does that fact not define me, per se, as "natural," i.e., "of God's nature"? Or are you implying me not to be one of His children but a bastard beyond the conceptualization-creation of the Universal Being to whom you sycophantically kowtow? Are you imposing limits upon His omnipotence?

...

No, I thought not. I am one of you. In a sense, I am you. This is what terrifies you most, Mr. Hahnemann, admit it. Were you able to dismiss me as an ungodly aberration, you might experience less fear. Your terror lies precisely in the knowledge that I and others like me might arise at any time from within your midst. (From within your very self?) Unpredictably. As undetectable as a latent virus lurking, waiting to garner strength and attack at will. Repress us with your theological rants, attempt to rout us with your undercover stings and relegations to prison. We're here, we're severe, get used to it.

. . .

Spare me your Psych 101 notions of self-hatred: I did not engage in the ecstatic murder and mutilation of gay men so as to extinguish the homosexual in myself. No. I chose gay men as prey because gay men are those whose psyches I understand and am able to predict and manipulate precisely because I am one of them. Had I been an octopus, I'd have wrung the life from other Cephalopoda molluscs; had I been a bumblebee, I'd have wreaked havoc in my hive.

. . .

And so, your final question, or at least the last to which I will respond. I have been awaiting this question. Anticipation of this question has kept me engaged in these interviews because I have grasped the extent to which it makes you uncomfortable. This question places you, yourself, on trial: was there anything you could have done to stop me sooner?

So very narcissistic of you, Mr. Hahnemann, to focus on yourself when those boys are dead or maimed, and I am in isolation in a German prison. Meanwhile, you are alive and at liberty to enjoy boundless wealth. Where is the justice?

You ask whether you could have stopped me. You know the answer, Mr. Hahnemann. You have known the answer for months or longer. Yet you have chosen to deny it, and your conscience now cries out in a last vestige of hope that I shall deny it for you. I shall not.

You could have stopped the competition at any point. You know that. You do not need me to inform you of this truth except to relieve you of the responsibility of drawing the self-incriminating conclusion yourself.

Admit it, Mr. Hahnemann, if you dare: had you canceled the post-Munich Grand Sex Tour FuckFests after what was obviously an intentional attack on Habsburg-jawed Mr. Arrogant, had you accepted the concomitant financial ruin and personal risk from disappointed investors, you would have succeeded in terminating my spree, and two of your boys—Freddy and Yuki—would still be alive. A week later, you had a second opportunity: had you stopped the Tour after someone obviously slit Freddy's throat intentionally, Yuki would still be alive. However, ardent capitalist that you are, you continued the Tour in both instances, thereby placing the surviving boys at additional risk. You are complicit in my crimes. You are my co-conspirator. In fact, if not for you and your entire enterprise, I might never have discovered certain repressed propensities nor experienced such heady erotic rushes. And so, before the world in this interview, I point my finger directly at your chest and declare: *J'accuse!*

At the same time, I thank you. I fully acknowledge having done the deeds and having exulted in the telling, in becoming known. Whether understood or misunderstood, I have been heard. Have not newspapers now dubbed me The Grand Sex Tour Stalker, thereby adding me to the rolls of the historically notorious? Surely, Hollywood will soon take note, and then—endless possibilities.

You and your readers might not comprehend my motivations, inspirations, reasonings, or inclinations, but I have now had the chance to articulate them, vent them, unleash them on the world. Who can know which of my words, thoughts, visions might one day drift into the mind of a contemplative soul inclined to take refuge in the legitimacy of my precedent?

Actually, I take comfort in the knowledge that my capture resulted from the arrogance of thinking myself smarter than you and the authorities, my *hubris*, a classical failing that places me alongside the mythical Greek greats. And I still have my eyes, to boot.

I take even greater comfort in the awareness that others' hostile responses to my actions will assure my legacy's extraordinary longevity. For hate never finds resolution, the urge for vengeance can know no satisfaction, rage fire burns in perpetuity. I will be the object of them all, so I shall be remembered. What more can any man ask of life, Mr. Hahnemann? What more?

But, will you be remembered, Mr. Hahnemann? Or will you be relegated to history's proverbial dustbin overflowing with generic nothings?

As we conclude this final interview, the thought occurs that you have never once addressed me by name. Because the spelling and pronunciation are somewhat irregular? As a farewell gift, Mr. Hahnemann, I shall pronounce and spell my name for you on this final recording so that your book can include my name with accurate precision. My name is—

Producer's Finale

Europol returned our passports and let us go after we signed statements that we'd be available online or by phone for any questions, and that we'd return to be witnesses at a trial if they wanted us. To keep track of us, they sent all our data to the FBI, CIA, Homeland Security, Alexa, and who the hell knows where else.

I crowned Yuki as Grand Prize winner with the most points during the entire competition, even without Berlin. The rest of the boys were happy with that. I sent the Grand Prize money to Yuki's folks in Frisco on his behalf "for performing outstanding international relations community service work at great personal risk to self." I also sent money to Little Frenchie's mom in Montreal and to Freddy's in Austin, giving the same reason. That dough came from the killer's profit share. He doesn't like it— let him sue me. Like any judge'd order me to pay him diddley squat.

Klíma helped me send Freddy's body home from Vienna and Yuki's from Prague.

After Dean got his dick sewed back on—he can't use it but to piss, but that's better than nothing, right?—we set up a giant group memorial service for the boys in NYC. St. Paddy's Cathedral was filled to bursting with so many fags it was like Catholic Priest Coming Out Day or something. Of course Burt filmed the service, and we included the footage as "behind-the-scenes" supplemental material in the director's cut film. It gave "gravitas" (Burt's word) to the whole project. And now we're up for a ton of film festival awards for "most innovative hybrid" film—the first-ever tear-jerker-porn-reality-travel-foodie-murder-mystery-killer-capture drama.

The money keeps rolling in. We paid off investors, subscribers, gamblers, the boys, and still made a shitload. Burt and I are set for life.

Note to Self: take a breather, Paulie boy, you've earned it.

So here I am, a year after The Grand Sex Tour, finishing up this one-of-a-kind book. You can be damn sure this book is the one and only there'll ever be because no way am I going through another Grand Sex Tour. First of all, my legal ability to film anything else in Europe is no-go from the get-go. I was lucky Klíma arranged permission for me to come back to interview that asshole killer in prison after the trial. Second, I kind of blew the chance for another Sex Tour somewhere else by giving in to the public's—your— begging for gossip. In other words, I shot myself in the foot by writing this book that's better than any how-to manual, especially the parts about the bogus point-scoring algorithm, and the way I put the fix on the gambling.

Not that any gambler lost much—there's been enough money to go around. But if anyone lost—hey, that's why they call it "gambling," right? So sue me.

But you gotta find me first. Burt and I aren't sitting still in any one place too long, so good luck with that.

Some of you been emailing I shouldn't ever be allowed to publish this book and make a fucking mint off the killer's interviews. First of all—fuck off because it's none of your goddamn business. Second—what makes you think it's his interviews'll sell this book and not my memories? Third, are you saying *he* should get to write a book so's *he* can pocket the dough? *He* should get rich off what he did? That murderer? I'm the one busted my ass to make The Grand Sex Tour happen, not him. The whole Grand Sex Tour was *my* idea. That killer just rode my coattails, so now *he* should get fame and fortune?

No fucking way.

I was gonna end this book with the killer's last interview because it's fucking creepy, right? Totally nuts. But then I figured hell no, this is my goddamn book, so I'll end it with my voice, not that asshole's. Like I'd let him call me out and throw me under the bus. Like I'd let the world think he wasn't fucking insane for trying to dump guilt on me when he's the one shoveled all the shit.

I won't even include his name in my book. Like I really want the world to remember him more than me. Fuck that shit.

…Oh, alright, I'll cry "uncle." Here's his name:

A-S-S-H-O-L-E.

But don't you worry—I'm no selfish asshole like him: I'm gonna share all book royalties with the living boys, and the families of the dead ones. You didn't expect that, did ya? You expected the worst from me, didn'tcha? Maybe that's what's wrong with our whole society, everybody assuming everybody else is out to swindle and make a fast buck no matter who suffers. Well, not me. I'm one of the good guys. I'm no pimp making gold off those boys' sweaty asses without paying 'em their fair share. I'm not the same as that asshole killer. I'm nothing like him. Go fuck yourselves if you say I am.

I really care about those boys and their families whatever their race or religion, whatever their hair or eye color. Whether they're top or bottom or versatile, they're all my boys. Now that you've read this book, I hope you understand that. My boys. My boys my boys my boys.

I wanted a reunion show with my boys. Just one evening together. A dinner, not a FuckFest. And of course, I'd foot the bill. A fancy dinner with everybody in tuxes, buckets of roses on the tables, a dozen frou-frou courses by reality TV cooking show award winners. A dinner with the survivor boys and portraits of those we'd lost so we could remember our buddies like war vets do. A private dinner just for us. Burt'd film it all, of course, because why shouldn't I live-stream it and make some final bucks after everything we suffered? Our last hurrah.

But none of the surviving boys would come to a reunion. After they watched the director's cut film and realized Burt and I'd filmed 'em secretly in their hotel rooms all along, they refused to come. They actually turned on me, can you believe it? Blaming me for what that asshole did. All of a sudden, my boys don't wanna have anything more to do with me.

That hurts.

None of it was my fault no matter what the boys or that asshole killer think. I didn't off anyone. You just read those interviews where the asshole confessed to everything, goddamn it! Why the hell do you think I included his interviews with my memories here except to show you how nuts he is and to prove to you and the boys it wasn't my goddamn fault? Like I'd share the spotlight with that asshole if I didn't really have to.

The biggest reason I know none of it was my fault is because Burt tells me so every night right before I go to sleep. When he pries away my empty Scotch bottle and holds my head on his chubby chest in bed. When he rocks me. When he hands me tissues to wipe away my snot dribbles. When he tells me I gotta stop blaming myself.

Because I'm not guilty. I'm not guilty. I'm not.

And don't you forget it, you motherfuckers. Don't you forget it.

Note to Self: don't you forget it.

ABOUT THE AUTHOR

Daniel M. Jaffe is a prize-winning writer whose short stories and personal essays have appeared in dozens of anthologies, newspapers, and literary journals in over half a dozen countries. His book, *Foreign Affairs: Male Tales of Lust & Love*, was selected by *Kirkus Reviews* as one of the Best Indie Books of 2020 and one of the Best Indie Short Story Collections of 2020. He is author of the novels *Yeled Tov* (2018: Rainbow Awards Finalist and Honorable Mention) and *The Limits of Pleasure* (2001; *ForeWord Magazine* Book of the Year Award Finalist; reprinted in 2010, 2019). He also wrote the novel-in-stories, *The Genealogy of Understanding* (2014; Rainbow Awards Finalist and Honorable Mention), and the short story collection, *Jewish Gentle and Other Stories of Gay-Jewish Living* (2011). He authored *One-Foot Lover*, the inaugural chapbook in the Seven Kitchens Press Editor's Series (2009). In addition, Daniel compiled and edited *With Signs and Wonders: An International Anthology of Jewish Fabulist Fiction* (2001) and translated *Here Comes the Messiah!* (2000), a Russian-Israeli best-seller by Dina Rubina. Profiled in *The Greenwood Encyclopedia of Multiethnic American Literature*, Daniel holds degrees from Princeton University (A.B.), Harvard Law School (J.D.), and Vermont College (M.F.A.). Read more at www.DanielJaffe.com.